I0551741

THE CRYPTOGRAM

A Story of Northwest Canada

By

William Murray Graydon

First published in 1897

Stillwoods Edition 2020

Stillwoods.Blogspot.Ca

Catalogue Information:
Title: The Cryptogram – A Story of Northwest Canada
Author: William Murray Graydon (1864-1946)
First Published 1897
This Edition by: Stillwoods 2020
ISBN Canada: 978-1-989788-03-5
Blog: Stillwoods.Blogspot.Ca
Storefront: http://www.lulu.com/spotlight/lulubook22

Keywords: Canadian, Hudson's Bay Co., Graydon

Description: Also known as "Our Lady of the Snows." This novel is a stirring romance of North-West Canada, published first in 1897. It tells the tale of a Hudson's Bay employee who becomes impossibly confused in romance and espionage in early Canada.

Introduction: I was surprised when I discovered that this was a story that took place in Canada. I had been working just a bit on 'The Curse of the Cardews' which starts out in South America, Guyana, or British Guiana as it was previously known. This was only published as a serial in 20 parts in newspapers only in Australia and New Zealand, so far as known. The web contents are horrific in quality; hence I suspect that I will never complete the story. Then I came across this one which has very few copies in Canada!

I hope you enjoy it.
Doug Frizzle

A few books available at:
http://www.lulu.com/spotlight/lulubook22

Bottom of Suez
Crooks' Vendetta
Voodoo Island
Five in Fear
The Grey Ghost
The Case of the Duplicate Key
The Temple of Many Visions
Gangland's Decree
The Clue of the Four Wigs
The Mystery of the Film City
The Black Abbot
Murder Ship
Spies Ltd.
A Mystery of the Big Woods
The Mystery of the Kidnapped Killer
The Secret of the Swamp
The Case of the Pink Macaw
The Terror of Gold-digger Creek
The Case of the Mummified Hand
Pearls of Doom
The Victim of the Gang
The Case of the Courtlandt Jewels
Nelson Lee and the Lhassa Red Menace
The Riddle of the Russian Gold
Voodoo Vengeance
Hounded Down
Bribery and Corruption
The Sacred Sphere
The Tiger of Canton
The Crook of Marsden Manor
The Affair of the Six Ikons
The Secret of the Coconut Groves
The Case of the Disguised Apache
Under the Eagle's Wing
The Rogues' Republic
The Mitcham Murder Mystery

CHAPTER I.   THE SAVING OF GRAY MOOSE.

I have long had in mind to set down the story of my early life, and now, as I draw pen and paper to me for the commencement of the task, I feel the inspiration of those who wrote straight from the heart. It is unlikely that this narrative will ever appear in print, but if it does the reader may rely on its truthfulness and accuracy from beginning to end, strange and incredulous though parts of it may seem.

Thirty years ago! It is a long time, but the magic power of memory laughs at wider gulfs. Every incident comes back to me with the vividness and clearness of yesterday. I hear the echo of voices that have been silent these many years. Dead faces, some smiling and some looking fierce-haired, take dim shape in the corners of the room.

Beyond the open window, where birds are twittering in the overhanging ivy, an English landscape of meadow and woodland, hills and hamlets, rolls far in the sunshine of a June morning. It is the year 1846, in the reign of her gracious majesty, Queen Victoria. I close my eyes, and I am back in another world. I see the Great Lone Land—its rivers and lakes, its plains and peaks, its boundless leagues of wilderness stretching from sea to sea. I sniff the fragrant odors of snow-clad birch and pine, of marsh pools glimmering in the dying glow of a summer sun. I hear the splash of paddles and the glide of sledge-runners, the patter of flying moose and deer, and the scream of the hungry panther. I feel the weird, fascinating spell of the solitude and silence.

The Great Lone Land! Truly, to those who have known it, a name to conjure with! As it was then so it remains to-day, that vast, mysterious, romantic realm of the Canadas. The territory of the Hudson Bay Company, chartered remotely and by royal warrant when Charles II was king; the home of the Red Indian and the voyageur, the half-breed trapper and hunter, the gentlemen adventurers of England, Scotland and France; a land of death by Indian treachery and grizzlies, starvation and freezing, snowslides and rapids; a mighty wilderness, with canoes and sledges for the vehicles of travel and commerce, and forest trails joining the scattered trading posts.

There I, Denzil Carew, was born. There was my home from the cradle to manhood, and there my story lies. In that wild country I was nurtured and bred, schooled in the lore of the woods, taught to shoot and swim, to bear fatigue and to navigate dangerous waters. Nor did I grow up in ignorance of finer arts, for my father, Bertrand Carew, was an Englishman and a gentleman, and he took pains to give me the benefit of his own education and culture. Who his people were, or what had brought him out to the Canadas, were things he never told me.

My mother was the daughter of a company factor in charge of Fort Beaver. I do not remember her, for she died when I was a year old. At the factor's death my father succeeded to the post, and ten years later he was killed by a treacherous Indian. Fort Beaver was then abandoned, a new post having been recently built, seventy miles farther north. This was Fort Royal, on the Churchill River, one hundred miles south of Hudson's Bay, and I went there as assistant factor—I had already worn the company's uniform for three years.

At that time I was twenty years old—very tall, and built in proportion, with light hair and eyes, and a mustache in which I took some pride. I knew as much of the wilderness and the fur trade as any voyageur, and I had been twice to Quebec and other towns of Lower Canada.

I liked the life at Fort Royal, and I liked the factor, Griffith Hawke. We got on well together, and I performed my duties to his satisfaction. Thus five years passed way, and the closing of that uneventful period brings me to the opening proper of my story—to the mission that sent me five hundred miles down country in the dead of winter to Fort Garry, where the town of Winnipeg now stands, and thence more than a thousand miles eastward to Quebec. Concerning the purpose of the journey I shall speak later, but it was not a thing to my taste or experience.

Distinctly I recall that frosty morning of March in the year 1815. The picture of life and color, breaking on a scene of wintry grandeur and solitude, rises before my eyes. I see the frozen, snow-covered waste of the Lake of the Woods, the surrounding evergreen forests and towering hills, the low leaden sky overhead. Along the edge of the scrubby-timbered shore, five husky dogs come at a trot, harnessed in single file to a sledge. The dogs are short-legged and very hairy, with long snouts, sharp-pointed ears, and the tails of wolves; the sledge is a simple toboggan made of two pieces of birch nine feet in length, their ends turned high in front. Buckskin thongs hold the load in place, and at either side of this vehicle of the woods a brightly-clad figure on snowshoes glides swiftly.

Of the two men, one was myself, and the other was my half-breed servant Baptiste. I wore the winter uniform of the Hudson Bay

2

Company—a furred leather coat lined with flannel, a belt of scarlet worsted, breeches of smoked buckskin, moccasins of moose-hide, and blue cloth leggings. A fur cap was on my head, and a strip of Scotch plaid about my neck. Baptiste was dressed like all the company's voyageurs and hunters, in a blue capote, red flannel shirt, beaded corduroy trousers and fringed leggings, and a cap decked out with feathers. We each carried a musket and a hunting knife, a powder horn, and a bullet pouch.

Fort Garry, where we had stopped for a few days after a fortnight's steady travel from the Churchill River, was a week's journey behind us, and we were likely to be another month in the wilderness before we should reach Quebec. But we liked the wild life better than the turmoil of towns, Baptiste and I, and we were in no haste to have done with it. The strange thing that was taking me to Quebec would not be ripe for accomplishment until the coming of the tardy June spring of the Canadas, which was as yet eight or nine weeks off.

The weather was bitterly cold that March day, and we kept the dogs at such a pace that by noon we had covered a matter of twenty miles. Then, as we were speeding along the frozen river that leads from the Lake of the Woods to Lake Superior, we heard the report of a musket, followed by the cry of a human voice and the growl of a beast. Baptiste and I stopped and at a word the dogs stood still and barked with uplifted snouts. The sound had come from close by on our left, but now we heard only a faint and receding patter on the snow crust.

"*Nom de Dieu*, there are two running!" cried Baptiste. "It is a chase."

"And the dogs smell a bear," I replied. "I am off to the rescue, Baptiste. Do you wait here with the sledge, and if I shout for help, come quickly."

With that I turned and made into the forest, unslinging my musket as I ran. Fifty yards through scrub and timber brought me to a spot that bore the imprint of big claws and moccasined feet. Here were a few drops of blood on the snow, and the parts of a broken gun lying near. I had no need to follow the trail, for as I pushed on with great strides the noise of a struggle guided me straight.

It was but a short distance further. Breaking from the trees into a rugged hollow, I came upon a thrilling scene. An Indian had sought

3

refuge in a shallow crevice between two tall bowlders, and he was in sore peril of his life from a monstrous grizzly that was striving to tear him out. The bear—I had never seen a larger one—was dealing blow after blow with his heavy paws, and the redskin was making the best use of his knife that his cramped position would allow. The clamor of beast and man made a blood-curdling din.

I mastered the situation at a glance and vowed to save the Indian. I was as likely to hit him as the bear from where I stood, so I circled quickly around to one side. But the grizzly both heard and smelled me, and I had scarcely lifted my musket when he turned with a snarl of rage, and came at me. I aimed and fired. Bang!

It is difficult to kill a grizzly with a single shot, and as the smoke drifted aside I saw the brute advancing on hind legs. His eyes were like balls of fire, his open jaws dripped foam, and he roared horribly with pain and anger. Blood was trickling from a wound close to the heart, made by my bullet, and there was another bleeding hole in his neck.

I had no chance to reload, and there was barely time to flee. But my temper was up, and it drove me to a reckless determination. I stood my ground for an instant, while the grizzly shambled on, pawing viciously at the air. Then I drew my long-bladed knife, darted out of the way, and as swiftly turned and struck under the sheltered fore feet. It was a foolish trick, and my agility barely saved me from a crushing blow. As it was, I had to leave the knife sticking deep in the wound. But the thrust had gone straight to the heart, and I gave a yell of delight as the great beast came down with a crash. He lay quite still after a brief struggle that churned the snow crust to powder.

The bear was dead, and my first step was to withdraw the knife and wipe it clean. Then, having shouted to Baptiste, I approached the crevice just as the Indian crawled out. Too weak to rise, he propped himself against a rock. He was bleeding profusely from a dozen wounds. His shirt of buffalo skin, his breech-clout, his fringed leggings of antelope, all had been ripped to tatters by the grizzly's claws; his feathered scalp-lock was half torn from his head, and one shoulder was mangled.

I was full of pity at first, but my heart hardened when I recognized the savage. He was Gray Moose, a Sioux of much influence, and he and his people were said to be carrying on underhand dealings with the Northwest Company, which was the

4

great and dangerous rival of the Hudson Bay Company. We were known to each other, having met before on several occasions. Whether the above rumor was true or not, I was aware to a certainty that he held the Hudson Bay men in no favor; and I half regretted that I had saved his life.

"How came you in such straits?" I asked coldly.

He explained in a few words, and in fairly good English. The grizzly had come upon him unawares, and in his haste to fire he had inflicted only a slight wound. Then he fled, and took shelter in the rock cranny as a last resort.

"The red man is grateful to Pantherfoot," he concluded, addressing me by a name which my skill at tracking game had won for me among the Indians. "Gray Moose will not forget. Now let white man go his way."

But it was not in my nature to leave the poor wretch wounded and helpless, and I told him so. On questioning him, I learned that a village of his people was within a few miles, and I decided to take him there. By this time Baptiste had arrived with the team, and after dressing the Sioux's injuries as well as I could, I fixed him comfortably on the sledge, the half-breed and I shouldering the displaced part of the load.

On the way my servant had picked up the broken musket, and when Gray Moose saw that the weapon was beyond mending—the grizzly had shattered it by a terrific blow—such a look of misery came into his eyes as softened my heart at once. I knew the value an Indian set on his shooting-piece, and I gave him an extra gun which I chanced to have on the sledge.

Baptiste upbraided me for my folly, and, indeed, I repented the act the next moment; but the savage's gratitude was so sincere that I could not bring myself to take back the gift.

An hour's tramp—the direction was quite out of our way—brought us to the Sioux village. We left Gray Moose with his friends, and pushed on, refusing an invitation to spend the night. I attached no significance to the affair at the time, nor did I give it much thought afterward, but the future was destined to prove that my trivial deed of kindness was not wasted, and that even a bad Indian will remember a benefactor.

I need make no further mention of our journey through the wilderness to Quebec, where we arrived safely in a little less than four weeks. But at this point, for the better understanding of my narrative, I must set down a brief statement of the ugly and threatening situation in the Canadas at the period of which I write. Long before—during many years, in fact—the Hudson Bay Company had vainly tried to obtain from the English Parliament a confirmation of the charter granted them by Charles II. But Parliament refused to decide the matter in one way or the other, and on the strength of this a number of French and Scotch merchants of Upper Canada formed themselves into the Northwest Trading Company in 1783. They established posts here and there, and in 1804 they erected one on the very shore of Hudson's Bay.

Within the next few years their forts grew to outnumber those of the older company, being scattered about in Prince Rupert's Land, and even across the Rocky Mountains in British Columbia. Then, in 1812, the Hudson Bay Company made a bold move. Lord Selkirk, a prominent official of the company in London, sent out a large colony of Scotchmen who had been evicted from their homes in Sutherlandshire. He hoped thus to build up a stronghold and seat of government that would brook no rivalry. The colonists came and settled at Fort Garry, at the forks of the Red River; but matters grew worse instead of better. Each company claimed to be in the right, and was resolved to drive the other out of existence. During the next few years the men of the Northwest Company and of the Hudson Bay Company came to blows more than once, and finally, in October of 1814, the Northwest Company were ordered to remove from the territory within six months—a mandate which they treated with contempt and derision.

It was early in the following year, the reader will recall, that Baptiste and I left Fort Churchill for Lower Canada, and from what we had seen at and about Fort Garry when we stopped there, we were satisfied that serious trouble was brewing, and that it would break out when navigation opened in the spring. We knew that the Northwest Company were plotting to secure the aid of the Indians, and we were also aware that the feeling throughout Lower Canada—even among the government officials—was strongly in favor of the Hudson Bay Company's enemies.

Such being the situation, I was naturally anxious to get back to my post as soon as possible; for though I was not so hot-headed as to wish for war, I was ready to fight for the supremacy of the company I

6

served, and which my father had served before me. But I foresaw with distaste that I should probably be detained in Quebec until the summer months—since I was to await the arrival of a certain ship from England—and I entered that town with but a poor zest for my task.

CHAPTER II.   THE HOTEL IN BONAVENTURE STREET.

It was nine o'clock on a Monday evening in the fourth week of June, and I was sitting, as was my nightly custom, in the cozy coffee room of the modest hostelry where I had taken lodgings when I first came to Quebec. This was the Hotel Silver Lily, kept by Monsieur Jules Ragoul and madame, his wife. It was a quiet little place in Bonaventure Street, which was one of the oldest and narrowest thoroughfares of the lower town.

I was alone in the room, save for an elderly man who was sound asleep in a big chair on the far side of the table, remote from the candlelight. He had been there when I entered, and I could not recall having seen him before about the hotel; but of this I was not certain, since his face was in shadow and half-covered by his hat. In the adjoining bar, to judge from the clinking of glasses and bottles and the hum of conversation, Madame Ragoul was busy with a few customers. The evening was warm, and as I sat by the open window sucking at my long pipe, I could hear on the one side the occasional challenge of the sentries high up on the ramparts of the citadel. From the other direction came the boisterous voices of boatmen and sailors down by the quays of the St. Lawrence.

Two long months had passed since my arrival in Quebec. I was heartily tired of its noisy, brawling life, hungry for the solitude of my native wilderness. At first I had found much to see and enjoy, but the novelty soon wore off. I had but few acquaintances in the town, and none of them were to my fancy. I preferred the seclusion of the hotel, and the company of the honest little Frenchman and his wife. Not so with Baptiste. He had fallen in with a loose set of his own kind, and frequented the low taverns by the riverside. That very evening I had brought him home helplessly drunk, and seen him safely abed.

But before I go on, if you please, a word or two concerning the business that brought me to Quebec. I have spoken of Griffith Hawke, the factor of Fort Royal. He was a man of fifty-odd years, simple-hearted, absorbed in his duties, and with not a spark of romance or sentiment in his being. Would you believe that such a one could think of marriage? Yet it was even so! A wife he suddenly resolved to have, and he sent for one to the head office in London, as was a common custom in those days. Many a woman was sent out by the company to cheer the lonely lot of their employees.

To be brief, a correspondence was carried on for two years between Fort Royal and London—that meant but a couple of letters on either side—and the result of it was that I was now in Quebec to meet the bride of Griffith Hawke and escort her to her distant home.

She was due in the early summer, being a passenger on the ship Good Hope. I was to put her in care of Madame Ragoul, and we were both to sail for Hudson's Bay at the first opportunity in one of the company's vessels. The factor had not been able to leave his post for so long a time, and he had sent me on this errand with evident reluctance. He would meet us at Fort York, where there was a priest to perform the marriage ceremony.

As I said before, the task was not to my liking. Love was a word without meaning to me. I knew nothing of women, and had reached the age of twenty-five without giving a thought to the other sex. I was completely ignorant of the purport of the letters that had passed between Griffith Hawke and the head office, and as I never questioned him about particulars, he never vouchsafed me any. I naturally expected to meet a middle-aged dame who would make a suitable partner for the prosaic factor, and would adapt herself to the crude life and customs of the lonely trading post.

A mission of adventure and deadly peril would have been more to my taste, but this strange enterprise was put upon me in the capacity of a company's servant, and I was resolved to carry out my instructions to the best of my ability. I was pondering the matter as I sat in the hotel that June night, and reflecting, with some relief, that I should not be much longer detained in Quebec, for the Good Hope was expected in port at any day or hour.

Having finished my third pipe, I knocked the ashes out gently so as not to disturb my still sleeping companion. I rose to my feet, stifling a yawn, and just then a man entered the room from the bar, closing the door behind him. While he stood hesitating, I took in his appearance by a brief glance. He was tall, slim and wiry, with tawny yellow hair worn long, and thick, drooping mustache. His eyes were of a cold steel-blue, and his face, though very handsome, had something sinister and fierce about it. From his attire I judged him at once to be a polished man of the world, who had seen other lands than the Canadas. He wore a lace-trimmed coat of buff, breeches of the same material, top boots of tanned buckskin, and abroad felt hat of a claret color. For the rest, a sword dangled at his side, and a brace of

9

pistols peeped from his belt. He looked about fifty, and by his flushed countenance I saw that he was more or less under the influence of liquor.

I noticed all this even before the man drew closer. Then seeing me clearly in the light shed from the candles, he gave a sudden start. The color left his cheeks, and he stared at me with an unmistakable expression of bewildered surprise, of something like sharp fear and guilt. I never doubted that he mistook me for another person.

"Have we met before, sir?" I asked courteously.

The stranger laughed, and his agitation was gone.

"Pardon my rudeness," he replied. "I had a spasm of pain, to which I am subject at times, but it has passed off." He pointed to my blue capote with brass buttons—the summer uniform of the company. "You are a Hudson Bay man," he added, "and I am another. That is a bond of friendship between us; is it not so?"

His manner was so captivating that I forgot my first unfavorable impression of him; moreover, I felt flattered by the condescension of so fine a gentleman. I was easily induced to state my name and the position I held at Fort Royal.

"We shall meet again," he cried, "for I shall be in those parts ere the summer is over."

"Are you indeed in the company's service?" I asked. "You do not wear—"

"The uniform?" he interrupted, with a touch of hauteur. "No; my duties are not the same as yours. But I will be as frank as you have been—" He handed me a folded paper. "Read that," he said in a confidential tone, leaning over me and exhaling the fumes of wine.

I opened the document, and scanned it briefly. The writing showed, beyond a doubt, that my new acquaintance was in the secret service of the Hudson Bay Company, and that he stood high in favor of the governor himself. I was glad that he had revealed as much to me—a thing he would not have done but for his potations; for it had dawned on me a moment before that I had been indiscreet to unbosom myself so freely to a stranger, who, for aught I knew to the contrary, might be a spy or an agent of the Northwest Company. I handed the paper back to him, and he buttoned it tightly under his coat.

"Is that credential enough for you?" he asked.

"I am more than satisfied," I replied.

"Then permit me to introduce myself. I am Captain Myles Rudstone, at your service—ex-officer of Canadian Volunteers, formerly of London and Paris, and now serving under the same banner as yourself. In short, I am a man of the world."

"I judged as much, sir," said I.

"Your perception does you credit," he exclaimed.

"I see that you are a gentleman. And now let us drink together to celebrate our first meeting."

"With all my heart!" I replied cordially.

I expected that he would ring the bell for madame, but instead of that he strode around the table to the sleeping stranger in the chair, and clapped him heavily on the shoulder. The man was roused instantly, and as he sprang to his feet I saw that he was tall and middle aged. His face was shrewd and intelligent, clean-shaven, and slightly wrinkled. He wore a white neck-cloth, antiquated coat and breeches of rusty black, and gray stockings with silver buckles at the knee; a cluster of seals dangled from his watch chain, and his fingers were long and white.

"What the devil do you mean by striking me, sir?" he demanded angrily.

"I merely gave you a tap," Captain Rudstone replied coolly. "I wish you to join this gentleman and myself in a drink."

"I have no desire to drink."

"But I say you shall!"

"And I say I shall not. I am a man of peace, but by Heavens, sir, I will swallow no affront tamely."

"I believe you are a spy—an emissary of the Northwest Company," cried the captain; and I knew by his manner that he had really suspected the stranger from the first.

"Then you lie, sir!" declared the man in black. "Here is my card."

He tossed a slip of pasteboard on the table, and picking it up, I read the following:

"CHRISTOPHER BURLEY.

"For Parchmont and Tolliver, Solicitors,

"Lincoln's Inn, London."

I handed the card to Captain Rudstone, and he glanced at it disdainfully.

"A law clerk," he sneered. "But come, I will overlook your menial position. I am not too proud to clink glasses with you."

11

"The boot is on the other leg, sir," cried the man of law. "I pick my company, and I refuse to drink with a swashbuckler and a roysterer."

"You shall drink with me," roared the captain, drawing his blade, "or I will teach you civil manners with the point of this!"

I judged that it was time to interfere.

"Captain Rudstone, you are behaving unseemly," said I. "There is no cause for a quarrel. You will think better of it in the morning. I beg you to drop the matter. Let us retire to the next room and have our friendly drink."

I thought he would have run me through for my interference, so blackly did he glare at me; but the next instant he sheathed his sword and laughed.

"You are right," he said. "I have had a drop too much for the first time for months. I offer my apologies to the offended law. Come, Mr. Carew, I will take another cup to your good health."

As he spoke he approached the door, and as I followed him the law clerk stopped me by a touch on the shoulder.

"My thanks to you, young gentleman," he said. "I like your face, and I put no blame on you for what has occurred. A word with you, if I may. I see that you are in the service of the Hudson Bay Company."

"Yes," I assented.

"And do you know the Canadas?"

"As well as you know London," I replied.

His face brightened at that.

"I came over a month ago on important business," he went on, "and I have been lately in Montreal and Ottawa. Did you ever, in the course of your wanderings, hear of a certain Osmund Maiden? He landed in Quebec from England in the year 1787."

"I never heard the name, sir," I answered, after a moment's thought.

As I spoke I looked toward the door, and encountered the gaze of Captain Rudstone, who was standing in a listening attitude with his hand on the latch. I scarcely knew him. His cheeks were colorless, his lips were half-parted, and a sort of frozen horror was stamped on his features. Had he been seized by another spasm of pain, I wondered, or was there a deeper cause for his agitation?

"So you can give me no information?" said Christopher Burley, in a tone of disappointment.

12

"I know nothing of the man you seek," I answered.

Just then the door was flung open, and Jules Ragoul burst excitedly into the room.

"*Bonne nouvelles!*" he cried. "News, Monsieur Carew! Good news! The Good Hope is in the river, and she will land her passengers early to-morrow!"

All else was forgotten, and I eagerly questioned the little Frenchman. When I was done with him I looked about for Captain Rudstone and the law clerk. Both had vanished, and I saw them no more that night.

CHAPTER III.   FLORA HATHERTON.

The next morning, at the hour of seven, I might have been found on the landing-quay by the river. The Good Hope, I was informed, still lay a short distance below the town, where for some reason she had anchored during the night. It was unlikely that I should be kept waiting long, yet I was in no haste to play the unaccustomed role of gallant. To conceal my nervousness I tried to affect an air of jaunty composure. I repeated over and over the words of greeting that I had chosen for the occasion.

It was as fine a day as ever dawned on Quebec. A crisp, cool air blew from the St. Lawrence, ruffling the water into little tips of foam. From a blue and cloudless sky the rising sun shone on the scattered shipping, on the green hills and islands, on the rugged and historical heights of the town. Many others besides myself were on the quay, doubtless drawn hither for the same purpose—priests, soldiers, soberly-clad citizens, several coureurs-de-bois, and a redskin or two. I had a distant view of Christopher Burley, and closer at hand I saw Captain Myles Rudstone in conversation with a group of men. By-and-by he discovered me, and strolling forward he gave me a pleasant word of greeting.

"It is quite an event, the arrival of a ship from England," said I.

"An event of importance," the captain replied. "But for the early hour the quay would be crowded."

His manner was reserved and dignified, and I liked him better in this mood. Yet I observed that his face wore a puzzled and uneasy expression as he glanced at me, and that he seemed disinclined to look me straight in the eyes. He ignored the events of the previous night, neither making any reference to them nor offering the slightest apology. He chatted indifferently for a moment or two, and then asked abruptly:

"You are waiting for the Good Hope, Mr. Carew?"

I nodded assent.

"Expecting a friend, perhaps?" he went on, carelessly; and I detected a masked note of curiosity in his voice. It put me on my guard.

"Not exactly a friend," I replied evasively. "I am to meet a person whom I have never seen."

"A strange coincidence, indeed!" said the captain, with a laugh. "That is precisely my situation." He bent his head a little closer. "I am on duty this morning," he added. "Secret work for the company, you understand."

If he hoped by this confidence to draw my own in return he was disappointed, though there was in truth no reason why I should not speak freely; but it pleased me to be as mysterious as himself, so I answered him by nodding my head wisely. Our eyes met, and he hastily turned and looked out on the river.

"The ship is coming!" he exclaimed; and with that he bowed curtly and strode away. He was soon lost to view in the crowd.

I gave him no further thought at the time. For a few moments I was all in a flutter, and half-minded to take to my heels like a foolish boy. But for very shame I presently plucked up courage and sought a point of vantage at the edge of the quay.

Now the people were cheering loudly, and joyous hails floated shoreward over the water. Nobly the Good Hope came in, her bulwarks and poop-deck crowded with figures, the breeze bellying her canvas and fluttering the flag of England at the masthead. I was fairly carried away by the novel excitement, and I only came to my sober senses when the vessel was at last moored alongside the quay and the gangway rattled down almost at my feet.

I stuck to my place in spite of pressure and crowding. The first to come ashore were all men—English merchants, returning Canadians, a couple of uniformed officers, Frenchmen decked out in lace and fine clothing, and a motley sprinkling of others. They passed on, some being met and embraced by waiting friends; and next came an elderly, sour-looking dame, who regarded me with ill-favor. I followed her a few paces beyond the crowd, never doubting that I was right. Then I stepped boldly up to her and doffed my cap.

"Do I address Miss Hatherton?" I began.

"No!" she snapped. "Wretch, how dare you?"

I fell back in confusion, with a titter of mocking laughter ringing in my ears. I longed to hide my face, and I vowed that I would make no more rash ventures. I was about to stride away when a hand touched me on the shoulder, and a sweet voice asked:

"Pardon me, sir, but did I hear you inquire for Miss Hatherton?"

I turned round quickly, and what I saw brought my heart to my mouth and the hot blood to my cheeks and temples. Before me stood a young girl of no more than nineteen, slight and graceful of figure, with eyes of a purple hue, a complexion like a ripe peach, and little

15

curls of brown hair straying from under her dainty bonnet. By her fine clothing and her clear-cut features I knew that her station in life was of the best. I, who had given no second thought to a woman in all my life, felt a thrill of admiration. I stared at this fair creature as though she had been a goddess, for I had never seen anything so lovely before. For a moment I was speechless, and the girl repeated the question with some spirit, accompanying it by a tap of the little foot.

"I—I did ask for Miss Hatherton," I stammered, "but surely you are not—"

"I am Flora Hatherton," she interrupted; and as she spoke she made a sudden and strange sign that puzzled me. "Who sent you to meet me, sir?" she added impatiently.

Again I was at a loss for words. A great pity and resentment swelled up in my heart. I still hoped that there might be a mistake somewhere. I shrank from picturing this young and beautiful girl as the wife of old Griffith Hawke, sharing with him the uncouth and half-barbarous life of a wilderness trading post. It was too cruel for belief!

"Who sent you, stupid?" she repeated.

"Are you truly Miss Hatherton?" I asked.

"Of course I am!"

"Then I am at your service," said I, "and I am here to meet you in behalf of the factor of Fort Royal."

Her eyes dropped and her face saddened.

"Oh," she exclaimed, "I thought you might be—"

But before she could finish the sentence a tall figure was thrust impetuously between us, and I looked up to recognize Captain Rudstone. He paid no heed to my presence, but made a swift sign to the girl. She answered it as quickly, and then said, with a smile:

"You are Captain Rudstone?"

"The same, mademoiselle," he replied, with a courteous bow.

They moved a few paces to one side, and began to talk in low tones. I hung back in confusion and anger, feeling bitterly the slight that had been put upon me, and quite at a loss to know what the affair meant. I overheard the words "Lord Selkirk" and "dispatches," and then I saw the girl draw the end of a sealed packet of papers from her bosom; but she thrust them out of sight again at a sharp command from Captain Rudstone. The latter looked round just then, and I could have sworn that he sneered contemptuously when he met my glance.

16

My temper was ruffled by the neglect and the sneer, and I stepped forward.

"Will Miss Hatherton permit me to escort her to the lodgings where she is expected?" I asked the girl.

"My claim to this young lady's attention is prior to yours, sir," broke in Captain Rudstone.

"I deny that, sir!" I cried hotly. "Will you be so kind as to state your claim?"

"My word is enough. Be careful lest you provoke me further, Mr. Carew."

"I beseech you not to quarrel on my account, sirs," exclaimed Miss Hatherton. "You are both right."

The captain scowled at me.

"Which of us is to have precedence, mademoiselle?" he asked curtly.

But before the girl could answer an abrupt and unexpected interruption fell upon us.

CHAPTER IV.   MUTUAL EXPLANATIONS.

From a distance a man had been watching us steadily—I had observed him before—and now he came quickly and with an air of bravado to where we stood. He was about my own age, but a little shorter and slighter, clean-shaven, with dark eyes and thick, black hair. Though handsome in a way, the stamp of an evil and unscrupulous nature was on his bronzed features. His dress was that of a gentleman.

"Can I be of any service to you, Miss Hatherton?" the fellow began, darting an impertinent glance at the captain and myself.

The girl shrank from him with aversion in her eyes.

"I need no assistance," she replied. "And I thought we had spoken the last word on the ship, Mr. Mackenzie."

"I was no party to that agreement, you will remember," the man answered, looking at her with fierce admiration. "I have been searching for you, and when I caught sight of you but a moment ago, I judged that these gentlemen were paying you unwelcome attentions. Certainly they were on the point of an altercation."

I looked to Captain Rudstone to take the matter up, but to my amazement he bowed and walked away, whispering at my ear as he passed me:

"Be prudent. I will join you at the Silver Lily."

To put his desertion down to cowardice was the only construction open.

I held my ground, wondering what strange thing would happen next. The dark man eyed me insolently for a moment, evidently expecting and hoping that I would follow my companion. Then he bent closer to Miss Hatherton.

"Why will you persist in this folly?" he asked. "You are alone in a strange land—in a strange town. I urge you to accept the shelter of my sister's house. It is but a short distance from here."

"And I refuse!" the girl cried indignantly. "I wish no further speech with you, Mr. Mackenzie. I am not friendless, as you think. I am going with this gentleman."

"It's a devilish bad choice!" the man exclaimed angrily.

"What do you mean by that?" I cried, ruffling up.

"Miss Hatherton, I beg you to listen to me," he went on, ignoring my demand. "It is for your own good—"

18

"Not another word, sir," she interrupted, edging nervously toward me as she spoke.

"You shall hear me!" he insisted; and with that he caught her brutally by one arm.

The girl struggled in his grasp and gazed at me with such mute and earnest pleading, with such fear and distress in her lovely eyes, that I must have been more than human to resist taking her part. I was in a hot rage, as it was, and I did not hesitate an instant. I shot out with my right arm—a straight, hard blow from the shoulder that took the ruffian between the eyes. He reeled and fell like a log.

The deed was no sooner done than I regretted—for Miss Hatherton's sake—that I had gone to such extremities. But I made the best of it by quickly leading the girl away, and she clung tightly to my arm as we hurried through the curious group of people on the quay. To my relief, no one stopped us, and indeed the incident had attracted little attention. Looking back, I saw that Mr. Mackenzie was on his feet, the center of a small crowd who were bent on preventing him from following us.

It was not long before we were off the quay, and in the shelter of the quiet streets of the town. By a few words Miss Hatherton gave me to understand that she was aware of the arrangements made for her, and that the trunk was to be sent to the Silver Lily. Then she looked into my face with a sad and grateful smile that set my heart to fluttering.

"I am glad to have found such a friend and protector," she said. "You have done me a great service, and one that I will not forget, Mr. Carew—I think that is your name. But I fear you have not seen the last of Mr. Mackenzie."

"He will be wise to let the affair drop," I replied. "I count it an honor and a pleasure, Miss Hatherton, that I had the opportunity of helping you. If the man seeks satisfaction, he shall have it."

She glanced at me with some surprise, and with a tinge of amusement, I fancied.

"Are you a Canadian?" she asked.

"A native-born child of My Lady of the Snows," said I.

"And you have never been in England?"

"No nearer than Quebec," I answered.

"I should not have believed it," she replied. Then, after a pause: "I met Cuthbert Mackenzie on board the Good Hope. He sailed with

19

me from London, and from the first I disliked him. He constantly forced his attentions upon me, though he saw that they were hateful to me; and when I refused to have anything to do with him, he even went so far as to threaten. I hope I have seen the last of him."

"He shall not annoy you again," said I.

She was silent for a moment.

"Shall we find Captain Rudstone at the hotel?" she asked.

"I believe so," I answered, hiding my annoyance at the question. "He made an abrupt departure, Miss Hatherton."

"Perhaps he had good reasons," she replied; and with that the matter dropped.

The rest of the distance was all too short for me. It was a novel thing that I, who had scarce spoken ten words to a woman before in my life, should be playing the gallant to as pretty a girl as could be found in Quebec. But she had put me quite at my ease, and mightily proud I felt when I gave her into the care of Madame Ragoul, though the thought that she was the promised bride of old Griffith Hawke seemed to bring a lump to my throat. I bade her good-by for the present in the upper hall of the house, and going downstairs, I sauntered into the room behind the bar. There sat Captain Rudstone, a glass of wine before him.

"You have just come?" said I.

"But a moment ago," he answered coldly, and with a sour look. "What is the meaning of this strange affair, Mr. Carew?"

"I had to knock the impertinent rascal down," I replied.

"I do not refer to that," said he, with a grim smile. "I witnessed the whole trouble."

"From a distance?" I ventured.

His eyes flashed.

"Have a care," he muttered. "I am not in a trifling mood. Tell me, what took you to the quay this morning to meet Miss Hatherton?"

"I might ask you the same question," I replied.

"Will you answer me, sir?"

"There is no reason why I should not," said I. "Miss Hatherton was sent over to become the wife of the factor of Fort Royal. I met her in accordance with my instructions, and we are to take the first ship that sails for Hudson's Bay."

Captain Rudstone's hard expression softened; he looked astonished and relieved.

20

"I am glad the matter is cleared up," he said. "It is plainly a case of killing two birds with one stone. I will be equally frank, Mr. Carew. I was directed by the governor of the company to await the arrival of the Good Hope, and to receive from Miss Hatherton a packet of important dispatches secretly intrusted to her in London by Lord Selkirk."

It was my turn to be amazed. I saw that each of us had suspected the other without cause.

"I also sail on the first ship for the Bay," the captain went on. "I am charged with the duty of delivering Lord Selkirk's letters of instructions to the northern forts. This is a serious matter, Mr. Carew. There is trouble brewing, and it may break out at any time. So the head office is zealously preparing for it. By the bye, do you know who this Mr. Mackenzie is?"

I shook my head.

"He is an official and a spy of the Northwest Company," said Captain Rudstone, "and he has been in London working for the interests of his people. I was aware of this when he approached us on the quay, and I hurried away so that he might be the less suspicious as to my dealings with the young lady."

"I did you an injustice," said I. What I had just heard caused me much uneasiness, and I foresaw possible unpleasant complications.

"It was a natural mistake," replied Captain Rudstone. "I overlook it. But speaking of Mackenzie—the letters would be of the utmost value to him if he could get hold of them. I don't believe he suspected the girl during the voyage, or he would have robbed her; but I am afraid he saw her withdraw the packet from her bosom. I made her put it back at once."

"He was standing near us on the quay for some time," said I, "does he know who you are?"

"It is quite likely! Hang it all, Mr. Carew, I don't like the look of things! I'm going to do a little spying about the town on my own account; but, first it is important that I should see Miss Hatherton."

I did not relish the idea of disturbing the girl so soon after her arrival, and I was about to say as much. But just then appeared Madame Ragoul with a request that my companion would accord an interview to Miss Hatherton. He departed with alacrity, and I took it with an ill grace that I should be left out of the matter. I waited for a long time, seeking consolation in the thought that I alone would be the girl's protector in future, and at length Captain Rudstone returned.

"I have the dispatches," he announced, tapping his breast.

"You were an hour about it," said I petulantly.

"Oh, ho!" he laughed; "so the wind blows from that quarter! But I am no lady's man, Mr. Carew. And Miss Hatherton is not for either of us, rare beauty though she is—ay, and a girl of pluck and spirit. She is bound by a sacred promise—a promise to the dead—to marry that old fossil, Griffith Hawke. I knew him seven years ago. A fine husband indeed for such a maid!"

The captain's foolish insinuation angered me, and I felt myself blushing furiously, but I said nothing.

"It is a sad story," he went on. "I persuaded the girl to give me her confidence. It seems that her father, a gentleman of good family, was a friend of Lord Selkirk. Some months ago he lost every shilling he had in the world through unwise speculation, and the shock killed him. On his deathbed he sent for Selkirk, and begged him to care for his daughter, who would be left quite alone in the world. The old rascal persuaded the father that the girl could not do better than go out to the Canadas and marry the factor of Fort Royal—he had received Hawke's application for a wife at about this time. The result was that Flora yielded and consented—I daresay there was no way out of it— and Selkirk took advantage of the opportunity to send these important letters with her; he knew she was the last person that would be suspected of having them. This much may be put in Selkirk's favor: he visited Canada some years ago, and took a fancy to Hawke."

"The factor is a gentleman born," said I, "but he is past fifty. And think of the life! It is a sad pity for the girl."

"She knows what is before her," replied the captain, "and she seems to be resigned. To tell the truth, though, I half-believe there is something at the back of it all—that some deeper cause drove her out here. Nothing to her discredit, I mean."

"What makes you think so?" I asked.

"A chance remark that she let fall," he answered.

I would have questioned Captain Rudstone more closely, but just then he drained his glass and rose with an air of sudden determination.

"I have work to do," he said gravely, as he put on his hat. "I must keep track of Cuthbert Mackenzie. Miss Hatherton knew nothing of his real character, and I am satisfied that he knew as little of her while

22

they were at sea. But what he may have learned since landing is a different matter. I will come back here this evening, and meanwhile I would advise you to remain in the hotel. There is a ship sailing for the Bay in a week as you probably know, and I shall be heartily glad when we are at sea. Cuthbert Mackenzie is a serpent that stings in the dark."

He bade me good morning and was gone.

CHAPTER V.   THE ALARM IN THE NIGHT.

It was about eleven o'clock of the forenoon when Captain Rudstone departed. I smoked a quiet pipe, and then sought out Baptiste; he had a little box of a room over the hotel kitchen. I found the rascal but half-sobered, so heavily had he liquored on the previous night, and I angrily bade him stay in bed for the rest of the day. Miss Hatherton did not come down to dinner, and I had for company in the coffee room Mr. Christopher Burley; there were no other guests in the house at the time.

Neither of us was in a talkative mood, and very brief speech passed between us. But shortly after the meal I met him again at the bar, where he was paying his account. He looked ready for a journey, having his hat on and a portmanteau in his hand.

"You are leaving, sir?" I asked politely.

"I return to Montreal to-day," he replied, "and later I go West. You, I believe, are bound shortly for the North?"

I nodded assent.

"We may meet in the future," he went on; "and meanwhile I trust you will remember that name—Osmund Maiden."

"I will bear it in mind," I promised, "and I wish you every success in your errand."

With that we parted, the law clerk thanking me warmly and giving me his hand. That I should ever see him again, or run across the man of whom he was in search, were things so utterly improbable that I gave them no second thought. But I was to learn in later days how small a place the world really was.

I spent the afternoon in the hotel, for I was satisfied that Captain Rudstone's caution against venturing in the streets was not to be despised. He had gone up several degrees in my estimation since the little cloud of mutual suspicion had cleared away. I did not doubt that he was as zealous for the interests of the company as myself, and, moreover, I felt that he would prove a trusty friend should Mr. Cuthbert Mackenzie try to give me any trouble. That the captain was to sail on the same ship to the Bay was a matter less to my liking, though I hardly knew why. He was of a type that a youngster like myself usually looks up to, and he had flattered me by giving me his full confidence: but he never seemed quite at ease in my presence, or inclined to stare me straight in the eyes, which I could not account for.

The time passed listlessly. I chatted for awhile with Monsieur Ragoul, and watched the customers who came in to drink. I could not put Miss Hatherton out of my mind. As often as I remembered that she was to share the long sea voyage with me, the joy of it was marred by the picture of old Griffith Hawke waiting at Fort York for his bride. I was angry at myself for taking the thing so much to heart—uneasy because a woman could thus interest me.

I had hoped to see her that afternoon, but she did not make her appearance until the late supper-time. We sat down to table together, and it gave me a strange thrill to see her sitting opposite. She looked more lovely than ever without her bonnet, and in a black gown relieved by some touches of creamy lace. I fear I stared at her stupidly, and was dull of conversation; but she chatted freely of the wonderful things to be seen in London, and I was sorry when the meal was over. Miss Hatherton then offered me a dainty hand and bade me good-night, saying that she had not been able to sleep all day, and intended to retire early.

I finished my bottle of wine, and went upstairs to my room on the third and top floor of the hotel—a meager little hole where I, used to a blanket and fir boughs, had always felt cramped and stifled. But now I wished to be alone, and for some hours I sat there without a light, smoking and thinking. A distant clock had just pealed eleven when I heard the unbolting of a door downstairs—the house had been closed for the night. A little later, after the stir and sound of voices had died away, light footsteps fell on my ear, and there was a rap at the door. I hurriedly lit a candle.

"Come in!" I cried, thinking I knew what it meant.

Captain Rudstone entered, closing the door softly behind him. With a nod he threw himself into a chair, helped himself to a pipeful of my tobacco, and looked inscrutably at me through a cloud of smoke.

"So you are still up?" he began. "I expected to find you in bed. Have you been away from the hotel?"

"Not outside of the door," I replied.

"I have left my old lodging," he went on, "and Monsieur Ragoul has given me a room next to yours."

"I rejoice to hear it," I said politely. "And have you learned anything to-day?"

"Mr. Mackenzie will demand satisfaction for that blow," the captain answered coolly.

"He shall have it," said I.

"He is a skilled swordsman and a deadly shot, Mr. Carew."

"I will meet him with either weapon," I declared hotly.

"There must be no fighting, if it can be avoided," replied the captain.

"That is a matter which rests with me," said I. "But how do you know all this?"

"I put a man on the track," was the reply. "He overheard Mackenzie talking with two boon companions who are as deep in the plotting of the Northwest Company as himself. Unfortunately, he learned no more than I have told you, and he lost the trail at an early hour this evening in the upper town."

"I shall depend on you to see me through the affair," said I.

"I fear there is mischief brewing in another quarter," the captain replied. "To be frank, Mr. Carew, you and I, and Miss Hatherton are in a decidedly unpleasant situation. Or, to leave the girl out of it, you and I must decide a very delicate question. Shall we stand by our honor, or shall we choose the best interests of the company we serve?"

"Make your meaning plainer," said I. "As yet I am in the dark."

"The point is this," the captain answered gravely. "If we wait for the company's ship, which sails in a week, serious things may happen—not to speak of the duel. I happen to know that a trading-vessel leaves the river to-morrow morning for the Bay. The captain is a friend of mine, and he will give the three of us a passage."

"This is the last proposition I should have looked for from you, Captain Rudstone," I replied indignantly. "Would you have me slink away like a thief in the night, giving Cuthbert Mackenzie the pleasure of branding me far and wide as a coward? It is not to be thought of, sir."

The captain shrugged his shoulders, and meditatively blew a cloud of smoke ceilingward.

"I admire your spirit," he said, "but not your discretion. Am I to understand, then, Mr. Carew, that you choose honor before duty?"

I looked at him speechlessly. He had a cutting way of putting things, and it dawned on me that there was indeed two sides to the question. But before I could find words to reply, the silence of the

26

June night was broken by a shrill scream directly below us. It was followed by a cry for help, and I was sure I recognized Miss Hatherton's voice.

With one impulse Captain Rudstone and I drew our pistols and sprang to our feet. In a trice we were out in the hall, and plunging recklessly down the stairs. We heard distant calls of alarm from the lower part of the house, and a woman's voice, ringing loudly and close at hand, guided us to Miss Hatherton's room. Captain Rudstone burst the door from its fastenings by a single effort, and I followed him over the threshold. The moon was shining through an open window, and by its pale light the girl darted toward us, her snowy night dress trailing behind her, and her disheveled hair flowing about her shoulders.

"Save me!" she cried hysterically. "Save me from Cuthbert Mackenzie!"

CHAPTER VI.   PREPARATIONS FOR FLIGHT.

When I heard Mackenzie's name pronounced by those fair lips and realized that the scoundrel had dared to force his way to Miss Hatherton's bedchamber, I was put in such a rage as I had never known before. I did not wait for further information, but, brushing past the girl, I leaped through the open window. There was a narrow balcony beyond it—as I knew—which ran along the side of the house, and looked down on a paved courtyard overshadowed by an adjoining building.

Being familiar with the hotel, I was at no loss to account for the means by which the villain had entered and fled. I dashed at once to the end of the balcony, which was within easy reach of the limbs of a tree that grew up from the court. As I peered down from the shadows, I heard a rustling noise, and the next instant I saw a man at the base of the tree; it must have taken him all this time to descend the trunk. I was sure that I recognized Mackenzie, and as he made off I took aim with my pistol and fired. A sharp cry and an oath followed the report, but the fellow sped on to the end of the court, where a passage led out to a back street. Here a voice hailed him; showing that one or more had shared his enterprise.

But a moment had passed since I leaped out of the window, and now I found Captain Rudstone at my side.

"Did you hit him?" he demanded.

"I think so," I replied; "but he ran like a deer."

"He'll not run far if I can get sight of him. To take the scoundrel will be a good card in our hands!"

With that the captain swung himself into the tree, and went down hand over hand, from limb to limb, with the agility of a cat. He was on the ground before I could have counted ten.

"Do not follow me," he called up, and then he vanished in the shadows across the court.

I would have preferred to take a part in the chase, but I swallowed my disappointment and returned along the balcony. The pistol-shot had raised some clamor in the neighborhood. I could hear men shouting, and several lights were moving in the opposite house. I climbed through the window into the room, where I found Monsieur and Madame Ragoul and their three servants all in a state of excitement. Miss Hatherton had by this time put on a dressing-gown

28

and slippers, and seemed to have entirely recovered from her fright. She blushed prettily as she saw me.

"You have not killed him. Mr. Carew?" she asked.

"I fear not," I replied; "but Captain Rudstone hopes to take him."

"It will be a shame if he escapes," cried Madame Ragoul. "Oh, the pig—the wicked robber! He might have strangled the pretty English mademoiselle!"

The servants were rolling their eyes and shivering with fear, and Monsieur Ragoul was dancing about, with his red nightcap hanging to one ear.

"I am ruined!" he wailed. "The good name of my house is gone! Never—never did such a thing happen before! The officers of the law will enter—they will demand why a pistol is fired to waken the quarter!"

"Coward, be quiet!" snapped his wife. "The affair is no fault of ours."

I judged it was time to interfere. The distant clamor had not perceptibly increased, and I saw some chance of keeping the matter a secret, which was a thing greatly to be desired.

"Monsieur Ragoul, I think there need be no publicity," said I. "Will you be so good as to close the window and draw the curtains, and also put out that candle you are holding?"

He obeyed me promptly, and just as the room was darkened Baptiste made a tardy appearance. I explained the situation to him in a few words, and then I turned to Miss Hatherton.

"I trust you are none the worse," I said. "I deeply regret that you should have suffered such an outrage—"

"And I am sorry to have put you to so much trouble on my account," she interrupted. "This is twice you have come to my help at a time of need."

"Then I am twice honored," I replied. "But, tell me, was the scoundrel indeed Mr. Mackenzie?"

"I am sure of it, Mr. Carew. I woke suddenly, and saw him standing in the moonlight at the foot of my bed. When I screamed the second time he vanished through the window. It was the shock that unnerved me. I beg you to believe that I am not ordinarily a coward."

"The adventure would have terrified the bravest of women," I answered. Bending to her ear, I added, in a whisper: "As for Mr. Mackenzie, I take it he was seeking the dispatches?"

"Yes, he doubtless thought I still had them," Miss Hatherton replied. "I am afraid he will pay dearly for his folly if Captain Rudstone overtakes him."

Even as she spoke a startling thing happened. In the silence of the room we all heard the faint report of a pistol. The sound came from some distance away, and in the direction of the upper town.

"That was the captain's shot," I declared.

"Or Mr. Mackenzie's," the girl suggested, in a tone of alarm.

"The saints save us!" cried Monsieur Ragoul. "This is worse and worse!"

I was for going out to investigate, but Miss Hatherton would have it that such a step meant danger, and I yielded reluctantly to her pleadings. However, I persuaded the little Frenchman to let me into the courtyard, by which way I knew the captain would return if he was able. We went downstairs, accompanied by Baptiste, and Monsieur Ragoul unbarred and opened the side door.

When I stepped into the court I was relieved to discover that the immediate neighborhood was comparatively quiet. But at a distance, in the direction whence the shot had come, a confused clamor was audible. I had been listening no more than a minute when I heard footsteps, and across the moonlit court came Captain Rudstone. My heart leaped for joy at the sight of him. Without a word he motioned us into the house, and closed and fastened the door. Then I knew that he had bad news.

"Monsieur Ragoul," he said, "will you go and tell Miss Hatherton to dress at once and to put in a parcel as many of her belongings as she can carry in one hand. Be quick!"

The Frenchman dared not ask any questions. He departed in a state of alarm and mystery, and Baptiste and I were left alone with the captain. The latter rested a hand on my shoulder.

"Mr. Carew," he said gravely, "you remember the question I put to you an hour ago? You have no longer any choice in the matter; we must leave Quebec at once—within a few minutes. That is, if we can."

"What do you mean?" I asked hoarsely. "What has happened?"

"Much," he replied. "In the first place, you wounded Mr. Mackenzie in the right arm. In the second place, I followed the ruffians for a quarter of a mile—there were two of them—and finally came up with them at a lonely spot. I tried to take them both, but they

30

resisted fiercely. To save my own life I shot and killed Mackenzie's companion, a Northwest man named Tredennis. Mackenzie fled, raising the alarm as he ran, and by a detour I got back to the hotel unobserved."

"There is likely to be trouble over the affair," said I; and indeed I felt more alarm than I put into my voice.

"Trouble?" cried the captain, with some irritation. "By Heavens, Mr. Carew, it's as black an outlook as I ever faced! Mackenzie knows his power, and he will hatch up a devil of a lie. In Quebec feeling runs high against the Hudson Bay people, and the authorities openly favor the Northwest Company. I tell you there will be warrants out for our arrest within the hour—perhaps in less time. And you must perceive what the result will be if we are taken. Lord Selkirk's dispatches will fall into the hands of our enemies; you and I will be thrown into prison. And God only knows what will become of Miss Hatherton!"

I felt a sensation as of a hand clutching at my heart. I knew that the situation was as dismal as Captain Rudstone had painted it—that we could not expect fair dealing from the authorities of Quebec. And the thought of the girl's peril, if she should be left to the wiles of Cuthbert Mackenzie, put me in a mind to accept any opportunity of escape that offered.

"What is your plan?" I asked.

"The Yankee ship Speedwell sails for the Bay in the morning," the captain replied. "She lies anchored a short distance down the river, and we must get on board as soon as possible. I have known her master, Hiram Bunker, of Salem, for several years."

I made no objection to the arrangement. Baptiste had been listening, and a few sentences put everything clear. He was trusty and I saw a way to utilize him.

"Off with you to the river—to the landing at the foot of Bonaventure Street," I directed. "There are plenty of boats about. Get possession of one, and wait for us."

Captain Rudstone warmly approved this step. We let Baptiste into the court, locked the door, and hurried upstairs. In the hall we encountered Miss Hatherton, fully dressed and carrying a small bundle. The brave girl had promptly obeyed instructions, though ignorant of what they meant. When we explained our purpose she showed an admirable pluck and spirit, putting herself entirely in our hands, and urging us to be off without delay. Monsieur Ragoul

31

seemed disposed to give us some trouble at first, but that blew over when we presented him with a few gold pieces, and pointed out to him that our departure was for his own good. Our destination, of course, we did not reveal.

In ten minutes more we were ready to start. My musket was strapped to my back, and the captain and I had each a bundle containing a change of clothes. We came quietly down the dark stairs, monsieur and madame leading the way, and the servants bringing up the rear—traversing the hall, we turned toward the side exit. And just then, on the front door of the hotel we heard a loud and sudden thumping.

CHAPTER VII.   THE SKIPPER OF THE SPEEDWELL.

The alarm took us by surprise, for we had expected to get the start on our enemies by at least half an hour. That the officers of the law were at the door none of us doubted. We stood still where we were, and in a whisper the captain admonished us to be quiet. There was a brief silence, and then the rapping began again.

"What am I to do?" whispered Monsieur Ragoul, and so loudly that his wife promptly clapped a hand over his mouth.

"They have come to seize us," said I, in a low voice. "I fear we are in a trap, with no choice but to yield or fight."

"Resistance would be folly," Captain Rudstone replied quickly, "and for Miss Hatherton's sake we must not be taken. There is a chance for us yet—it is possible that the back way of the house has been left unguarded."

"Then let us be off at once," I urged, taking courage from his suggestions.

As I spoke, a lull came in the pounding, and a voice cried loudly, "Open! Open!"

Monsieur Ragoul was fairly beside himself with terror and the servants were as helpless as himself; so the captain and I had to act for ourselves, and that without the loss of another second. We found the side door, opened it, and closed it softly behind us when we stepped into the court. The pounding at the front of the house had started afresh, and there was a clamor off in the distance; but so far as we could see by the moonlight this rear avenue of escape was open.

The captain led the way forward, and I followed with Miss Hatherton at my side; her hand rested on my arm, and I could not detect the slightest tremor in her touch. We glided swiftly across the court, and entered a narrow passage leading to the street beyond. We were just at the end of it when a man appeared abruptly from one side and barred the way.

"Not so fast!" he exclaimed, with a movement to draw a weapon. "Stop, in the name of—"

The fellow got no further, for quickly the captain had him pinned by the throat. The two fell after a brief scuffle, and I heard somebody's head give the stone an ugly rap. The captain jumped to his feet, but the other man lay motionless and quiet.

"Is he dead?" Miss Hatherton asked, in a horrified whisper.

I bent over the fellow, and recognized him as one of the town watch.

"He is only stunned," I replied, "but he got a bad fall, and won't know anything for a couple of hours."

Meanwhile Captain Rudstone had ventured out of the passage to reconnoiter, and he called to us sharply to join him. We did so, and were relieved to find that the street was dark and empty.

"I feared the man would have companions with him," said I. "It seems he came round here alone."

"Yes, luckily for us," the captain replied. "There will be a pretty row before long; that scoundrel Mackenzie has wasted no time in showing his hand. But I think we are fairly safe, and if the skipper of the Speedwell is open to reason we shall be going down the river under full sail within the hour."

"I hope so, indeed," I replied. "You say the man is a friend of yours?"

"He owes me more than one service, Mr. Carew, but enough of speech! Do you and Miss Hatherton follow me closely, and avoid any appearance of alarm or haste."

We had already crossed the street that lay in the rear of the Silver Lily, and entered one at right angles to it. There was a great deal of noise behind us, and for this reason there was the more danger to be apprehended from the front, since the alarm had roused some of the inhabitants of the quarter from their beds. Here and there men passed us with sharp glances, and curious faces stared down at us from open windows. But none stopped us, so boldly and with such unconcern did we comport ourselves, and after treading a maze of the straggling and dirty little thoroughfares, we came out on Bonaventure Street at a point close to the river.

And now we made a discovery that was very discomforting. Looking up in the direction of the hotel, we could see vaguely-moving figures, and there was a sound of shouting and running that swelled louder on the air.

"Our escape has been discovered," said I.

"Without a doubt," replied Captain Rudstone; "and what is worse, the chase is coming this way. Some persons whom we met have given information. But the river is close at hand, and our pursuers have barely started from the Silver Lily."

"Will we escape them?" Miss Hatherton inquired anxiously.

34

"Assuredly," said I, in spite of a lurking doubt. "Keep up your courage. We are almost within reach of safety."

We quickened our pace—this end of the street was deserted—and fifty yards more brought us to the water's edge. The captain and I felt a fear that neither of us put into words, but happily it proved unfounded; for at the landing-steps, a short distance below, the faithful Baptiste was waiting with a boat—a deep, roomy little craft which he had found near by. At once we got in, Baptiste retreated to the bow, and Miss Hatherton and myself occupied the stern seat. The captain took the oars, and he wisely made the most of the opportunity by pulling straight out from shore and in between the shipping that was anchored hereabouts. It is a wonder we fared so well, for swinging lanterns shed their light upon us, and we passed under decks where men were pacing their night watches. But no inquisitive voices hailed us, and we glided safely through to the open river and turned downstream with the current. The tangle of masts and spars receded behind us, hiding the spot where we had embarked, and for five minutes we drifted on in the moonlight, our hearts too full for speech. Then Miss Hatherton broke the silence.

"Is the ship that we are seeking near or far?" she asked.

Captain Rudstone turned in his seat, and pointed to a dark object about half a mile below us.

"There lies the Speedwell," he replied, "a quarter of a mile out from shore, and by herself."

This was reassuring news, but there were perils to be reckoned with. A great hue and cry was spreading along the town's edge, mainly in the direction of the landing-stairs, and we looked for a boat to appear behind us at any moment. Also, to my mind, there was some uncertainty as to the reception the Speedwell's skipper would give us.

However, there was no sign of pursuit within next five minutes, and by that time we were alongside of the ship, which was a tidy brig of some hundred and fifty tons burden. Her sea gear was rove and her sails stowed. Several heads looked over her bulwarks as we made fast, and a voice hailed us sharply.

"That you, Bunker?" the captain replied.

"Yes. Who are you?" came suspiciously.

"Myles Rudstone."

There was an exclamation of surprise, and a moment later a rope ladder was thrown down to us. Baptiste and I and the girl preceded the captain, and as he followed us he cast the boat adrift. At the first sight, seeing him on deck by the glare of a lantern, I was favorably impressed by Hiram Bunker. He was a short, thick-set man, with a sandy beard and a shrewd, good natured face. He scanned Miss Hatherton and myself with open amazement, and shook hands heartily with Captain Rudstone.

"Glad to meet you again, sir," he cried in a nasal voice. "My mate wakened me up to listen to the row over yonder," pointing to the shore, "and that's why I'm on deck at this hour. I might have guessed you had a hand in the rumpus. But what does it mean, anyway?".

The captain explained, making the situation thoroughly clear, and the little skipper listened with thoughtful attention.

"It's an ugly scrape," was his grave comment.

"It is that; but you can get us out of it. What do you say?"

"I say I'll do it," cried the skipper. "I'm a Hudson Bay man at heart, and I'll save the lot of you—hang the risk!"

"And you will sail at once?"

"At once. I've got my full cargo on board, and I was only waiting for daylight to start. It's not far off that now. But, shiver my timbers, if there don't come the rascals you thought you had slipped!"

He pointed up the river, and I saw a longboat approaching swiftly. It was still a good distance off, but there was not a moment to lose, and the skipper was aware of the fact. He hastily roused the crew, and I never saw a more pleasing sight than that hardy lot of men as they set to work to unfurl the sails and get the vessel under way.

Miss Hatherton stood with me at the bulwark, holding to my arm, and asking me what I thought of the situation. I hardly knew how to answer her, for there was no telling as yet what was going to happen. A stiff breeze was blowing ready for the canvas, and when the anchor was lifted we began to drift. But meanwhile the boat had come up close, and with evident determination to board us. It held ten men, and they were mostly at the oars.

"Sheer off, there!" cried the skipper. "What do you want?"

"You are sheltering fugitives from the law," a harsh voice replied. "Give them up. It's a case of murder!"

The skipper refused in plain terms, and catching a sudden gleam of steel, he shouted savagely:

"If you come any nearer or fire a single shot I'll give you a volley of ten guns!"

36

By this time the ship was under way and moving with full canvas spread. The pursuing boat fell back, its occupants yelling curses and threats; and so the danger passed. The Speedwell bore swiftly on, leaving a foamy wake dancing on the bosom of the St. Lawrence, and in my delight I felt tempted to throw my arms about Miss Hatherton. Captain Rudstone joined us, and with thankful hearts we watched the lights of Quebec fading in the distance.

CHAPTER VIII.   CLOSE TO PORT.

I need make but brief mention of the long cruise that followed our escape, of the days that passed slowly while we worked our way down the mighty St. Lawrence, out to the open Atlantic by the rocky gates of Newfoundland, and thence up the coast of Labrador to Hudson Straits. For the most part wind and weather favored us, yet it was a matter of six weeks before we got into the bay and made sail across that inland waste of water toward our destination, Fort York, which was far down in the southwestern corner. The distance from Quebec by land would have been far less. Our course, as a map will show, was along the three sides of a square.

The Speedwell was a sound little ship, and carried a mixed cargo to be delivered at the Hudson Bay posts. We were well fed and snugly berthed, Miss Hatherton having a cozy cabin all to herself. The crew were good fellows, and Hiram Bunker was a typical New England skipper—bluff, honest and popular. I did not see very much of him, for he and Captain Rudstone became boon companions and stuck well together. It was the same with the captain. Indeed, he seemed to take pains to avoid me, except when others were present, thereby causing me some perplexity and chagrin. And if we happened to find ourselves alone he appeared ill at ease, and would look at me in a strange and shifty manner, as though he had something on his mind. But for all that the time did not hang heavily on my hands, nor was the voyage an uneventful one to me, as I shall relate in a few words.

It came about naturally enough that Miss Hatherton and I spent the long days together. In less than a fortnight we were calling each other by our Christian names. Secluded in some nook of the deck, we would talk for hours, or I would read aloud from one of the few volumes that the skipper's cabin afforded. She told me much of her life in London. Her father had been a gentleman of some means until speculation wrecked him, and later she confided to me the whole of her sad story.

There was more than I had known before, as Captain Rudstone suggested. It seems that prior to her father's death the only son of Lord Selkirk fell in love with the girl. She did not return his affection, and, indeed, she disliked the young man. But the old lord was either ignorant of this fact or would not believe it. He had higher matrimonial views for his son, and so, in order to get Miss Hatherton out of England, he hatched the plot that resulted in the poor girl

38

making her father a sacred promise that she would go to the Canadas and marry Griffith Hawke. She had no relatives to interfere, and a cruel disadvantage was taken of her helplessness and poverty. She spoke of the matter only on the one occasion, and it did not come up between us again. Nor had I the heart to mention it, since she was clearly resigned to her future.

But I pitied the girl deeply, and I would have been more than human, with the opportunities afforded, had I not fallen a victim to her charms and loveliness. I did not perceive where I was drifting. I did not realize my danger until it was too late. In short, I, who had hitherto felt but contempt for all womankind, suddenly discovered that I was a slave to the great passion. It was a sharp awakening, and it destroyed my peace of mind. To me Flora Hatherton was a divinity, a goddess. It gave me the keenest torture to think that she would soon be the wife of old Griffith Hawke. I knew that she was as far out of my reach as the stars above, and yet I felt that I should love her passionately all my life—that the memory of her sweet face would shatter all the joys of existence for me.

I could have cursed myself for being such a fool, and I hated the factor for sending me on such a mission. It never entered my head to play him false and try to win Flora, nor did I believe there was any chance of doing so. Day after day we were together, and with Spartan courage I hid my feelings—or, at least, I thought I was hiding them. It was a hard task, for every word or look that the girl gave me seemed to turn my blood to fire. That she was indifferent to me—that she regarded me only as a friend—I was convinced. I was a youngster and inexperienced, and so I was blind to the girl's pretty blushes, to the averting of her eyes when they would meet mine, and to other signs of confusion that I remembered afterward. To remain at Fort Royal, a witness of Griffith Hawke's domestic happiness, I knew to be impossible. I determined to seek a new post, or to plunge far into the northern wilderness, as soon as I should have delivered Flora at her destination.

The days slipped by fraught with mingled joy and bitterness, and at sunset one chilly August evening I stood alone on deck by the port bulwark. The wind was rising, and there was a clammy mist on the gray, troubled waters. We were nearly across the bay, and in the morning we expected to sight the marshy shores that lay about Fort York. Flora was in her cabin. She had seemed depressed all day and I

39

remembered that an hour before, when the skipper told her how near we were to land, she had smiled at me sadly and gone below. I had no wish for the voyage to end. The thought of the morrow cut me like a knife, and I was lost in gloomy reflections, when a hand clapped me on the shoulder. I turned round with a start, and saw Captain Rudstone.

"A few hours more, Mr. Carew," he said, "and we shall have dropped anchor under the walls of the fort. Do you expect to meet your factor there?"

"It is doubtful," I replied. "He will hardly look for our arrival so soon. We took an earlier ship, you will remember, and our passage has been a swift one."

"It was a dangerous passage," he said meaningly—"at least, for you. I take it you will be glad of a few days of grace. But may I ask— I happen to have a curiosity—how this thing is to end?"

"What thing?" I cried, ruffling at once.

"You love Miss Hatherton," he answered with a smile.

I felt my face grow hot.

"Does that concern you?" I demanded curtly. "I will thank you to mind your own affairs, Captain Rudstone."

"The girl loves you," he replied calmly.

"I don't believe it," said I.

"Bah! you are a blind fool," he muttered. "I gave you credit for more perception. But it is just as I said—the girl returns your affection. What are you going to do about it? Will you allow her to marry Griffith Hawke?"

I could have struck the captain for his jesting tone, and yet at the same time I detected a ring of truth in what he had said. It flashed upon me that I had indeed been blind, and the revelation thrilled my heart.

"Miss Hatherton is the promised wife of Griffith Hawke," I answered hoarsely; "and Griffith Hawke is my superior officer. I am acting under his orders, and I dare not betray my trust. I am a man of honor, and not a knave. I scorn your suggestion, sir."

"Do you call it honorable," sneered the captain, "to help this innocent girl, whose heart belongs to you, to marry another man?"

I looked at him with some confusion for, to tell the truth, I had no answer ready to my lips. And just then Hiram Bunker strode up to us, his countenance unusually grave.

"It's going to be a nasty night, or I'm no mariner," he exclaimed. "There's a storm brewing, and we are perilously near the coast. I don't like the prospect a bit, gentlemen."

Captain Rudstone made some fitting reply, but I was in no mood to heed the skipper's words, or to give a second thought to the prophecy of a storm. I left the two together, and with my brain in a whirl I crept down to the seclusion of my cabin.

CHAPTER IX.   AT THE MERCY OF THE SEA.

For an hour or more I sat on the edge of my berth, pondering the matter first in one way and then in another. The captain's plain speech had opened my eyes, as it were, and as I recalled many little incidents of the past, looking at them now in their true light, I saw that I had indeed been dull-witted and slow of comprehension. I had won Flora's heart—she returned my affection. That was the meaning of her frequent blushes and confusion—signs which I had interpreted as indifference when I thought of them at all.

The discovery both caused me an exquisite joy and added to my wretchedness. At the first I painted a bright and glowing picture of the future. Flora should be mine! I would make her my wife, and carry her off into the wilderness or to one of the lower towns. I was young and strong. I had some money laid by, and it would be but a delightful task to carve a home and a fortune for the two of us. So I reasoned for a time, and then a more sober mood followed. I saw that I had been indulging in an empty dream.

"There is no such happiness for me!" I groaned aloud. "I was a fool to think of it for a moment. The girl loves me, it is true, but no persuasion of mine could ever induce her to break her promise. She belongs to Griffith Hawke, and she will marry him. And even if it were possible to win her, honor and duty, which I have always held sacred, would keep me from such a knavish trick. If I proved unfaithful to my trust, could I ever hold up my head among men again?"

Thus I revolved the matter in my mind, and I confess that I was sorely tempted more than once to stake all on the chance of making Flora my own. But in the end I resolved to be true to my manhood— to the principles my father had been at such pains to teach me. Without taking the trouble to undress, I stretched myself on my bed— the hour was late—and for a long time I dozed or tossed restlessly at intervals. At last I fell into a sound sleep, and it could have been no great while afterward when I was rudely awakened by a crash that pitched me out of my bunk to the floor. A second and far louder crash followed at once, immediately overhead, and then a shrill commotion broke out. I knew the ship had struck, and I lost no time in getting to my feet. Luckily no bones were broken, and with some difficulty—for the vessel was pitching heavily—I groped my way through the darkness to the deck.

42

Here I beheld such a scene as I trust I may never see again. The mainmast had fallen, tearing a great gap in the bulwark, and crushing two sailors under its weight. Hiram Bunker and some of his men were rushing to and fro, shouting and yelling; others were gazing as though stupefied at the wreckage of shattered spars, flapping canvas, and twisted cordage. The ship was plunging fore and aft—a sure sign that she was not now aground. The mist had partly cleared, and the air was raw and cutting. A storm of wind and rain was raging, blowing from the starboard or seaward side. Several of the crew had followed me above, but most of them had evidently been busy on deck at the time of the disaster.

A single lamp was burning, and at first none observed my presence. All was seemingly confusion and panic, and the skipper's orders were being tardily obeyed. I moved forward a little, and recognized Captain Rudstone holding to the snapped-off end of the mast.

"What has happened?" I demanded anxiously. "Are we in danger?"

"Little doubt of it, Mr. Carew," he answered calmly. "The ship struck on a submerged rock—probably the side edge of it—and immediately sheered off into deep water. It was a hard blow to shatter the mast, which crushed two poor fellows to death in its fall."

"What is the time?" I asked.

"Two o'clock in the morning, and we are close to the shore."

"The vessel might have fared worse," said I. "But is she leaking?"

"Ay, there's the rub," the captain replied. "The water is pouring in, and the ship is already beginning to settle."

"God help us," I cried, "if that is true!"

I wanted further confirmation, and I hurried away to seek the skipper. I found him close by, and as I hurried up to him he was joined by another man, a bearded sailor, who called out excitedly:

"There is four feet of water in the well, sir, and it is steadily increasing. We can't keep afloat long."

"Stick to the pumps, Lucas, and do what you can," the skipper directed. "Get some food ready, men, and prepare to lower the boats," he shouted loudly to the crew. Then he turned to me.

43

"'Tis is a bad business, Mr. Carew," he said hoarsely. "It's all up with my ship, and I'm a ruined man. But I'm going to save all hands, if it is possible. Where is Miss Hatherton?"

"In her cabin," I replied.

I had not forgotten the girl, but I had felt reluctant to rouse her until I knew what danger threatened us. Now there was no time to lose, and I hastened to the companion way. At the foot of it, where there was some depth of water, I dimly perceived Flora wading toward me. She uttered a little cry of joy and clasped my arm.

"So you are up and dressed," I exclaimed. "I was just coming for you."

"I was awakened by the crash," she replied, "and I prepared for the worst at once. Is the ship sinking, Denzil?"

"She will go down ultimately," I answered; "but there is plenty of time for all hands to escape. Do not be alarmed."

"I am not frightened," she said bravely. "I know that I am safe with you."

There was a tenderness in her voice that tempted me to some mad reply, but I checked the impulse. I bade her stay where she was while I went to my cabin for some articles of value. I was quickly back, and as soon as the companion was clear—the skipper and some of the crew were swarming down—I helped Flora up. We went forward to the bulwark, Captain Rudstone joining us, and there we waited for a quarter of an hour of suspense and anxiety.

In spite of the sucking of the pumps, the ship settled steadily, bows first, and rolled less and less to the waves. It was very dark, and the wind shrieked and whistled dismally; the rain fell unceasingly, soon drenching us from head to foot. The worst of it was that we had shortly to face a deadly peril. The boats were frail, the sea rough, and the storm-beaten coast of the bay was no great distance off. I had not the heart to tell Flora how slight was our chance of life, and I do not know if she suspected it. At all events, she was perfectly calm and collected.

The men were under control now, and there was little confusion. They promptly obeyed orders, and Hiram Bunker seemed to be everywhere at once. We could do nothing but look on, with a growing uneasiness, for which there was good cause. But at last all was in readiness, and none too soon, for the bows of the sinking ship were

44

close to the water. It was from this quarter that the two boats—the longboat and the jolly-boat—were lowered.

The latter was the smaller, and it was quickly filled by Miss Hatherton, Captain Rudstone, Baptiste, and I, and four seamen. The first mate, who had a lantern lashed to his waist, let down some food and then followed us. The skipper and the rest of the crew occupied the long boat, which was lowered at the same time from the opposite side. Both craft were hurriedly thrust off by the aid of boathooks, and there we were on the open surface of Hudson Bay, exposed to the fury of the storm, and drifting away into the black maw of the night.

How narrow an escape we had made of it we were quickly to learn, for we had gone no more than a hundred yards when I heard a bitter cry from Hiram Bunker, followed by shouts of "Look! Look!" I glanced back from the stern seat, and at that moment the Speedwell went to her doom. There was a sound of creaking planks, her bow dipped under and her stern rose high the air, and then the waves closed over the poop-deck and blotted out the swinging lantern.

We were beyond the reach of the vortex, and our men pulled hard away from the fatal spot. The sea grew rougher, and the rain poured in torrents; we were compelled to keep bailing the water out. The wind-lashed gap between the two boats widened swiftly, and in a short time the long boat was lost to sight in the darkness. Again and again we shouted at the top of our voices, but no reply came back. The wind shrieked, the billows roared and crashed, and the shadow of death seemed to be lowering on us from the black sky overhead.

"How are we going?" Captain Rudstone asked of the first mate, who was at one of the oars.

"Badly enough, sir," the man replied. "It's no use trying to keep off the shore, pull as hard as we may."

"Is there no hope?" Flora asked of me in a whisper.

"Very little," I replied hoarsely. "It is better to prepare for the worst."

I put one arm round her, and she voluntarily snuggled closer to me. Thus we sat for twenty minutes or half an hour, expecting constantly to be capsized and flung into the sea. The storm still raged with undiminished violence, but it was growing a little lighter now, and as often as we rose to the top of the swell we could see the faint blur of the land far off. It was an ominous sight, for most of us knew

45

what the shore of the bay was like in a tempest. Wind and tide were drifting us steadily nearer.

"Look! Look!" Captain Rudstone suddenly shouted. "Pull hard about, men! Quick, for your lives!"

But it was too late to avert the danger. I had scarcely glanced behind me, where I saw a mighty wave, yards high, rolling forward swiftly, when the jolly-boat was pitched far into the air. It hovered an instant on the crest of the wall of water and then turned bottom up, shooting us all down the slope into a foamy trough.

I lost my grip of Flora—how I do not know—and was sucked deep below the surface. When by hard struggling I came to the top and looked about, I experienced a moment of sickening horror, for I could see nothing of the girl; but suddenly she rose within a few feet of me, her loosened hair streaming on the water, and by a desperate effort I reached and caught hold of her.

It was just then, as we were both at the mercy of the sea, that a strange and providential thing happened. A heavy spar, which had doubtless been washed from the sinking ship, floated alongside of us. I seized it firmly with one hand, while I supported Flora with the other. We were hurled up on a wave, and from the crest I saw the capsized jolly-boat some distance off. Two men were clinging to the keel, but I was unable to recognize them. The next instant the wind seemed to fall a little and shift to another quarter, bringing with it a gray fog that settled speedily and thickly on all sides of us. But I had caught a glimpse of the coast, and above the gale I could faintly hear the muffled pounding of the surf.

The spar drifted on for several minutes, now high in the air, now deep in the greenish hollow of the sea. Flora was perfectly conscious, and partly able to help herself. We were in such peril that I could offer her no words of comfort, and she seemed to understand the meaning of my ominous stillness.

"Are we going to be drowned?" she asked.

"We are in God's hands, Flora," I answered huskily. "The shore is very close, and we are drifting straight in. A tremendous surf is breaking and it will be a miracle if we live through it."

"Then we will die together, Denzil," the brave girl whispered; and as she looked up at me I read in her eyes the confession of her heart—the pure depth of a love that was all my own.

46

CHAPTER X.   THE DAWN OF DAY.

Flora's words, and the meaning glance that accompanied them, melted the resolve I had made but a few hours before. There was no reason, indeed, why I should keep silence at such a time. I believed that we were both in the jaws of death, with not the faintest chance of escape. To lift the cloud that was between us—to snatch what bliss was possible out of our last moments—would be a sweet and pardonable thing. So, while the spar bore us lightly amid the curling waves, I drew the girl more tightly to my breast with one arm, and pressed kisses on her lips and eyes, on the salty, dripping hair that clustered about her forehead.

"My darling, I love you!" I whispered passionately in her ear. "You must let me speak; I can hide it no longer. I lost my heart weeks ago, but honor held me silent."

What more I said I do not recall, but I know that I poured forth all my burning, pent-up affection. When I had finished, Flora lifted her tear-dimmed eyes to my face and smiled; she put a trembling arm about my neck and kissed me.

"And I love you, Denzil," she said softly. "Oh, I am so glad that I can tell you; it seems to take away the sting of death. I would have hidden the truth from you; I would have kept my promise and married Griffith Hawke. But now—now it is different. In death we belong to each other. You made me love you, Denzil—you were so kind, so good, so brave!"

"If we could only live, and be happy together!" I replied hoarsely.

"Hush! God knows best," she whispered. "In life we must have been apart. Kiss me again, Denzil, and hold me tight. The end will not be long!"

I kissed her passionately, and drew her as close to me as I could with one arm, while with the other I took a firmer grip on the spar. I had my heart's desire, but already it was turning to ashes. I could not reconcile myself to so cruel a fate. As I looked into Flora's eyes, shining with the light of love, I felt a bitter resentment, a dull, aching stupor of despair.

We were both silent for a few moments, and then of a sudden a rising wind scattered the gray fog. From the top of the swell we had a glimpse of the low, rugged shore, less than half a mile distant.

Monstrous waves were rolling toward it, and the angry bellowing of the surf was like continuous thunder.

"I am growing weaker," Flora whispered, "and I am so cold. Don't let me slip, Denzil."

I assured her that I would not, but I doubted if I could keep my word. I, too, was beginning to succumb to the effects of the long struggle with the raging sea and the driving storm. I was almost exhausted, and chilled in every limb. I feared that before long we must both be washed from the spar.

But during the next minute it grew a little lighter, and I made a discovery that caused me a strange agitation. Over on the shore, and slightly to our right, a promontory of rock and bushes jutted out some distance. It was to leeward of the wind, which was blowing us perceptibly that way, while at the same time the waves swept us landward. I knew that if we should drift under the promontory, where doubtless the surf was less violent, there would be some faint hope of escape. I said nothing to Flora, however, for I thought it best to let her continue to believe the worst. She was much weaker now, and made no effort to speak; but the look in her half-closed eyes was more eloquent than words.

On and on we plunged, gaining speed every instant—now deep down between walls of glassy water, now tossed high on the curling swell. At intervals I sighted the shore—we were close upon it—and there was no longer any doubt that we should strike to leeward of the promontory. Faster and faster! The spar spun round and round dizzily. I gripped it with all my strength, supporting Flora's half-insensible form with the other arm.

For a minute we were held in a watery trough, and then a huge wave, overtaking us from behind, lifted us high on its curling, hissing crest. I had a brief, flashing vision of a murky strip of sand and bushes washed by milky foam. It looked to be straight below me, and on the instant I let go of the spar. I strained Flora to my breast, and made a feeble attempt to swim. There was a roaring and singing in my ears, a blur of shadows before my eyes, and the next thing I remembered was a tremendous crash that I thought had shattered every bone in my body.

The instinct of life was so strong that I must have scrambled at once to my feet. I had been flung into a hillock of wet sand and grass, and with such force that the deep imprint of my body was visible. I

48

looked about me, dizzy and stunned, and immediately saw Flora lying huddled in a thick clump of bushes a few feet to the left. I knew not if she was dead or alive, but as I staggered toward her I discovered a great foaming wave rolling up the beach. Rallying what strength I could, I seized the girl and dragged her back as far and as quickly as I was able. The wave broke with a crash, hurling its curled spray almost to our feet. I dropped my burden, and reeled over in a deathly faint. When I came to my senses—I could not have been unconscious more than a few minutes—the chilly gray dawn had driven away the shadows of the night. A bleak and disheartening prospect met my eyes in every direction. Straight in front the sea rolled to the horizon, still tossing and tumbling. Behind me, and to right and left, stretched a flat, dreary, marshy coast, scarred with rocks, thickets and evergreens.

It was a familiar enough scene to me—I had often visited the shores of Hudson Bay—and I gave it but a glance. Flora lay close beside me, her head and shoulders pillowed on a clump of weeds, and at the first I thought she was dead. But when I had risen to my knees with some pain and difficulty—I was as weak as a cat—I found that she was breathing. I set myself to restore her, and chafed her cold hands until the blood began to circulate freely. Then I poured a few drops of brandy between her lips—I fortunately had some in a small flask—and it was no sooner swallowed than she opened her lovely eyes. I could see that she was perfectly conscious, and that she knew me and remembered all; but when I lifted her gently in my arms she made a weak effort to draw back, and looked at me with a sort of horror.

"My darling, what is the matter?" I cried.

"Hush, Denzil, not that name," she replied faintly. "Oh, why were we spared? You must forget all that I told you, even as I shall forget your words. It was only a dream—a dream that is dead. We can be nothing to each other."

I knew in my heart that she was right, but the sight of her beauty, the memory of her confession, put me in a rebellious mood. I drank what was left of the brandy, and rose dizzily to my feet.

"I will not give you up," I said in a dogged tone. "You love me, Flora, and you are mine. Providence saved us for a purpose—to make us happy."

She shook her head sadly.

49

"Denzil, why will you make is so hard for me?" she replied. "I must keep my promise—you know that. Be brave, be honorable. Forget what has happened!"

The appeal shamed me, and I averted my eyes from her. In my wretchedness I felt tempted to throw myself into the sea.

"Where are the rest?" she asked in a different voice.

"I fear they are all drowned," I answered gloomily. "Fate has been less kind to us."

"Do you know where we are?" she continued.

"Not exactly," I said, looking about, "but we can't be a great distance from Fort York—and from Griffith Hawke."

I was sorry for the cutting words as soon as they were spoken, and I would have made a fitting apology. But just then I heard voices, and two voyageurs, in the blue capotes of the Hudson Bay Company, came out of the timber about twenty yards off. They saw us at once and ran toward us with eager shouts.

CHAPTER XI.   A COPY OF "THE TIMES."

I was both glad and sorry for the interruption. In our forlorn condition we needed assistance badly enough, but I would have preferred to have Flora all to myself for some time longer. However, I made the best of it, and gave the voyageurs a warm greeting. They were from Fort York, and they told me that they and half a dozen more had been on a week's hunting trip, and that they had spent the night in a sheltered spot near by. They added that when they were about starting for the fort, half an hour previously, two survivors of the wreck had straggled into their camp.

This was pleasing news, but before I could glean any further information, the rest of the party made their appearance from the timber—three more voyageurs and three of the company's Indian hunters. And with them, to my great delight, were Captain Rudstone and Baptiste. Both walked with difficulty and were sorely bruised. It seems they had come ashore clinging to the jolly-boat—the rest of the crew were drowned—and had been cast on a sandy part of the coast. They knew nothing of the other boat or its occupants, and there was reason to believe the worst.

"I fear they are all lost," said Captain Rudstone. "The longboat was heavily weighted and it probably capsized soon after it left the ship. We four have had a truly marvelous escape, Mr. Carew. I judge that Miss Hatherton owes her life to you."

"We came ashore together," I answered.

"Mr. Carew is too modest," Flora said quietly. "But for him I should have been drowned when the boat upset. I was helpless all the time, while he held me on the spar."

The captain looked queerly from one to the other of us, and I was afraid he would say some awkward thing; but he merely shrugged his shoulders, and turned to another subject.

"We might be in a worse plight," he remarked. "We are sound of limb, and Fort York is but six miles away. And I have saved Lord Selkirk's dispatches, which is a matter to be thankful for." He patted his breast as he spoke. "A drying at a good fire is all they will need," he added.

After some discussion, it was decided that two of the voyageurs should remain behind for the present and search the coast on the chance of finding trace of the longboat and its crew. The rest of us started for the fort, but first a rude litter was constructed on which to

51

carry Flora, who was too weak and bruised to walk so great a distance.

The captain, Baptiste, and I were not in much better condition, and we were heartily glad when, after a weary tramp of under three hours, we arrived at Fort York. This was and still is, the main trading-post of the Hudson Bay Company. It stood close to the bay and to the mouth of the Nelson River. It was larger than the other forts, but in every respect like them—a fortified palisade surrounding a huddled cluster of buildings, in which live a little colony of men, from the factor and his assistants down to the Indian employees.

Captain Rudstone and myself were well known at the fort—we had both been there before—and we received a cordial greeting from old friends. We were soon provided with dry clothes and a stiff glass of liquor, and then, little the worse for our hardships, we sat down to a plentiful breakfast. Baptiste had fared worse than either of us. It turned out that one of his ribs was broken, and he went straight to the hospital. The factor's wife took charge of Flora, and I saw her no more that day. One thing sadly marred our spirits—we had no hope that Hiram Bunker or any of his crew had been saved, and the disaster cast a gloom on all in the fort. I may add here that the two voyageurs found the bodies of the kind-hearted American skipper and six of his men, and that they were buried the following day on a low bluff overlooking the scene of their death-struggles. Peace to their ashes!

I slept soundly until late in the afternoon, and when supper was over, and I had visited Baptiste in the hospital, Captain Rudstone and I spent a quiet evening with the factor. Over pipes and brandy we told him the story of the wreck, and of the circumstances that led to our hurried flight from Quebec. He agreed that we had acted wisely, and he had some remarks to make to the disadvantage of Cuthbert Mackenzie.

"He is a revengeful man," he added, "and he will leave no stone unturned to settle with you for that night's work. I have no doubt that the theft of Lord Selkirk's despatches was his aim."

"He did not get them," the captain laughed.

"It would have been a most unfortunate thing if he had," the factor replied gravely. "One of the letters in the packet was for him and he had already received it. Lord Selkirk is a shrewd and determined man, and I am glad to know that they understand the danger at the head office in London. My instructions are just what I

52

have wished them to be, and I suppose the import of all the letters is about the same."

"Very likely," assented Captain Rudstone. "I am glad you are pleased. Trouble has been brewing this long time, and the crisis can't be far off. By the by, have you had news from Quebec later than the date of our sailing?"

"Not a word. The last mail, which brought me some London papers, left Fort Garry at the close of June."

The factor sighed. He was fond of the life of towns and he had been buried in the wilderness for ten years!

"Gentlemen, fill your glasses," he added. "Here's to the prosperity of the company!"

"May it continue forever!" supplemented the captain.

I drank the toast, and then inquired what was the state of the lower country.

"There have been no open hostilities as yet," the factor replied, "but there are plenty of rumors—ugly rumors. And that reminds me, Mr. Carew, a half-breed brought me a message from Griffith Hawke two days ago."

"I rather expected to find him here," said I, trying to hide my eagerness at the opening of a subject which I had wished to come to.

"He has abandoned that intention," the factor stated. "He is afraid to leave at present. The redskins have been impudent in his neighborhood of late, and he thinks their loyalty has been tampered with by the Northwest people. He begged me to send you and Miss Hatherton on to Fort Royal at the first opportunity after your arrival, and there happens to be one open now."

"How is that?" I asked.

"My right-hand man, Gummidge—you met him at supper—has been transferred to Fort Garry," the factor explained. "He is married, and he and his wife will go by way of the Churchill River and Fort Royal. Mrs. Gummidge will be a companion to Miss Hatherton. They expect to start in a week, so as to cover as much ground as possible before the winter sets in."

"The sooner the better," said I.

"And what about the marriage?" Captain Rudstone inquired carelessly.

"There will be a priest here—one of the French fathers—in the course of a month," said the factor, "and I will send him on to Fort Royal."

I tried hard to appear unconcerned, for I saw that Captain Rudstone was watching me keenly.

"I trust I shall be present for the ceremony," he remarked. "I go south by that route when I have finished with the business that brought me to the bay. I have three forts to visit hereabouts first."

The factor sucked thoughtfully at his pipe.

"Hawke is a lucky man," he said. "By gad, I envy him! Miss Hatherton is the prettiest bit of womanhood I ever clapped eyes on."

"She is too young for Hawke," said Captain Rudstone, with a sly glance in my direction.

"She will make him a good wife," I replied aggressively.

"There is another who wishes to marry her," he answered.

"What do you mean by that?" I cried.

"I refer to Cuthbert Mackenzie," said the captain.

I gave him an angry look, for I knew he had been purposely drawing me on, and to hide my confusion I drank a glass of brandy and water. There was a pause, and then, to my relief, the factor turned the conversation on the prices of furs.

The next five days passed slowly and uneventfully. Baptiste came out of hospital, and was pronounced fit for travel. Flora was none the worse for her exposure and suffering; I saw very little of her, for she lived in the married men's quarters and was looked after by the factor's wife and Mrs. Gummidge. But when we found ourselves alone together, as happened several times, her guarded conversation gave me to understand that the past must be forgotten, and she showed plainly that she was deeply grateful to me for not bringing up the subject that was next my heart. And indeed I had no intention of doing so. I realized that the girl could not be mine, and that what had occurred between us, when we believed ourselves to be on the edge of the grave—was the more reason why I should remain true to faith and honor. But my love for her was stronger and deeper-rooted than ever, and I still adhered to my resolution to take myself out of temptation's way at the first opportunity—to begin a new life in the wilderness or the towns of Lower Canada. I would have evaded the journey with her to Fort Royal had it been possible to do so.

Captain Rudstone made no further mention of the girl, and during the time he remained at the fort we were on the best of terms, though I observed that he took no pains to seek my company, and that he often looked at me with the puzzled and uneasy expression which I had noted from the first. On the morning of the fourth day he left for a fort some miles to the eastward, and on the night before an incident happened which I must not forget to mention.

We were sitting in the factor's room after supper—the captain and I—and he was reading an English paper that had come up with the last mail. Suddenly he uttered a sharp cry of surprise, and brought his tilted chair to the floor with a crash. When I inquired what was the matter he looked at me suspiciously, and made some inaudible reply. He tossed the paper on the table, gulped down a stiff brandy, and left the room.

As he did not return, I ventured to pick the paper up and examine it. It was a copy of the London Times, dated a year back. I scanned the page he had been reading, but could find nothing to account for his agitation. Where his hand had rumpled it was a brief paragraph stating that the Earl of Heathermere, of Heathermere Hall, in Surrey, was dead; that his two unmarried sons had died during the previous year—one by an accident while hunting; and that the title was now extinct, and the estate in Chancery. I read it with momentary interest, and then it passed from my mind. The notice of deaths was close by, and I concluded that it contained the name of one of the captain's English friends. I remembered that he had resided in London for some time.

Early the next morning Captain Rudstone departed, expressing the hope that he would see me within a month or six weeks. Two days later—on the morning of the sixth day after the wreck of the Speedwell—I was on my way to Fort Royal. Our party numbered eight, as follows: Jim Gummidge and his wife, Miss Hatherton and myself, Baptiste, and three trusty voyageurs. Gummidge was a companionable fellow, and his wife was a hardy, fearless little woman of the woods.

Our course was to the west, across a seventy-mile stretch of waterway, formed of connecting lakes and streams, that would bring us to the Churchill River, at a point a few miles above Fort Royal— the Churchill, it may be said, empties into Hudson Bay more than a hundred miles to the northwest of Fort York. We traveled in one long, narrow canoe, which was light enough to be portaged without difficulty, and on the evening of the second day we were within thirty-five miles of our destination.

CHAPTER XII.   A WARNING IN WOODCRAFT.

That night we pitched our camp on a wooded island in a small lake, erecting, as was the usual custom, a couple of lean-tos of bark and fir boughs. Gummidge owned the traveling outfit and the factor of Fort York had provided Baptiste and myself with what we needed in the way of weapons and ammunition. We were all well armed, for none journeyed otherwise through the wilderness in those days. But at this time, and from the part of the country we had to traverse, it seemed a most unlikely thing that we would run into any peril. However, neither Gummidge nor I were disposed to relax the ordinary precautions, and when we retired we set one of the voyageurs to watch.

This man—Moralle by name—awakened me about two o'clock in the morning by shaking my arm gently, and in a whisper begged me to come outside. I followed him from the lean-to across the island, which was no more than a dozen yards in diameter. The night was very dark, and it was impossible to make out the shore, though it was less than a quarter of a mile away. A deep silence brooded on land and water.

"What do you want with me?" I asked sharply.

"Pardon, sir," replied Moralle, "but a little while ago, as I stood here, I heard a low splash. I crouched down to watch the better, and out yonder on the lake I saw the head and arms of a swimmer. Then a pebble crunched under my moccasins, and the man turned and made off as quietly as he came."

"You have keen eyes," said I. "Look, the water is black! A fish made a splash, and you imagined the rest."

"I saw the swimmer, sir," he persisted doggedly.

"You saw a moose or a caribou," I suggested.

"Would a moose approach the island," he asked, "with the scent of our camp fire blowing to his nostrils?"

This was true, and I could not deny it.

"Then you would have me believe," said I, "that some enemy swam out from the mainland to spy upon us?"

"It was a man," the voyageur answered, "and he was swimming this way."

"I will finish your watch, Moralle," said I. "Give me your musket, and go to bed. Be careful not to waken the others."

He shuffled off without a word, and I was left to my lonely vigil. I had detected a smell of liquor in Moralle's breath, and I was disposed to believe that his story had no more foundation than the splashing of a fish. At all events, while I paced the strip of beach for two hours, I saw or heard nothing alarming. There was now a glimmer of dawn in the east, so I wakened Baptiste, bidding him without explanation to take my place, and returned to the lean-to for a half-hour's sleep.

It was broad daylight when Gummidge roused me. The fire was blazing and the voyageurs were preparing breakfast. Flora and Mr. Gummidge were kneeling on a flat stone, dipping their faces and hands into the crystal waters of the lake. The wooded shores rose around us in majestic solitude, and I scanned them in all directions without discovering any trace of human occupation. I made no mention of the incident of the night, attaching no importance to it; nor did Moralle have anything to say on the subject.

Sunrise found us embarked and already some distance down the lake. We were in the heart of the woods, and the wild beauty of the Great Lone Land cast its mystic spell upon all of us.

The morning was yet young when we passed from the lake into one of its many outlets. This was a narrow stream, navigable at first, but quickly becoming too shallow and rocky for our further progress. So we left the water, and there was now a portage of two miles over a level stretch of forest, at the end of which we would strike the Churchill River at a point twenty miles above Fort Royal.

We started off rapidly, Baptiste and the three other voyageurs leading the way with the canoe on their shoulders. The paddles and a part of the load were inside, and Gummidge and I carried the rest. The women had no burdens, and could easily keep pace with us.

"Have you passed this way before?" asked Gummidge.

"Only once," I replied, "and that was some years ago."

"The place reminds me of the enchanted forests one reads of in old fairy tales," said Mrs. Gummidge.

"I wish we were out of it," exclaimed Flora. "It has a sad and depressing influence on me."

Something in her voice made me turn and look at her, and she quickly averted her eyes.

"What's that?" cried Gummidge, an instant later. "Don't you see? There it lies, shining."

58

I darted past him to the left of the path and at the base of a tree I picked up a hunting knife sheathed in a case of tanned buckskin. We all stopped, and Lavigne, one of the voyageurs, left the canoe to his comrades and took the weapon from my hand. He examined it with keen and grave interest.

"It is just such a knife as the men of the Northwest Company carry," he declared.

"Yes, you are right," assented Gummidge; and I agreed with him.

For a minute or more Lavigne searched the ground in the vicinity, creeping here and there on all-fours. Then he rose to his feet with the air of one who has made an unpleasant discovery.

"Indians have passed this way within a few hours," he announced, "and a white man was with them. They went toward the northwest."

Gummidge and I were fairly good at woodcraft, but the marks in the grass baffled us. Yet we did not dream of doubting or questioning Lavigne's assertion, for he was known to be a skilled and expert tracker. Redskins and a Northwest man together! It was a combination, in these times of evil rumor, that boded no good. I remembered Moralle's tale of the swimmer, and I felt a sudden uneasiness.

"We must be careful," said Gummidge. "This is a fine neighborhood for an ambuscade."

I glanced at Flora, and by her pale and frightened face I saw she was thinking of the same thing that was in my own mind.

"Do you suppose he is near us, Denzil?" she asked, stepping close to my side.

"Impossible," I replied. "Cuthbert Mackenzie is hundreds of miles away in Quebec. Do not be afraid. There is no danger, and the river is not far off."

But my assuring words were from the lips only. At heart I felt that Mackenzie was just the sort of man to have followed us to the North—a thing he could easily have done by land in this time. Gummidge took as serious a view of the matter, though for different reasons, and he approved the precautions I suggested.

So when we started off again, our order of march was reversed and otherwise changed. Gummidge and I went ahead single file, with our muskets ready for immediate use. The women came next, and then the canoe; we had put the luggage into it, and the voyageurs did not grumble at the extra load.

Less than a mile remained to be covered, and I was alert for attack with every foot of the way. But no Indian yells or musket-shots broke the stillness of the forest, and I was heartily glad when we emerged on the bank of the Churchill. Only twenty miles down stream to Fort Royal! No further thoughts of danger troubled us. Swiftly we embarked, and swung out on the rushing blue tide.

After the first five miles the scene changed a little. The river narrowed, and grew more swift. The hills receded right and left, and a strip of dense forest fringed the banks on either hand. A dull roar in the distance warned us that we were approaching well-known and dangerous falls, where it would be necessary to land and make a brief portage through the woods.

Closer and closer we swept, and louder and louder rang the thunder of the rapids. The voyageurs began to make in a little toward the left shore, and just then a musket cracked shrilly from the forest on that side. Gardapie, who was immediately in front of me, dropped his paddle, and leaped convulsively to his feet He clutched at his bleeding throat, gave a gurgling cry of agony, and pitched head first out of the canoe, nearly upsetting it as he slid off the gunwale.

CHAPTER XIII.   THE AMBUSCADE.

The attack was so sudden and unlooked for, and took us at such a disadvantage, that it was a mercy the half of us were not killed by the enemy's first straggling volley. For on the instant that Gardapie fell dead into the river two more shots rang out, and then a third and a fourth. A bullet whistled by my ear, and another flew so close to Baptiste that he dropped his paddle and threw himself flat, uttering a shrill "*Nom de Dieu!*" The women screamed, and Lavigne cried out with a curse that he had a ball in his right arm.

"Redskins!" I yelled. "Down—down for your lives!"

The canoe was luckily of a good depth, and we all crouched low and hugged the bottom. The firing had ceased as abruptly as it opened. Not a shot or a yell disturbed the quiet of the woods on either hand, and but for poor Gardapie's vacant place, and the splash of blood where he had been kneeling, I might have thought that the whole thing was a hideous dream. We drifted on with the current for a moment, while the roar of the falls swelled louder. Our loaded muskets were in our grasp, but we dared not expose our heads above the gunwales.

I looked back toward the stern, and saw Moralle tying a bandage on Lavigne's wounded arm. Gummidge was bareheaded, and he told me that a ball had carried his cap into the river.

"We're not done with the red devils," he added. "It's a bad scrape, Carew. I've no doubt the Indians have been won over by the Northwest people, and hostilities have already begun."

On that point I did not agree with him, but I was unwilling to speak what was in my mind while Flora was listening. We were between two perils, and I called out to Moralle for his opinion.

"If the redskins are in any force it will be impossible to land and make the portage," I said. "We are within a quarter of a mile of the rapids now. What are the chances of running them safely?"

"I have taken a canoe through them twice," replied Moralle, "and I could do it again. That is, provided I can paddle and look where I am going. Shall I try it, sir?"

"No, not yet; wait a little," I answered.

"I don't like this silence," exclaimed Gummidge. "Why did the redskins stop firing so suddenly? Mark my word, Carew, there's a piece of deviltry brewing. I'm afraid not one of us will—"

I stopped him by a gesture, and spoke a few comforting words to Flora; her face was very white, but beyond that she showed no trace of fear. Then I crept a little past Baptiste, and with the point of my knife I hurriedly made two small holes below the gunwales of the canoe, one on each side. I peeped through both in turn, and the curve of the bow gave me as clear a view ahead as I could have wished.

What I saw partly explained the meaning of the brief silence— scarcely more than a minute had elapsed since the musket volley. Here and there, in the leafy woods to right and left I caught a glimpse of dusky, swiftly moving bodies. We were close upon the falls, and but for the noise of the tumbling waters I could have heard the scurrying feet of our determined foes.

"What do you make out?" Gummidge whispered.

"The Indians are running ahead of us through the forest," I replied. "They expect that we will try the portage, and then they will have us in a trap. Our only chance is to dash down the rapids."

"It's a mighty poor one," murmured Gummidge; and as he spoke I heard an hysterical sob from his wife.

"We are not going quite straight," I called to Moralle. "If we keep on this course we will hit the rocks. A few strokes to the left—"

"I'll manage that, sir," the plucky voyageur interrupted.

I glanced over my shoulder, and saw him rise to his knees and begin to paddle. He was not fired on, as I had expected would be the case, so Baptiste and I ventured to lift our heads. As we watched, we held our muskets ready for the shoulder.

The current was bearing us on swiftly. A short distance below, the river narrowed to a couple of hundred feet, and here stretched the line of half-sunken rocks that marked the beginning of the falls. In the very center was a break several yards wide, and straight for this the canoe was now driving. There was no sign of the enemy, and it was difficult to realize that such a deadly peril awaited us.

Bang went a musket, and a puff of bluish smoke curled from the forest on the left. The ball passed over Moralle's head; he ceased paddling and dropped under cover. Baptiste did the same, but I kept my head up, looking for a chance to return the shot. My attention had just been attracted by a movement between the trees, when Gummidge cried, hoarsely:

"Keep down, Miss Hatherton! That was a mad thing to do!"

I turned around sharply as Gummidge released his hold of Flora, who, I judged, had been exposing herself recklessly. I was startled by her appearance. She looked at me with frightened eyes and parted lips, with a face the hue of ashes.

"Save me!" she gasped. "I saw him! I saw him!"

"Saw who?" I cried.

"Cuthbert Mackenzie! I am sure it was he, Denzil!" And she pointed to the right.

I looked hard in that direction, scanning the woods right and left. By Heavens, the girl had not been mistaken. Through a rift in the foliage, nearly opposite the canoe, peered a swarthy, sinister countenance and I recognized the features of Cuthbert Mackenzie. I took aim at him, but before I could fire he was gone. My brain seemed in a whirl. I had found the clew—the fiendish clew—to the attack that threatened to cost us our lives. Bent on revenge, Mackenzie had traveled up country to intercept us on the way to the fort—to kill me, and to capture Flora. He had bribed the savages to help him, and he and his ruthless allies had been in the vicinity of our camp on the previous night.

Swiftly these things coursed through my mind. I tried to speak to Flora, but my tongue seemed to be held fast. I heard a shot—another and another. The bullets sang close to my ear.

"Down—down!" warned Gummidge.

"Keep low!" shouted Moralle and Lavigne in one breath.

My brain grew suddenly clear, but I did not heed the friendly advice. Three shots had missed me, and I knew that the canoe was jerking about too much with the current to admit of a sure aim the savages.

"Paddle on, Moralle!" I cried. "Faster—faster!"

Meanwhile I watched the right flank, hoping to get another chance at Cuthbert Mackenzie. Baptiste—brave fellow!—was on the alert with me but he was scanning the left shore, and a sudden exclamation from him drew my eyes in the same direction. Ten yards in front, on the edge of the timber, a redskin thrust his coppery face from the leaves. I fired as quickly and the savage vanished with a yell of pain.

We were almost upon the rapids, and half a minute more would see us plunged into the seething, foaming slide of angry waters. To right and left, where the jagged reef touched the forest, stood three or four painted redskins, with muskets to their shoulders. And some distance below the falls, where the water broadened and shallowed, I made out the feather-decked heads of more Indians. This was a dread and significant discovery, and I instantly perceived the trap that had been laid for us.

"Keep under cover!" I shouted at the top of my voice.

"Be ready to fight when we pass the rapids! The devils are waiting for us below, blocking the way! Don't try to paddle, Moralle. The canoe is headed straight for the rift in the middle. It's sure death if you show yourself."

CHAPTER XIV.   AN INDIAN'S GRATITUDE.

Above the thunder of the falls my warning was heard and understood. Glancing back to make sure, I saw the startled faces of the two women, and the grimly-set countenance of Jim Gummidge. From the stern Moralle half-rose, looked this way and that, and made two daring strokes with the paddle. He dropped under cover again just as a volley of musket balls swept close over the canoe.

"You fool!" I shouted at him.

"I had to do it," he yelled back. "We were swinging to the left. It's all right now."

"Steady! Here we go!" cried Gummidge.

I gave Flora a brief look that brought a dash of hot color to her pale cheeks, and then I turned quickly to one of my loopholes— Baptiste was gazing from the other. There was scarcely time to see anything. Like a flash I made out the little knot of painted savages on the reef to the left, and caught a blur of scarlet and copper from the shallows beyond the rapids. The next instant the turbulent waters leaped up and hid the view, and we struck the verge of the falls.

The Indians to right and left of the channel had evidently been posted there to prevent us from landing, and they did not fire on us as we shot by, but they yelled and screeched like fiends, their comrades below joining in, and above the horrid din of voices I heard the roar of the great waves that now surrounded us.

For a few seconds—it could have been no more—we hugged the bottom tightly. Spray and foam dashed over us; the frail craft pitched and tossed, swung round and round; billows and rocks smote the toughened birch-bark. Then came a sudden crash, the canoe turned over in the twinkling of an eye, and out we went into the raging falls, studded thickly with sunken bowlders and jagged, protruding reefs.

I was whirled about by the angry waters as though I had been a mere chip, sucked deep down, hurled to the surface, and bruised against rocks. I fought hard for life and held my breath, and when a spar of moss-grown bowlder loomed suddenly in front of me, I caught it with both arms and held it fast.

At the first I was grateful to Heaven for this mercy, and thought of nothing else. I filled my lungs with air and took a tighter grip of the rock. Then a burst of shrill yells and a couple of musket shots, ringing above the clamor of the rapids, roused me from my semi-stupor. I remembered that the canoe had capsized, flinging us all to the flood or to the waiting savages. And Flora! What was her fate? The dread that she had perished sickened my heart.

I shook the water from my dripping hair and eyes, and looked about me. There was little of cheer or hope in what I saw. I was stuck midway in the falls, with my face downstream. Many yards below, where the foaming slide of water broadened into choppy waves and swirling shallows, Baptiste was splashing hip-deep for shore. Three redskins were dashing after him with drawn tomahawks, and I gave the poor fellow up for lost.

Moralle had been carried through the cordon of savages, and had reached the farther bank. There, on the edge of the forest, he was locked limb to limb with a stalwart warrior. The two were down, rolling amid the grass and gravel, and three Indians were watching for a chance to shoot the voyageur without injuring their comrade. Off to my right, in a deep, whirling eddy formed by a big bowlder, Gummidge was struggling hard to save himself and his wife; he had the use of but one arm, for the other was fastened around the little woman's waist. A short distance beyond them, Lavigne, in spite of his wounded shoulder, was clinging in the bushy limb of a tree that overhung and dipped to the surface of the stream.

All this I observed at a sweeping glance—scarcely a moment could have elapsed since the upsetting of the canoe—and in vain I sought further for trace of Flora. That my companions were in peril of their lives, that death by drowning or the tomahawk must be my own fate—these things seemed of slight importance to me at the time. The canoe I discovered readily enough. It was wedged broadside to the stream no more than four yards above me, creaking and bending with the fierce current, its bow and stern jammed against half-submerged pinnacles of rock.

"Flora—Flora!" I shouted, loud and hoarsely.

Above the thunder of the waters, above the yelling of the bloodthirsty savages, I fancied I heard an answering cry. Again I called her name.

Just then I saw two white hands gripping the gunwale of the canoe, and Lavigne, who was still clinging to the tree, nodded his head in that direction, and shouted something I could not understand. The next instant the shattered canoe was torn loose by the rush of the current. It shot toward me, turned over twice, and sank from sight. And close behind it—she had been clinging to it all the while—my

66

darling rose out of the greenish water. Swiftly she drifted on, the folds of her dress inflated with air, her hands beating feebly, and her white, agonized face staring at mine.

I saw that she must pass beyond me, at least an arm's length out of reach. I did not hesitate an instant. Letting go of my precious rock, I struck out across the current. I swam alongside of the helpless girl, and caught her slender waist tightly.

Escaping the network of bowlders and reefs as by a miracle, we were swept down the remainder of the tumbling rapids. At the bottom I found a footing, and with my burden I struggled on, now slipping and floundering, now breasting the furious current, half-blinded at every stride by the dashing spray that beat in my face. But I was alive to the danger that awaited below, and I felt that there was no hope for either of us.

"Save me, Denzil! Don't let me die!" Flora murmured faintly in my ear.

"I will save you," I cried, "or I will perish with you."

I had hardly spoken when a voice—an English voice—rang loud and sharp from the forest:

"Don't harm the girl! Take her alive!"

I knew that the command came from Cuthbert Mackenzie. He was hidden by the trees, and I vainly tried to catch a glimpse of him while I fought my way through the boiling current. A moment later the stream grew suddenly calmer and more shallow, and few feet below me, on a reef that jutted out into the water I saw an Indian standing. The sunlight shone on his feathered scalp-lock, on his breech-clout and fringed leggings, on his hideously painted face. With a whoop of triumph he leveled his musket and pointed it straight at my head.

I heard the click of the hammer as it was drawn back, and knew that I must die—shot down like a dog. Life was sweet, and I could have cursed my bitter fate as I stood there, breast-deep in the water, trying to shelter Flora with my body. She uttered a heart-rending cry, and clung to me tightly.

"Save the girl, but kill the Englishman!" Mackenzie yelled again from the shelter of the forest.

The savage seemed to hesitate, still keeping his finger on the trigger of his weapon and the muzzle pointed at my head and as I stared at him, and noted the purple scars on his breast, I suddenly

67

recognized him beneath the war-paint that wrinkled his face. A wild hope flashed to my mind.

"Gray Moose!" I cried hoarsely. "Is this your gratitude? Don't you know me?"

The merciless aspect of the savage's countenance softened. With a guttural grunt he leaped forward and gazed at me hard. Then he lowered his musket and said quickly:

"Pantherfoot!"

"Ay, Pantherfoot," I replied. "Do I deserve death at your hands?"

"The white man is my brother," said the Indian. "I knew not that he would be here, else I would have refused to take the war-path. I have listened to words of evil."

"And you will save us all?" I cried.

For answer, Gray Moose turned to his braves, who were whooping like fiends and firing an occasional shot, and shouted a few words to them in the native tongue. In a moment more—almost before I could realize my good fortune, every Indian had melted away into the forest. I heard Mackenzie cry out with baffled rage and furiously curse his recreant allies. Then a silence fell, broken only by the dull roar of the falls.

I waded to the shore, and placed Flora's trembling and half-unconscious form against a tree. Baptiste quickly joined me; he had escaped from his pursuers, and had seen the whole affair from his hiding-place in the thick timber. Gummidge and his wife were clinging to the bowlders in midstream, and with some difficulty they joined us. But Lavigne had disappeared and poor Moralle lay motionless on the opposite bank, apparently dead. Cuthbert Mackenzie's villainy had cost us dear.

68

CHAPTER XV.   FORT ROYAL.

At first, huddled there together on the rocky spit of land, we stared at one another in dazed silence. It had been so sudden a transformation that we could not comprehend it all at once. A moment before while the horrid chorus of war-whoops rang in our ears we had each of us been marked out for death by tomahawk or bullet. Now our red enemies had vanished as swiftly and noiselessly as the deer; there was no sound but the droning chant of the rapids, and the singing of the birds in the forest trees.

But five of us were left; we had been eight that morning. As I thought of the three brave fellows we had lost, I made a vow that sooner or later I would avenge them. Then I knelt beside Flora, and by comforting words sought to banish the look of frozen horror from her lovely face. Mrs. Gummidge had fainted, and her husband was dashing water on her temples. Baptiste was wringing his dripping clothes and bemoaning the loss of his prized musket. We were all drenched to the skin, and it behooved us to mend our sad plight as quickly as possible.

"Our lives are safe Gummidge," I said, rising, "and that is something to be thankful for. We must have a fire to dry our clothes, and then we will be off on foot for the fort. The canoe is at the bottom, and crushed beyond repair."

"But why did those red varmints spare us?" Gummidge cried hoarsely. "They melted away like chaff. What does it mean, Carew?"

"The leader of the Indians was Gray Moose," I replied. "I saved him from a grizzly last winter, and this was his way of paying the debt. The moment he recognized me he called off his braves."

"Then they were not on the war-path against the company? There was a white man with them."

"I know that," I answered, "and it was he who hired the savages."

I briefly explained my view of the situation to Gummidge, who was aware of all that had happened in Quebec.

"It is a clear case," I concluded, "and the motive was revenge and the capture of Miss Hatherton. Mackenzie chose this spot so that he could drive us over the falls. No doubt he intended to kill all of us but the girl."

By this time Mrs. Gummidge was sitting up, and the color was returning to her cheeks. Baptiste set to work with flint and steel to light a fire, and meanwhile Gummidge and I waded through the

69

shallows to the opposite side of the stream. To our surprise, we found Moralle lying unconscious, but breathing. He had two ugly tomahawk wounds on the head and shoulder, but I judged that he had a fighting chance for life. Gardapie had gone to the bottom above the falls, and doubtless Lavigne's body had been sucked into one of the deep holes below, for we could find no trace of it.

We called Baptiste over, and he helped to carry poor Moralle back. We put him down by the fire, which was blazing cheerily, and Gummidge started to dress his wounds. Flora was standing alongside the flames. She was shivering with cold, and her face looked blue and pinched. I made her swallow some brandy—I had a flask in my pocket—and the fiery liquor warmed her at once.

"Denzil, was Cuthbert Mackenzie with the Indians?" she asked.

"Yes," I admitted.

"We have not seen the last of him!" she cried. "He will come back."

"I only wish he would," I replied. "But don't be alarmed. You are quite safe. We shall soon be at the fort."

"The fort!" she murmured. "Then we are near it?"

"Very near," said I. "It will be a couple of hours' tramp, and then—"

I was interrupted by a shout from Gummidge and Baptiste. Hearty cheers answered them, and when I looked around I saw four men, with a big canoe on their shoulders, coming up the shore at a trot. And the foremost of them was the factor of Fort Royal.

Flora divined the truth instantly, and all her self-control could not prevent an agitated heaving of her bosom and a sudden pallor of the cheeks.

"Oh, Denzil, is it—" she began.

"Yes; it is Griffith Hawke," I broke in savagely.

"Be brave!" she whispered. "Our paths lie apart—do not make it harder for me."

Our eyes met in a look that spoke volumes, and then there was a sudden uproar as the factor and his companions joined our party. I heard my name called and soon Griffith Hawke's hand was locked in mine and he was pouring out a torrent of eager words.

"And is this Miss Hatherton, my boy?" he asked suddenly.

I introduced him briefly and he made her a low and respectful bow. What he said to Flora or how she greeted him I do not know.

70

But as I turned on my heel I stole a glance at the girl and I saw that she was struggling hard to keep her composure. The sun was shining brightly but the world looked dark and black to my eyes.

As soon as the excitement of the meeting was over Gummidge and I gave the factor a coherent story of our adventures; and the narrative brought a grave and troubled expression to his face.

"I will speak of these matters later," he said. "The first thing is to get back to the fort. The wounded voyageur needs immediate attention. My canoe is a large one and will hold us all."

"But where were you bound?" I asked. "To Fort York? You sent word that you were not coming."

"Yes; but affairs grew more quiet," Hawke replied, "and I concluded that I could be spared for a week or two. I was on my way to meet you, Denzil, and it is fortunate that we did not miss each other."

A few moments later we were all tucked into the canoe. Moralle was still unconscious, and the paddles of the voyageurs swept us down the foaming current of the Churchill River. It was shortly after noon when on turning a bend we saw below us the towers and palisades, the waving flag of the Hudson Bay Company's post of Fort Royal. Since I had last seen it months before what a change had come into my life! It was a sad and bitter home-coming for me.

So our journey through the wilderness ended and now there was a lull before the threatened storm broke in all its fury—before the curtain rose on new scenes of excitement and adventure. I will pass briefly on to the things that followed soon after our arrival at the fort, the events that far surpassed in tragedy and bloodshed, in sorrow and suffering, all that had happened previously; but first I must give the reader a peep at a northern Hudson Bay Company's post as it was in those remote days—as it exists at the present time with but few changes.

Fort Royal was a fair type of them all though it was much smaller than some. It was built mostly of heavy timbers and stood in a little clearing close to the river. The stockade was about six feet high, and had two corner towers for lookout purposes. Inside, arranged like the letter L, were the various buildings—the factor's house, those of the laborers, mechanics, hunters and other employees; a log hut for the clerks; the storehouses where were kept the furs, skins and pelts, and the Indian trading house where the bartering was done. Some smaller

71

buildings—the icehouse, the powder house and a sort of stable for the canoes—completed the number.

Nearly every man had a little bedroom meagerly furnished with pictures from old illustrated papers adorning the walls. The living room where they sat at night or on off days, yarning, smoking, and drinking, was a great hall. A big table in the center was strewn with pipes and tobacco, books and writing materials; on the walls hung muskets and fishing tackle. All the houses had double doors and windows; and in the winter tremendous stoves were kept burning. The food varied according to the season, ranging from pemmican and moose-muffle—which is the nose of the moose—to venison and beaver, many kinds of fowl, and fresh and salted fish.

A word as to the Indian trading house. It was divided into two rooms, the inner and larger one containing the stores—blankets, scalping knives, flints, twine, beads, needles, guns, powder and shot and other things too numerous to mention. To the outer room the Indians entered and through a square iron-barred hole they passed their furs and pelts, receiving in exchange little wooden castors, with which they purchased whatever they wanted.

Fort Royal, as I have said, was not so large as some. It held at this time about forty men, all trusty, good-hearted fellows. It was regarded as an impregnable post; but little did any of us dream how soon our flag would be lowered amid scenes of flame and shot, of carnage and panic.

CHAPTER XVI. A RESOLVE THAT FAILED.

Two things were clear to my mind—first, that Flora was lost to me, and that honor forbade me to speak one word of love to her again; second, that I could not remain permanently under the same roof with her, whether she was married or single. The latter was a delicate and difficult affair, and I had some misgivings as to how it could be arranged; but, fortunately, chance came to my aid, as I shall show.

The factor's house was shared by several other non-commissioned officers of the company, one of whom was married. The single spare room was assigned to Mr. and Mrs. Gummidge. I saw my opportunity, and eagerly volunteered to give my own apartment to Flora, whose proper place was with the women. The matter was easily arranged, and within two hours of our arrival at the fort I was installed in a little room in the men's quarters.

I was sitting there after supper, gloomily smoking my pipe, when I received a visit from Griffith Hawke. The sight of his rugged, kindly face gave me a keen twinge of conscience. He had been like a father to me in the past, and I hated to think how nearly I had done him a foul injury.

"All going well?" I asked.

"Within the fort, yes," he replied gravely, as he sat down. "Miss Hatherton is quite recovered, and has an appetite. She seems to be a brave and spirited girl."

"She is," I assented. "You knew they were sending her, I suppose?"

"Yes, Lord Selkirk forwarded me a little water color sketch of her months ago. I am afraid there is a considerable disparity in our ages, but that can be overcome. I shall make her a good husband, and a steady one—eh, Denzil?"

With a forced smile, I pretended to appreciate the jest.

"How is Moralle?" I asked abruptly.

"He is a very sick man," said the factor; "but it is not a hopeless case. With care, he may recover. But I came to have a serious talk with you, my boy. First of all, tell me everything that happened from the time you met Miss Hatherton in Quebec until I ran across you up the river this morning. I have heard only fragments of the narrative."

I did as he requested, and he hung on my words with close attention and with a deepening look of anxiety in his eyes. When I

73

had finished, he asked me numerous questions, and then pondered silently for a few moments.

Finally he leaned forward and began to fill his pipe. By this time my mind had strayed from the subject, and on a sudden impulse I plunged into the thing that I was so anxious to have done and over with.

I grew confused from the start—a lie was so foreign to my nature—and I fear I made rather a mess of it. What words I used I cannot recall, but I incoherently told the factor that I wished to leave the fort at once and go down country, pleading as an excuse that I was tired of the lonely life of the wilderness and had taken a fancy to carve a future for myself among the towns.

By the expression of his face I was certain that he suspected the truth, and I could have bitten my tongue off with chagrin and shame. He looked at me hard.

"You would leave the service of the company?" he asked. "And with your fine chances!"

"I might be transferred—Fort Garry would suit me nicely," I blundered, quite forgetting what I had said previously.

"This is not the time to make such a demand," Griffith Hawke replied, not unkindly. "I want you here. There will be trouble in the North before many days."

"I am very anxious to go," I persisted doggedly.

"I can't spare you," he said sharply. "Let that end the discussion for the present. In the spring if you are of the same mind—"

"I will wait until then," I broke in.

I saw that all was against me, and that there was nothing to do but make the best of it.

"I can hardly believe," continued the factor, "that Cuthbert Mackenzie would have undertaken so desperate an affair, or that the Indians would have taken service under him, unless both he and they knew that they had the Northwest Company back of them. I am of the opinion that the redskins have been bought over—that hostilities are about to begin. What do you think?"

"I am inclined to agree with you," I replied.

"My duty is plain," said Griffith Hawke. "I have already despatched a full report of the matter by messenger to Fort York. To-morrow I shall send a dozen men out to scour the country to the east, west and south. They are not likely to find Mackenzie—he is

74

doubtless safe in one of the Northwest Company's posts by this time—but they may run across some of Gray Moose's braves, and ascertain from them what is brewing."

"I hope they may," said I.

"There is a chance of it," replied the factor. "Will you take charge of the expedition, Denzil?"

I had been waiting craftily for this offer, which meant a prolonged absence from the fort. Nothing could have suited me better—short of transference to another post—and I accepted without hesitation. We talked the matter over together until it was time to turn in for the night.

I was off two hours after sunrise the next day, in command of twelve of our best men. I did not see Flora before I started, nor did I wish to. And I fervently hoped, as we plunged into the forest and lost sight of the fort that the priest would have arrived and the marriage be over before I returned.

I do not intend to write at length of the expedition, and indeed but little could be said of it. We scoured the wilderness in three directions, but we found no trace of Cuthbert Mackenzie or of his hired band of savages. They had melted away mysteriously, and the empty fastnesses of the Great Lone Land told us nothing of what we sought to learn. The Indians of those parts we met in abundance, but they were peacefully engaged in trapping, and denied that any overtures had been made to them by the Northwest Company.

We were gone a fortnight, and covered some hundreds of miles. Meanwhile the winter had set in, and we returned on snowshoes. The weather was bitterly cold, the streams and lakes were frozen, and the snow lay two feet deep. Away from the fort I had been in better spirits. When I entered the stockade again, and realized that I was near Flora my heart began to ache as before.

I was soon informed of what had taken place during my absence. Gummidge and his wife had departed for Fort Garry a week previously. Moralle was out of danger, and was mending slowly. The messenger was back from Fort York, bringing news that Captain Rudstone had not yet returned there—as was his intention before coming south—and that matters were quiet. Moreover the priest had not yet arrived at Fort Royal, and there had been no marriage. Flora was still single, and likely to remain so for a time.

75

A week slipped by rapidly. The winter raged in all its severity, and there was a steady influx of Indians laden with furs and pelts. I had much to do, and was kept busy. I did not return to the factor's house, as I might have done, but stuck to my new quarters. I saw Flora occasionally, but at a distance. By mutual consent we seemed to avoid each other.

Then a memorable day dawned—a day fraught with a series of events that stamped themselves indelibly on my memory.

CHAPTER XVII.   A STRANGE WARNING.

I had been up late the night before, going over some tedious accounts with the clerks, and it was by no means an early hour when I opened my eyes and tumbled out of bed. It was a clear morning, but bitterly cold. I hurriedly drew on my thick clothing, and was about to leave the room, when I caught sight of an object sticking under the bottom crevice of the door which opened on the fort yard.

I picked it up, and looked at it with interest and curiosity, not unmixed with a vague alarm. What I held in my hand was a flat strip of birch bark about six inches square, containing some rudely-painted scrawls, which I at first took to be hieroglyphics, but which quickly resolved themselves into the uncouth figures of two men. The one was clearly a white man, wearing on his head what was evidently intended to represent the odd-shaped cap of the Northwest Company. The other was an Indian in leggings, blanket and feathers.

Here was a puzzle, indeed, and I could make nothing out of it. I was satisfied, however, that it was meant to warn me—to indicate some danger that threatened myself or the fort.

"It is a mysterious affair altogether," I reflected. "I can't fathom it. Gray Moose may be the sender, but how did he get the bark under my door? Ah, perhaps he conveyed it by some of the Indians who came to trade; they must have been admitted to the inclosure an hour ago."

But this explanation was not plausible enough. After some further thought, I concluded that the warning came from some of the Indian employees within the fort, who had learned from their own people of some threatening danger, and had chosen this means of communicating it. Then, looking more closely at the bark, I discovered in the background a few rude lines that had escaped my notice before. They were unmistakably intended for the barred window of the trading room, and of a sudden the solution to the problem flashed upon me.

"I was right in the first place," I muttered. "This is the handiwork of Gray Moose, after all. And now, to make sure, I'll set about it quietly, and won't say anything to the factor until my suspicions are confirmed."

I hastened from my quarters, forgetting that I had not yet breakfasted. I was so intent on my task that I did not even glance toward the upper windows of the factor's house, where I usually

77

caught a glimpse of Flora's pretty face at this hour. The birch bark I had tucked out of sight in my pocket.

The gates of the stockade were wide open, and within the inclosure a number of Indians—a dozen or more—were standing in groups around sledges packed with furs waiting their turn to be served. They had left their muskets outside, as was the rule when they came to trade. I glanced keenly at them from a distance, and passed on to the trading house, entering by the private door in the rear.

Here, looking from the storeroom into the common room beyond, the scene was a noisy and brilliant one. Half a score of gayly-attired savages were talking in guttural tones, gesticulating, and pointing, demanding this and that.

Griffith Hawke greeted me with a nod. He and two assistants were busily engaged at the barred window of the partition, receiving and counting bales of skins, passing out little wooden castors, and taking them in again in exchange for powder and shot, tobacco and beads, and various other commodities.

For a few moments I watched the scene sharply, though with an assumed air of indifference. I was satisfied that no Sioux were present. They were all wood Indians—as distinguished from the fiercer tribe of the plains—but they were in stronger numbers than was customary at this time of the year.

What I was seeking I did not find here. I scanned each face in turn, but all present in the outer room were unmistakably redskins.

"You are doing a lively business this morning," I remarked to the factor.

"Yes; I am having quite a run," he replied. "I can't exactly account for it." In a lower tone he added: "Every man of them is purchasing powder and shot, Denzil."

This seemed a partial confirmation of my suspicions.

"It's queer, to say the least," I answered. "I wouldn't sell them much. Tell them you're running short."

"They won't believe that," said Griffith Hawke.

"Stay and lend me a hand, Denzil, if you've nothing else to do."

"I'll come back in a moment," I replied. "I've got a little matter to attend to. I may want you to help me. If I shout for you, close the grating and run out."

Griffith Hawke's eyes dilated, and in a tone of astonishment he demanded to know what I meant. But I did not wait to answer him. I

78

slipped unheeding out of the trading house, turned the corner and almost ran into a big savage who was coming from the rear of the inclosure—a place in which he had no business to be.

He was apparently an Assiniboin brave, decked out in cariboo robe and blanket, fringed leggings, and beaded moccasins. But his cheek bones were not prominent enough for an Indian, and when he saw me a ruddy color flashed through the sickly copper of his skin and a menacing look shone in his eyes.

And I, at the first glimpse, knew that the fellow was no more of a redskin than myself. I had rightly interpreted the bit of birch bark, which meant that a white man—a spy of the Northwest Company— would be found within the fort disguised as an Indian. I was convinced that the object of my search stood before me, and I even had a lurking suspicion that the rogue was none other than Cuthbert. Mackenzie, though he was too cleverly disguised for me to feel certain of that fact.

All this passed through my mind in much less time than it takes to tell. I was on the alert, and let slip no sign that might betray my quest. And no sooner had our eyes met than the Indian's agitation vanished, and he looked at me with a proud and stolid expression.

"What are you doing here?" I demanded roughly. "This is not the way to the trading house. You have no business in this part of the fort."

The brave's only reply was a guttural "Ugh!" Folding his blanket closer about him, he began to stride off. This did not suit my purpose.

"Stop!" I cried. "I want to know what you were doing here."

"Indian mean no harm," he replied. "Heap nice fort—white man build many houses."

The moment he spoke the last ray of doubt fled from my mind, for to my trained ear the fellow's voice and accent were but feeble imitations of what they ought to be, and I fancied I could detect a little trick of mannerism I had observed in Cuthbert Mackenzie. It was time for me to show the iron hand, and I did not hesitate a second.

"You may be telling the truth," I said, "but you must give an account of yourself to the factor. Don't make any disturbance. Come along with me quietly or—" I finished the sentence by displaying a pistol which I had dexterously slipped from my belt.

I had expected some resistance, and was prepared for it. The Indian's eyes gleamed with anger, and from under his blanket he

79

whipped out a knife. As quickly I struck the weapon from his hand and grappled with him. He gave a shrill cry, and I followed it with a loud shout for help.

What happened next, though it proved to my discomfiture, was as neat and swift a thing as I have ever seen done. From the front of the trading house, and from the inside of the building the Indians came dashing in a body. They made no use of any weapons, but by sheer muscular force they wrested my captive from me and beat me cruelly on the head.

The thing was over before a man could come to my assistance, though plenty were within sight and hearing. Rising dizzily to my feet—I had been knocked down and trampled upon—I saw the daring band of savages swarming toward the open gates, taking with them the disguised spy, their sledges of furs, and the powder and shot they had just purchased.

"Help—help!" I shouted, running in pursuit. "Stop them! Don't let them get away!" With shrill cries, the redskins pushed on, and the single sentry at the gates deserted his post and fled. I heard an outcry behind me, and turning I saw that the factor and half a dozen others had come up. Griffith Hawke was the only armed man among them.

"What is the trouble?" he demanded.

"A spy!" I shouted incoherently. "A Northwest man in the fort, disguised as an Indian! I am certain it was Mackenzie! They tore him from me—don't let them get him away!"

"Stop, you rascals!" the factor yelled loudly. "We must have that man!"

No attention was paid to the command, and lifting his musket, he pointed it at the squirming mass of savages in the gateway. There was a sudden flash, a stunning report, and one of the rearmost Indians dropped.

"My God! what have I done?" cried Griffith Hawke, his face turning pale. "It was an accident—my finger slipped. Don't fire, men!"

The dead or wounded Indian had already been picked up by his comrades, and only a crimson stain was left on the snow to mark where he had fallen. The next instant the whole band were outside the stockade yelling like fiends, and with a crash some of our men flung the big gates to and barred them. A couple ran to the loopholes and peered out.

80

"The varmints are in retreat," cried one—"making for the woods on the north."

"And it's a dead body they're carrying with them, sure enough," shouted the other.

By this time the fort was in a tumult, and a crowd surrounded the factor and myself, clamoring to know the cause of the disturbance. So soon as Griffith Hawke could quiet them a little, I told all that I knew, and produced the strip of birch bark. It was passed about from hand to hand.

"You read the message right—I know something of Indian character writing," said the factor. "Doubtless Gray Moose sent it. A Northwest Company's man in the fort as a spy! It is a thousand pities he got away! But are you certain, Denzil, that he was a white man?"

"I am sure of it," I replied, "and the fact that the Indians rescued him so promptly—"

"Yes; that proves the existence of some sort of a conspiracy," the factor interrupted. "But do you know that the spy was Cuthbert Mackenzie?"

"I could not swear to it," I admitted, "but I am pretty well satisfied in my own mind."

Some of the men were for sallying out to pursue and capture the Indians, but Griffith Hawke prudently refused to permit this.

"Let well enough alone," he said. "A large force of savages may be lurking in the forest, and there will be trouble soon enough as it is. I regret the unfortunate accident by which I shot one of the Indians, for it will inflame them all the more against us. It is certain, I fear, that they have been won over by the Northwest people, and that they meditated an early attack on the fort. Thank God, that we got wind of it in time! Come what may, we can hold out against attack and siege! And at the earliest opportunity we must send word to the south and to Fort York."

There were sober faces and anxious hearts behind the stockade that day, for there could be no longer any doubt that the long-threatened storm—the struggle for supremacy between the rival fur companies—was about to break. Nay, for aught any of us knew, open strife might already be waging in the south, or up on the shores of Hudson Bay; a lonely and isolated post was ours on the Churchill River.

We held a consultation, and decided to omit no precautionary measures. Our store of weapons was overhauled, the howitzers were loaded, the gates and the stockade were strengthened, and men were posted on watch.

The day wore on quietly, and no sign of Indians was reported. I saw nothing of Flora, but I thought of her constantly, and feared she must be in much distress of mind. I confess, to my shame, that it caused me some elation to reflect that the marriage was now likely to be indefinitely postponed, but there I erred, as I was soon to learn.

At about four o'clock of the afternoon, when darkness was coming on, I was smoking a pipe in the men's quarters. Hearing shouts and a sudden commotion, I ran out in haste, thinking the Indians were approaching; but to my surprise, the sentries were unbarring the gates, and no sooner had they opened them than in came a couple of voyageurs, followed by two teams of dogs and a pair of sledges. The two occupants of the latter, in spite of the muffling of furs, I recognized at once. The one was my old Quebec acquaintance, Mr. Christopher Burley, the London law clerk; the other, to my ill-concealed dismay, was an elderly priest whom I had often seen at Fort York.

CHAPTER XVIII.   A STOLEN INTERVIEW.

The news of so unexpected an event spread quickly through the fort, and by the time the gates had been closed and barred again, men were hurrying forward from all sides. They surrounded the travelers, greeting them eagerly, and plying them and their guides with rapid questions.

I held aloof, for I was in too bitter a mood to trust myself to speech. The reasons that had brought the London law clerk to Fort Royal—a journey of hundreds of miles through the wilderness—gave me no concern; but I knew what Father Cleary's visit meant, and what would follow speedily on his arrival. Surely, I reflected, there could be no man living more wretched than myself. I thought I had become resigned to the loss of Flora, but now I knew that it was a delusion. I could not contemplate her approaching marriage without grief and heartburning—without a mad desire to dare the worst and claim the girl as my own.

The dogs and sledges were going to the stable, and the travelers, still hemmed in by a crowd, were moving toward the factor's house. Griffith Hawke caught sight of me, and made a gesture; but I pretended not to see him, and turning on my heel, I strode away to a far corner of the yard.

An hour of solitude put me in a calmer frame of mind—outwardly, at least. The supper horn drew me to quarters. I had little appetite, but I made a pretense of eating, and tried to answer cheerfully the remarks that my comrades addressed to me.

By listening I learned much of interest. The men kept up a ceaseless chatter and discussion, and the sole topic of conversation was the arrival of Christopher Burley and the priest. The travelers, it appeared, had come together from Fort York—where all was quiet at the time of their departure—and by the same roundabout road our party had traversed some days before. Strange to say they had encountered no Indians, either on the way or when near the fort, and for this the men had two explanations. A part asserted that the redskins had moved off in the direction of Fort York, while others were of the opinion that they had purposely let the travelers enter unmolested in order to deceive our garrison.

The discussion waxed so hot that no reference was made to the motive of the priest's visit, for which I was heartily thankful. I was anxious to get away from the noise and the light, and as soon as I had finished my supper I rose. Just then Andrew Menzies, a non-commissioned officer of the company, entered the room.

"Carew!" he called out; "the factor wants to see you when you can spare the time."

"All right; I'll go over to the house presently," and lighting my pipe, I sauntered out of the quarters.

Why the factor wanted me I could not readily conceive, unless it was for some detail connected with his marriage. There were several things that I wished to turn over in my mind before presenting myself to Griffith Hawke, where I would be likely to meet Flora.

A sound of low voices at the gates, and the rattle of a bolt, drew me first in that direction. A little group of men were standing at the loopholes, peering out.

"What's up, comrades?" I inquired in a whisper.

"Ah, it's you, Denzil?" replied one looking around. "Didn't you know? Vallee and Maignon, the voyageurs who came in a bit ago have just started back to Fort York on snowshoes, taking a letter from the factor in regard to the row here this morning."

"They will go as they came," added another, "and I believe they will get through all right. They are out on the river by this time, and they would scarcely have been permitted to pass yonder timber had any Indians been on the watch."

"I agree with you," said I. "Let us hope that the brave fellows will meet with no mishap."

I lingered for a moment, but the quiet of the night remained unbroken. Then I turned back across the yard, taking care that none observed me, and made my way to a small grove of fir trees that lay in the rear of the trading house and some distance to the right of the factor's residence. In the heart of the copse was a rude wooden bench, built some years before by the factor's orders. I made my way to it over the frozen snow crust, and sat down to meditate and smoke.

I had no more than settled myself when I heard the light, crunching patter of feet. The sounds came nearer, and of a sudden, by the dim glow of the moon, I saw the figure of a woman within six feet of me. It was Flora Hatherton. She was bareheaded, and a long cloak was thrown over her shoulders. As she advanced, her hands clasped in front of her, a stifled sob broke from her lips.

I had been on the point of retreating, but the girl's distress altered my mind. By an irresistible impulse I rose and stood before her.

84

"Flora!" I exclaimed.

She shrank back with a smothered scream.

"Hush! do not be alarmed!" I added. "Surely you know me?"

"Denzil!" she whispered. "Oh, what a fright you gave me!"

"Why are you here?" I asked.

"The house was so warm—they have the stove red hot," she stammered confusedly. "I slipped out for a breath of fresh air. And you?"

"I came for the same purpose," said I. "This is a favorite spot of mine. But you have been weeping Flora."

"No—oh, no," she answered, in a tone that belied her words. "You are mistaken, Denzil. I—came here to think."

"Of what?"

"Of my wedding day," she replied half-defiantly. "Surely you know that the priest has arrived. I am to be married to-morrow morning."

"To-morrow morning!" I gasped.

"Yes, unless the world ends before then. Oh, Denzil, I have such wicked thoughts to-night! It is in my heart to wish that the Indians would take the fort—that something would happen before to-morrow."

"Nothing will happen," I said bitterly. "The fort can stand a siege of days and months. So you are determined to wed Griffith Hawke—to forget what we have been to each other in the past?"

"Denzil, you have no right," she said sadly.

The words stung me, and I suddenly realized the depths of shame to which I had sunk. She saw her advantage, and pressed it.

"I have lingered too long," she said. "I fear I shall be missed. This is our last meeting. Farewell, Denzil!"

"Farewell!" I answered bitterly.

She held out her hand, and I pressed it to my lips. It was like marble. Then she turned and glided away, and I heard her light footsteps receding among the trees.

The next instant I regretted that I had yielded and let her go. The thought that I might never see her again maddened me. Without realizing the recklessness and folly of it, I started in pursuit, calling her name in a hoarse whisper.

But I was too late, swiftly as I moved. I reached the edge of the trees in time to see a flash of light as the rear door of the factor's house opened and closed.

I stood for a moment in the moonlight and solitude and then something happened that cooled my fevered brain and put Flora out of my thoughts. Loud on the frosty night rang the report of a gun; two more followed in quick succession. From the nearest watch-tower the sentries shouted a sonorous alarm, and their voices were drowned by a shrill and more distant burst of Indian yells.

CHAPTER XIX.   ANOTHER VISITOR.

That the redskins were making an attack in force on the stockade was my first and immediate conclusion, but it gave me no great uneasiness since I knew how stoutly we were protected. On second thoughts, however, I observed that the shots and yells—which were keeping up lustily—came from a considerable distance, and I began to suspect that something else was in the wind.

Meanwhile, I had not been standing idle. As soon as I heard the alarm I ran like a deer across the yard. It was the work of an instant to dash into the quarters and seize my musket. Then I sped on, with a great clamor rising from every part of the fort and armed men hastening right and left of me.

When I reached the gates, where a little group was assembled, no more than a minute could have elapsed since the outbreak. I passed on to the nearest watch tower—it was near by—and darted up the ladder which led to the second floor. Here there were good-sized loopholes commanding a view of the north and east fronts of the stockade. Half a dozen men were watching from them, and above their excited voices I heard the crack of muskets and the whooping chorus of savages.

"What's going on?" I demanded. "They are not attacking the fort?"

"No, not that, Carew," cried one. "The redskins are chasing some poor devils who were bound here. Ah, they have turned on them! Plucky fellows!"

"Will you stand here, sir? Look yonder—quick!"

It was the voice of Baptiste, who was at one of the loopholes. He made room for me, and I peered eagerly out. The view was straight to the north, and what I saw turned my blood hot with anger.

Less than a quarter of a mile away, where the white, moonlit clearing ended at a narrow forest road running parallel with the river, the sorely-harassed little group was in plain sight—a sledge, a team of dogs, and three men kneeling on the snow. They were exchanging shots with a mass of Indians, who were dancing about on the verge of the timber, and were for the moment being held at bay. I could see the red flashes, and the wreaths of gray smoke against the dark green of the trees.

"They had better make a dash for it," exclaimed Baptiste.

"Now is their chance."

"We are all cowards," I cried indignantly. "A party could have dashed out to the rescue by this time."

"Just my opinion, Carew," said a man named Walker. "But who was to give the orders? They must come from the factor. He's down at the gates now, and plenty with him."

"Then I'll get his permission to go out," I cried hotly. "Will you volunteer, men?"

But as I spoke—I had not taken my eyes from the loophole—the situation suddenly took a different turn. The Indians yelled with triumph, and I saw one of the three white men toss up his arms and fall over. At that his companions wheeled about, the one leaping upon the sledge, while the other ran toward the dog leader of the team.

"Only two left!" I shouted. "They are coming! Now for a lively race! God help them to reach the fort!"

"By Heavens, sir! they'll get in if they are quick!" cried Walker, who was on the other side of the tower. "Hawke knows what to do; he is opening the gates! The men are loading their muskets! They are bringing up the howitzer."

His last sentence I scarcely heard, for I had already left the loophole and was scrambling down the ladder. The next instant I was at the double gates, one of which had been unbarred and thrown wide open. A dozen men were lined up on each side of the entrance, among them Menzies and the factor.

"Stand back," Griffith Hawke shouted at me. "Keep the way clear!"

But I edged up to the front, where my view was uninterrupted. How my heart leaped to see the sledge gliding over the snow, the man inside and the one on snowshoes shouting at the plucky, galloping dogs! But they still had one hundred and fifty yards to come, not far behind them, whooping and yelling, firing musket and hurling tomahawks, were at least two score of redskins—the most of them on snowshoes. Crack, crack, crack! They seemed to be aiming poorly, for the sledge swept on, dogs and men uninjured.

"Be ready!" cried the factor: "make room there! The moment the sledge dashes in let the red devils have a volley—muskets and howitzer!"

What happened next, though it was all over in the fraction of a minute, was intensely exciting and tragic. The tower being high up,

88

the men posted there were now opening fire; lusty cheers rose as we saw a couple of Indians go down in the snow.

Bang, bang! a hit this time. The man on snowshoes staggered, reeled, fell over. His comrade turned and shot as the sledge swept on—more than that he could not do. Whether the poor fellow was dead or living we never knew; but nothing mattered the next instant, for the foremost savages reached the spot, and there was the quick gleam of a descending tomahawk.

Fifty yards now to the stockade! In spite of the fire from the tower, the Indians bore on. They let drive another straggling volley, and with a convulsive spring in air, the leading dog of the team dropped dead. In a trice the rest of the dogs, pulled up abruptly, were in a hopeless tangle. The sledge dashed into them, grated sidewise, and tipped over, sending its occupant sprawling on the snow.

I gave the poor fellow up for lost, but his pluck and wits were equal to the emergency. He sprang to his feet, and without looking behind him or stopping to pick up his musket, he struck out for the fort. On he sped, running in a zigzag course, while the now halted Indians blazed away at him, and our men cheered and shouted.

"Watch sharp!" cried Griffith Hawke.

As he spoke the fugitive swerved a little, and ten strides brought him to the gates. He rushed safely past me, and staggered into the inclosure.

Already the baffled redskins had scattered in flight, but they were not to get off so easily. From the marksmen in the watch-tower and at the stockade loopholes, from as many of our eager men as could line up outside the gates, a hot and deadly fire was poured. A way was cleared for the howitzer, and the roar that burst from its iron throat woke a hundred forest echoes.

A great cloud of bluish smoke hid the scene for a moment, and when it drifted and rolled upward, our short-lived opportunity was gone. With almost incredible speed the savages had melted away, and were safe in the shelter of the adjacent timber. They had taken some of their dead and wounded with them, as well as the dogs and sledge; but six or seven bodies lay sprinkled darkly here and there on the snow crust.

Nor were the casualties all on one side, as we now had time to observe. The last volley delivered by the Indians had killed one of our party and wounded two more. The men were for sallying out against the foe, but Griffith Hawke would have none of it.

"The devils are in ambush," he cried, "and would give us the worst of it. We'll need our powder and ball later, I'm thinking. Make all secure yonder, and be quick about it."

I helped to close and bar the gate, and then pushed into the thick of the clamorous crowd that surrounded the escaped traveler. I had fancied I recognized him when he shot by me, and now the first glimpse told me I was right, for the fugitive was none other than Captain Myles Rudstone.

CHAPTER XX. THE LOST LOCKET.

Captain Rudstone was in a temper, and but for the press in front of him he would have dashed at the gates.

"What are you afraid of?" he cried. "Why don't you pursue the red devils? make an end of them? They've killed two of the best voyageurs that ever tramped the woods. My God! what does it all mean?"

"It means war, sir," answered the factor. "The Northwest Company is at the bottom of the mischief. I entreat you to be calm, Captain Rudstone. The Indians are in force, and it would be sheer madness to try to track them down. I am responsible for the safety of the fort."

These sober words brought the captain to his senses.

"You are right, Hawke," he admitted. "I see there is nothing to be done at present. But, by Heaven! sir, I'll have the blood of a score of redskins for each of those poor comrades of mine. And you say war has broken out? I don't understand—"

Just then his eyes fell on me, and he held out his hand with a stern smile of welcome. I clasped it warmly.

"So we meet again, Mr. Carew?" he exclaimed.

"I wish it had been under happier circumstances," said I; "but I am heartily glad to see you."

"Thank you," he replied, and his eyes shifted from mine as they had been wont to do formerly. "I have much to be grateful for," he added, "I might be lying yonder with a bullet in my back and a tomahawk in my skull. It was a narrow escape."

"You did not come from Fort York?" I inquired.

"No, from the north—from Fort Churchill, at the mouth of the river. I am finished with my errand in this part of the country, and am bound south. I had no idea that trouble had broken out until I was attacked on the edge of the timber."

"I fear you will be detained here for many a day, Captain Rudstone," said Griffith Hawke. "But come to my quarters, and when you have fed and rested I will give you a full report of all that has happened."

Turning to me the factor added:

"See to the wounded, Denzil, and make sure that the sentries are properly posted. Then let me know how matters are going. I don't anticipate any further trouble."

That Griffith Hawke should put me in virtual command of the fort at such a time and in preference to several officers who were older and of superior rank, caused me some pride and satisfaction; for just now my mind was taken up with sterner things than my hopeless passion for Flora, and what martial spirit was in me had been fired by the prospect of an Indian siege.

After attending to my duties I strode on to the house and entered the cozily-furnished living room. Here logs were blazing in a great fireplace, at opposite sides of which, talking in low tones, sat Father Cleary and Andrew Menzies. The latter's wife, it may be observed, was Flora's companion.

At a table in the middle of the room, with lighted pipes between their teeth and their glasses of grog handy, were Griffith Hawke and Captain Rudstone. The latter was as handsome and dandified as ever, and by the litter of dishes at one end of the table I knew he had just finished supper. Both had been discussing the Indian troubles, to judge from their grave and thoughtful faces.

The factor's eyes seemed to read me through and through, and there was something in the scrutiny that disturbed and puzzled me. He motioned to a chair and I sat down awkwardly.

"All quiet?" he asked. "You have omitted no precautions?"

I told him what I had done, and he and the captain nodded approval.

"A bad storm has set in?" the latter said interrogatively.

"The worst kind of a one," I replied. "The wind is high, and the snow will drift heavily. The Indians are not likely to attack us in such weather."

"I wish I could feel sure of that," Griffith Hawke said doubtfully. "By the way, Denzil, I have reason to believe that white men are among the savages."

"I am pretty certain that Cuthbert Mackenzie is with them," said I.

"And others," broke in Captain Rudstone. "I heard more than one English voice when I was fighting and running for my life yonder."

"Northwest men!" exclaimed the factor. "By sir, I tell you I am right. To-day's events amount to an open declaration of war."

Captain Rudstone blew a thick cloud of smoke and smiled grimly through it.

92

"I don't agree with you," he said, in the tone of one who knows his ground. "The Northwest Company will not come to open hostilities—they are too crafty for that; but they are at the bottom of this trouble. Their agents have persuaded the Indians to rise, are fighting with them, and Mackenzie is determined to take the fort. Whether he fails or succeeds, his participation will not be proved. The blame will be thrust on your shoulders, Hawke, because of the Indian you shot this morning."

"That was an unfortunate accident," the factor admitted uneasily, "and it may serve the purpose you suggest. But I am not afraid that the fort will fall; we can hold out against big odds."

"You'll have them," said the captain. "I've no doubt there will be five hundred redskins before the stockade within a day or two, and then they'll give you sharp work. And a drifting snowstorm will be in their favor."

"I don't see it," replied Griffith Hawke. "What do you mean?"

The captain shrugged his shoulders. "Nothing in particular," he answered evasively. "By the way, Hawke, when are you to marry Miss Hatherton?"

As he spoke he jerked one arm toward the priest, who was still talking by the fire, and then gave me a swift glance of amused contempt. The factor also turned his eyes upon me, and I felt my face grow hot.

"I am to be married to-morrow," he replied half-sadly. "At least, that is the present arrangement. But I have been thinking of late—"

He was interrupted, to my vast relief, by the sudden opening of a door behind him. Mr. Christopher Burley entered the room, looking as if he might have just stepped from the legal chambers in Lincoln's Inn. He had evidently made a careful toilet, his traveling costume being discarded for a suit of sober black.

He nodded severely to Captain Rudstone, who he had seen earlier in the evening, and I observed a slight confusion in the bearing of both, clearly due to the recollection of their quarrel at the Silver Lily. Then, with an affable smile, the law clerk offered me his hand.

"I am pleased to see you, Mr. Carew," he said. "I learned from the factor that you were here. I predicted that we might meet again, if you remember."

"I remember well," said I. "This is a small world, after all. I take it that the quest you spoke of has brought you to the north?"

93

"You are right, sir," he replied. "It has led me hundreds of miles through the wilderness, from one fort to another of the Hudson Bay territory—truly a weary round of travel."

"And with what success?"

"None as yet; but I am not discouraged. From here I go southwest. I feel that I shall succeed in the end. I find that the factor is unable to help me, and it is no doubt needless to ask you—"

"Quite so," I interrupted. "Osmund Maiden is still an unfamiliar name to me."

"Captain Rudstone knows the Canadas thoroughly," said Griffith Hawke. "Perhaps he has run across your man in the past."

My eyes were on the captain just then, and I fancied he gave a slight start; certain it is that a sudden flush colored his bronzed face a darker shade, and I remembered that this was not the first time he had shown agitation at the mention of the man Christopher Burley was seeking. But he was instantly himself again, and he calmly twisted his long mustaches as he answered:

"Osmund Maiden! I fancy I have heard the name somewhere in my time. May I ask, sir, what object you have in desiring to find this man?"

"That I may reveal to none save Osmund Maiden himself," Christopher Burley replied. "But I beg of you to refresh your memory. It will be greatly to your advantage if you can give me any information—"

"Denzil, I have been thinking of something," the factor interrupted suddenly. "Forgive me, my boy, for alluding to a personal and delicate matter; but I have always fancied that there was some mystery about your father—that his name might have been assumed. I speak thus frankly because Mr. Burley has honored me in part with his confidence—"

"There was no mystery," I broke in sharply. I was angry with Griffith Hawke, though I knew that he meant well. "My father's name was Carew," I went on, "and he had a right to it. Why he left England I cannot say, but his home was in Yorkshire and his parents were dead when he came to the Canadas."

"Then I am mistaken," said Griffith Hawke.

"There are Carews in Yorkshire," added the law clerk. "It is doubtless the same family. Did your father leave no papers?"

"None," I replied.

94

"He used to wear a small gold locket about his neck," declared the factor. "Surely you have seen it, Denzil?"

"I remember it," I said curtly; "but I do not know what was in it, or what became of it. It was missing when my father's body was found in the woods."

"That is unfortunate," said Christopher Burley in a tone that showed a lack of further interest in the matter.

"Very!" assented Captain Rudstone, who was watching me curiously.

I made no reply. I had just recollected that I had in my pocket a seal ring—a trifle too large to wear—which had been my father's. I fumbled for it, hoping to put an end to a controversy that was distasteful to me. But before I could find and produce it there were hurried steps outside the house and the door was thrown open with a crash.

CHAPTER XXI.   THE BEGINNING OF THE END.

We all turned round and then with one accord sprang to our feet The horror of what we saw held us spellbound and speechless. We did not feel the icy air, the swirl of fine snowflakes that came driving into the room, for in the doorway stood Baptiste, his honest face almost unrecognizable with hot passion, and in each hand he thrust out a ghastly, gory, red-dripping thing of hair and flesh. They were human scalps, and we knew at once from whose heads they had been torn.

"*Nom de Dieu!*" cried the priest. "The poor wretches!"

"Yes, Valle and Maignon!" Baptiste said thickly, grinding his teeth. "They did not get far, sir, Heaven rest their souls! But a moment ago the red devils flung these bloody trophies over the stockade—none can tell how they crept so near! It is a warning, messieurs, that we are all to be served the same way."

"My poor voyageurs!" groaned Christopher Burley. "That they should come to such an end! Oh, this barbarous country!"

He suddenly turned sick and faint, and dropping into a chair, he sat there trembling, his face buried in his hands. Father Cleary was crossing himself and muttering piously.

"A thing like this," cried Captain Rudstone, "is enough to turn a man into a fiend. By Heaven! Hawke, if you say the word, I'll lead a party out against the savages!"

But the factor did not seem to hear him. He was leaning heavily on a chair, his face the hue of ashes. "My fault—my fault!" he said hoarsely. "I sent the poor fellows to their death. But God knows I believed they would get through safely!"

"We all believed that," broke in Andrew Menzies.

"Compose yourself, sir! No blame can possibly attach to you."

Meanwhile Baptiste had been standing in the same attitude. I sharply bade him close the door, and he did so. Then he stepped forward, tossed the reeking scalps on the table, and with a shaking hand helped himself, unbidden, to a stiff glass of rum.

"You need not have brought those hideous things here," said I.

"I did not come for that alone, Monsieur Carew," he replied. "I was sent with a message. The Indians intend shortly to attack. It will be well to prepare."

"We are all ready," exclaimed Griffith Hawke, roused from his dejection by this intelligence. "But what do you mean, my man? Why do the sentries look for an attack?"

96

"Sir, the Indians have been making strange signals," Baptiste answered, "and they were seen from the loopholes and the tower creeping along the edge of the timber in force."

"The warning is timely," said Captain Rudstone. "If the savages are prowling about it means mischief, otherwise they would be rigging up a camp against this bitter weather. And no doubt they reckon the storm will be to their advantage, since the driving snow thickens the air."

The rest of us were of the same mind, and to a man we thirsted for a chance to avenge the foul murder of the two voyageurs. We eagerly donned our fur coats and caps, and began to examine our weapons.

"Mr. Menzies, will you speak to the women before you go," said the factor. "Tell them not to be alarmed if they hear firing—that there is no danger."

"And perhaps they will take consolation from your company, Father Cleary," he added, when Menzies had left the room.

The priest was wrapping himself in furs, and before replying he took his musket from a rack over the fireplace.

"If the women folk need me, I will not refuse," he said quietly. "I am a man of peace first, but I can fight when occasion requires, and my choice lies that way now, Mr. Hawke."

"Then come with us, by all means," assented the factor.

"Nor shall I be left behind," cried Christopher Burley, showing a spirit that I did not think was in him. "I can handle a gun, sir."

He did not wait for permission, but borrowed a spare coat that hung on the wall and helped himself to a serviceable musket and a supply of powder and ball.

"Denzil, you had better go ahead and turn the men out," said the factor. "We will follow shortly."

I was eager to do this, and, accompanied by Baptiste, I hurried from the house. I thought with uneasiness, as I plodded across the inclosure, that I had seen few worse storms. The snow was falling fine and thick, and a stinging, shrieking wind was already heaping it in drifts.

"The redskins will give us trouble, sir," Baptiste said ominously.

"No doubt," I assented sharply; "but we could beat off double their numbers. Don't go and croak among the men, Baptiste."

The quarters were quite deserted, tidings of the expected attack having emptied them, and I found all the inmates of the fort—save those on duty—assembled near the northeast tower. These included the few Indian employees, who were to be fully trusted. I made a quick round of the loopholes, and learned that all was now quiet, and that no signals or movement had been observed for several minutes. When I returned Griffith Hawke and his little party had arrived, and I communicated the state of affairs to them.

"It is the calm before the storm," remarked Captain Rudstone. "I'll wager anything you like the savages are going to rush us."

We waited five minutes, standing about in scattered group, and listening for some warning from the watch tower. It was the eve of the factor's wedding—a fact that I recalled with bitter irony as I noted him posted alertly in the pelting snow, musket in hand, expecting shortly to be plunged in the thick of a bloody fray. Far across in the distance a gleam of light twinkled in the window of Flora's room. What were her thoughts?

A hand tapped me on the shoulder; I turned and saw Christopher Burley.

"It is worse than a London fog, this cold," he said, with chattering teeth. "I seem to feel it in my bones. How long will we wait, Mr. Carew?"

"That is hard to tell," I replied. "If you are freezing, go indoors."

I think he would have taken me at my word, but I had hardly spoken when the brooding silence was shattered by a cry from the watch-tower:

"Look sharp! They are coming on two sides! To the loopholes!"

Here and there a shout was heard, but for the most part the warning was received with a grim calmness that spoke well for the fighting temper of our men. The next instant the air was full of Indian war-whoops—and a more blood-curdling and fearful sound I have yet to hear. Then the savages fired a continuous volley, and the bullets came rattling like sleet against the stockade; some entered at the loopholes, and a cry arose that a half-breed was down.

At the first—such trivial things will a man do at critical times—my attention was taken by Christopher Burley. Elevating his musket in air, he pulled the trigger, and was flat on his back before you could count two. I helped him to rise, and he began to rub his shoulder ruefully.

98

"It was too heavy a charge," he said. "Did I kill any one?"

"It's a mercy you didn't," I replied.

I gave him a word or two of instruction, but did not wait to see how far his pluck would carry him. I left him in the act of reloading, and sped to a loophole near the gates, which faced eastward.

The east and north sides were the ones chosen for the assault, and here a good third of our men had already posted themselves. They, and the marksmen in the corner tower were firing steadily. The fusillade, blending with Indian yells and volleys, made an indescribable din. I took a hasty glance without. Through the driving snow, I saw a horde of warriors dashing swiftly forward. There must have been a hundred in sight on that one side, and I knew that we were in for hot work if as many were attacking from the north.

On they rushed, and now some dropped craftily behind lopped-off trunks of trees which were sprinkled plentifully about the clearing. Others sought shelter from the wind-blown heaps of snow, but the greater part made for the stockade. The powder smoke would hide them for an instant, and then I would see them a dozen feet nearer.

The patter of bullets close to my head warned me of the danger I was in, and stirred me to action. I thrust out my musket and fired. I looked in time to see an Indian fling up his arms and fall; right and left of him dark blotches stained the snow. I reloaded, and fired again, shouting with excitement.

To the north and east, and where the tower rose between, was one blaze and crackle of muskets. Smoke hid the snow and savage yells drowned the shrieking of the wind. In spite of the terrific fire, the redskins poured on. A ball sang by my ear, and another sent a shower of splintered wood into my very face. Close on my right a man was shot through the chest; farther to the left I saw a half-breed stagger and fall.

"Steady, men!" rang out the factor's voice. "Stand firm and make every shot tell!"

I poked my musket through the loophole and pulled trigger. It was next to impossible to miss, so near was the foremost line of savages. I was reloading in frantic haste, when the stockade in front of me creaked and rattled. Above the top rose the heads and shoulders of three painted warriors, and the next instant, with shrill cries, they had leaped into the inclosure.

99

CHAPTER XXII.   HOT WORK.

I was standing so near that the three daring redskins all but fell upon me. As I dodged quickly back, one let fly a tomahawk. I felt it graze my head, and the next instant I had smashed the skull of the howling wretch with the butt end of my musket. Already three more were over the stockade, and the five fell upon our men with desperate fury. The yelling and whooping, the cries of the wounded, made an infernal din. A comrade on my left was shot in the mouth, and dropped writhing to the ground; a half-breed at my very side clapped a hand to his arm and spun round.

But by this time the scrimmage had been seen at a distance, and there was a rally to the spot. Two savages were clubbed to death, and a third fell by Captain Rudstone's musket. I shot a fourth through the chest, but in spite of the wound, he made at me, and I had to settle him with a blow above the ear.

For one Indian that was slain, however, two fresh ones scrambled into the inclosure. There were as agile as cats, and as daring as panthers. With bullet and tomahawk they assailed us, and we were soon hard-pressed all along the line. There was fierce fighting on the north as well, and so no help could be spared from that quarter. Indeed, I began to fear that the fort would be taken by sheer numbers; and even while I was engaged hand to hand with the painted fiends, I was meditating what steps to take to save Flora.

But when the situation was most critical, several things befell to turn the tide. At great risk a couple of plucky fellows loaded the howitzer—it had been discharged once—and thrusting the muzzle out of one of the boles provided for that purpose, they fired it point-blank into the mass of savages who were coming on to the assault. At the same moment a swivel gun roared a few yards to the left, and the two tremendous reports were followed by shrill yells of agony and consternation.

This appeared to check the rush from without, and of a sudden the top of the stockade showed empty against the skyline. Seeing this, we took heart, and attacked the savages who were inside more furiously than ever. Just then we were joined by half a dozen men from the watch-tower and by four others led by Griffith Hawke. The redskins wavered, fell back, and bolted in panic for their lives. Ten of them we shot down or clubbed, and as many succeeded in scrambling

100

over the stockade. It had been a close shave, but the fort was saved for the present.

"Blaze away, or they'll be in again!" cried the factor. "Give them a steady volley!"

With ringing cheers we sprang to the loopholes, and fired as fast as we could load and empty. A vigorous fusillade was returned at first, but it soon slackened and straggled, and the whooping of the savages ceased entirely.

It was the same on the north side of the fort. The Indians had not retreated, but they were repulsed and disheartened, and were in no mood for further sacrifice. They lay hidden behind drifted snow and stumps, taking wary shots whenever they fancied they saw an opportunity.

Now we had time to breathe—time to take a welcome spell of rest after our hard struggle. We were all parched and powder grimed, and some of us were bandaging slight wounds. And the victory had cost us dear. Three sorely-hurt men had been carried off to the hospital, and among the dozen or more slain savages who lay in ghastly attitudes on the trampled, blood-soaked snow were four of our plucky defenders, who would never lift musket again. It was a hideous, revolting sight, and the raging storm, the murky gray of the night, lent an added horror to it.

The semi-lull continued, and little attention was paid to the straggling fire of the Indians, though sharp eyes were watching from the tower. Griffith Hawke came up to where I was leaning, breathing hard, on the barrel of my musket.

"Thank God you are all right, my boy!" he said hoarsely. "I never expected those devils would get over the stockade. It was Heaven's mercy that enabled us to drive them off; but we have lost heavily."

"Severely, indeed," I assented. "And so have the Indians. I doubt if they will try that game again. And what was the result at the north side, sir? I believe you had desperate fighting there at the same time."

"Not so bad as here," the factor replied; "but pretty nearly. The Indians broke in, but our fellows were getting the best of it when I left to help you. Menzies was in charge, and—ah! here he comes now."

The big Scotchman was loading his musket as he approached. He limped badly—a gunstock had struck him on the thigh—and he had a flesh wound in his left arm. He anxiously inquired how many we had lost, and when I told him, he shook his head gravely.

"I have three dead over yonder," he replied, "and twice as many disabled. The garrison is reduced by nearly a third, and the savages are fighting recklessly! I greatly fear, Hawke, that if they rush the stockade again—"

"We'll beat them off twice, thrice, four times if need be," the factor interrupted. "At the worst, we are likely to have a long siege of it."

He spoke cheerfully and confidently, but none the less I saw a haggard, strained look in his face, as he glanced toward the flickering light in Flora's window.

By this time the firing was taking a brisker turn, and the three of us separated, Hawke and Menzies striding across to the north side of the inclosure. I went to my old place, and there I remained for a trying half-hour.

Trying is a poor word for the sort of warfare the Indians carried on during that interval. They were scattered about thickly to north and east of the fort, and within close range, but each warrior was cunningly concealed behind a stump or a snow hillock.

How they could see so well is a mystery, but certain it is that they brought their muskets to bear on every loophole of the stockade and the tower. The storm was raging bitterly, but in their furred garments, their hide moccasins and leggings, they defied the exposure.

At the first we lost a man killed, and had three wounded. Then we grew more careful, and reconnoitered from what little crevices we could find before we ventured on a shot. Those who had no loopholes kept loading spare muskets and passing them to us, taking our own as soon as we fired. I had several narrow escapes, but by watching for the spurts of flame and smoke and for the limbs that now and then showed darkly against the snow, I killed or disabled half a dozen of the enemy. Baptiste was on my right, and just beyond him was Captain Rudstone.

There was one diversion during the time I speak of, and that from the west side of the fort, where a great clamor of firing and whooping suddenly broke out. I did not dare to leave my post—I was virtually in charge of the east stockade—but Captain Rudstone led half a dozen men to the disturbed quarter. The scrimmage was quickly over, and when the captain returned I got a report from him.

"It's all right," he said. "The devils rushed us, but we drove them back by volleys from the loopholes, killing half a score and losing one

102

ourselves. The ground dips down to the fort there, and we had a clean sweep. They won't molest us on that side again—it was a half-hearted attack, anyway."

"I wish they would drop the whole thing," I replied bitterly.

Captain Rudstone shrugged his shoulders.

"You would be a fool to expect it, Carew," he said. "I am not a bird of ill-omen, but, by Heaven! the redskins are determined to hang on till they take the fort."

"They'll have a wait," said I.

"That's as maybe," the captain rejoined. "If there were only the Indians to reckon with! But Northwest men are among them, cleverly disguised; and I doubt not Cuthbert Mackenzie is one of them."

"I am sure of it," I asserted.

"He is after revenge—and Miss Hatherton," the captain went on. "And to my mind, it is a toss up which will make the girl the happier—Mackenzie or Hawke."

I turned on him fiercely, and I could have struck him with pleasure; he seemed to take a malicious delight in probing my heart wound.

"Is this a time to talk of such things?" I cried. "I wish to hear none of it, Captain Rudstone. Miss Hatherton is nothing to me!"

The captain laughed—a low, sneering laugh—and just then an Indian bullet sang between us.

"A close shave!" he muttered, as he strode off to his loophole.

I turned to mine, and it partly relieved my feelings to get a shot at a feathered scalp-lock, that was bobbing behind a tuft of bushes twenty feet away. I aimed true, and with a convulsive leap a warrior fell sprawling in the open.

My success stirred the savages up a little, drawing a chorus of vengeful whoops, and a straggling shower of lead that pelted the stockade like hail.

Then the fire ceased almost entirely, and after waiting and watching for five minutes, I concluded to leave my post temporarily and have a look about the fort.

CHAPTER XXIII.   THE SECOND RUSH.

I went first to the highest watch-tower, the occupants of which had been better protected than those at the stockade, but for all that I found one poor fellow dead and another badly wounded. Such a true and steady fire had been poured at the loopholes, I was told, that it was as much as the men's lives were worth to expose themselves sufficiently to take aim. I looked out for a moment, but though I could see vaguely through the driving snow to the dark line of the forest, not an Indian was in sight.

"They have not retreated?" I asked.

"Not them, sir," a grizzled voyageur remarked, with emphasis. "Every clump of bushes, every stump and snow heap, has a lurking redskin behind it. And the woods yonder are full of 'em, too."

He had hardly spoken when there was a flash and a report off to the left, followed quickly by one from the right. Both shots were aimed at the stockade loopholes, but they seemed to strike harmlessly, and drew no reply from our men.

"Consarn the devils!" growled the voyageur as he peered into the night. "They don't show as much as a feather tip."

"They ain't lying so long in the snow for nothing," added another man. "They'll be at us again with a rush presently."

"I am afraid they will," I assented. "Keep a sharp lookout and give us timely warning."

With that I left the tower and walked along the north side of the fort. I was glad to observe that the men were in confident and even cheerful spirits. Some were loading muskets, while others were bringing bullets and canisters of powder, and, what was more urgently needed at present, pannikins of steaming hot coffee. The latter, I ascertained, came from the factor's house, and I had no doubt that it was due to the womanly forethought of Flora and Mrs. Menzies.

I could not find Father Cleary, and on making inquiries I learned that he was with the wounded, who had all been taken to the hastily improvised hospital in the men's quarters. I was told that he had stuck to his post through the fighting, and had done as good and valorous service as any man in the fort.

Mr. Christopher Burley I came upon seated astride of an empty cask, with his musket across his knees. His cap was gone, and his hair was awry; he was scarcely recognizable for a mask of perspiration and powder grime.

104

"I congratulate you," I said, "on keeping a sound skin."

"The same to you," he replied. "It was indeed a severe and bloody fight. I bore your advice in mind Mr. Carew, and I have fired six shots without discomfort."

"To what purpose?" I inquired.

"I hope at least that I have hit none of our own men," he answered with a touch of humor. "I confess I am more handy with a quill than a musket. I have friends in London, sir, who will not believe me when I relate my adventures in this barbarous country. But, alas! I may not live to see England again."

I thought this more than likely, but did not tell him so.

"Come, come, Mr. Burley!" I replied, "keep up your spirits; don't yield to depression. You will be spared to stamp many a blue document—to entangle scores of luckless litigants in the meshes of the law."

I slipped on without waiting to see how he took this sally, and went as far as the northwest angle of the fort. Here I stopped to talk with some comrades who were drinking hot coffee flavored with a dash of rum.

Close by, other men were watching alertly at the loopholes. Occasionally they would fire at some partly exposed Indians, and then dodge back as a straggling volley of bullets pelted the stockade. Over on the east side muskets were cracking in the same desultory fashion. The storm showed no signs of abating. On the contrary, the snow was falling more thickly and in finer flakes, and a bitter wind was constantly heaping it in higher drifts, and blowing it in blinding, eddying showers about the inclosure.

I was about to return to my post, warmed and strengthened by a pannikin of coffee, when a couple of shots rang out. One of the very men to whom I had been talking—a young Scotchman named Blair— reeled and fell heavily, hit by a ball that had entered at a loophole. I bent over him, and saw at once that he was badly hurt. He was shot in the left breast, and blood was oozing from his lips.

"It's all up with me, Carew," he moaned. "Let me lie here."

"Not a bit of it," I replied. "You'll pull through, take my word for it. But you must be in the doctor's hands without delay."

Three of us picked the wounded man up, and bore him across the yard to the hospital. At the door I relinquished my share of the burden, for the firing had suddenly recommenced so briskly that I feared the savages were meditating a rush.

But the fusillade dwindled to a few shots before I was halfway to the east side, and the next instant, as I was pushing along leisurely, I saw a dark object looming out of the snow twenty feet to my right. It was the figure of a woman. Her back was toward me, and she seemed to have halted in perplexity.

Suddenly she moved forward a little, and with that I was in pursuit, my heart beating fast. As I overtook her she turned round with a start.

"Denzil!" she gasped.

As I had suspected, it was Flora Hatherton. She was muffled in a cloak, a fur cap crowned her pretty face, and in her gloved hands she held a light musket.

"You here!" I exclaimed. "Are you mad, to expose yourself to such danger? Go back!"

"I don't want to go back," she said. "Please don't make me, Denzil."

"You must," I answered sharply. "Is it possible that Mrs. Menzies allowed you to do this rash thing?"

"I came without her permission. She thinks I have retired," Flora replied in a spirited tone. "Let me help to defend the fort, Denzil. I can fire a gun, and I am not a bit afraid, and it is my duty, I feel like a coward these brave men fighting and dying."

What could I say? The girl's rashness angered me, but I admired her pluck and courage. I had never loved her so much as I loved her that instant—never so fully realized what the barrenness of my life would be without her. And she was Griffith Hawke's!

"Flora—" I began.

She seemed to divine my feelings, and of a sudden she shrank a little from me.

"Hush!" she said. "I have been foolish and impulsive, Denzil. I am going back to Mrs. Menzies."

The mad words were checked on my lips.

"Yes, go!" I answered hoarsely. "Go at once—"

There was the sound of a footfall to one side, and I glanced around to see the factor. How much he had heard I could only surmise; but he stood in silence for a moment, looking from one to the other of us.

106

"Flora, why are you here?" he asked, and to me his voice seemed cold and harsh.

"I wanted to help to defend the fort," she answered in faltering tones, "but Mr. Carew stopped me—"

"I fortunately met Miss Hatherton," I broke in, "and urged her to go back."

"Quite right," said the factor. "It is not a woman's part to fight. Your place is in the house, Flora."

Without a word she turned and glided rapidly through the snow. Griffith Hawke hesitated, and then started to follow her; but he had not made two steps when a cry rang loudly from the northeast watch-tower:

"The redskins are coming! The clearing is alive with them! Every man to his post!"

The alarm was not a false one, for immediately a fiendish clamor and whooping broke out and scores of musket shots blended in a rattling din. The attack seemed to be directed entirely against the east side, and to that quarter the two of us ran fleetly.

"Spare guns this way!" the factor shouted at the top of his voice. "Stand firm, men!"

The scene that followed baffles description. There was no panic or fright, nor did the men entirely desert the other sides of the fort for the threatened point; but all who could be spared rallied to the north. I felt sure that this second rush would be a more serious business than the first, and I was not mistaken.

I quickly reached the stockade—I did not see what had become of Griffith Hawke—and managed to squeeze my way through to one of the loopholes. At grave risk—for the fire was already heavy on both sides—I peered briefly out. Through the smoke and snow I saw the dusky warriors advancing in great numbers and at close quarters, filling the air with their infernal yells. Some carried felled saplings with the branches lopped off short, the purpose of which was plain.

One glimpse was enough. I began to fire with my comrades, reckless of the bullets that whizzed about me. From angle to angle of the north stockade, from the embrasures of the tower, poured a deadly sheet of flame. A howitzer crashed, and then a swivel gun. I fired three times—spare muskets were passed to me—and I drew back from the loophole to reload. By the ruddy flashes I recognized

107

friends—Baptiste and Captain Rudstone, Griffith Hawke and Andrew Menzies, the excited countenance of Christopher Burley in the rear.

"Rake them down," the factor cried shrilly. "Beat them off if you can. Don't let them get a footing inside!"

The words were hardly uttered when the stockade groaned and rattled. The savages had reared their rude scaling ladders against it, and by these means some gained the top, while others clambered up with the agility of cats.

It was a most desperate and daring assault, but we met it with the dogged pluck of men who fight for a last chance. We shot half a score of the devils as they clung to the top of the stockade, and speedily finished others who dropped down among us.

They poured over thicker and faster, screeching like fiends, and now we were driven back a little. We fired as long as we could load, and then made an onset with clubbed muskets. The advantage was on our side, the Indians being mostly armed with tomahawks, and though more than a score of them were inside at once, we soon sent them scrambling back, and so checked the incoming tide.

A little handful stuck out to the last, disdaining to flee. They came at us ferociously, and nearly broke through our line. I finished one, and Captain Rudstone and Baptiste killed two more. A fourth Indian—a stalwart, hideously painted savage—carried a musket. He suddenly leveled it and fired, and I heard a sharp cry behind me. I looked round in time to see Griffith Hawke stagger, clutch at the rail and fall heavily.

CHAPTER XXIV.   A BLACK NIGHT.

At the time, so exciting and dangerous was the situation, I scarcely realized what had happened. The fight was still raging, and I was in the thick of it. Leaving others to render aid to the factor, I sprang with clubbed musket at the redskin who had shot him. I struck hard and true, and I yelled hoarsely as he dropped with a shattered skull. My comrades finished several more, and now the survivors—four in number—turned and fled. One scrambled safely over the stockade; the other three were cut down as they ran.

That ended the struggle. Again, and with terrible loss, our desperate foes had been repulsed. The moaning of the wounded was drowned in hearty cheers, and the musketry fire had dwindled to a few straggling shots. There was a sudden cry from the watch-tower that the enemy were in full retreat, and I ran to a loophole to see if this good news could be verified. It was true enough! The Indians were fading away into the curtain of snow, and in a manner that showed they had no intention of stopping short of the forest, since none took to shelter in the clearing.

I peered out for a few moments, until not a savage was in sight. Then the triumphant clamor within the fort seemed to change to an angry and mournful key, and I heard the factors name called from mouth to mouth. As I turned from the loophole, Captain Rudstone met me face to face.

"He wants you," he said. "Come at once."

"Who?" I asked mechanically.

"Griffith Hawke, of course. Surely you knew he had been shot. He is dying, I believe."

I tried to speak, but the words stuck in my throat. The captain looked at me keenly for an instant, and then strode off. I followed at his heels, reeling like a drunken man, and with my thoughts in such a whirl as I cannot describe.

Griffith Hawke dying! It was difficult to grasp the meaning of the words. At first I felt bitter grief and remorse for the untimely end of the man who had been my greatest benefactor; I remembered his many kindnesses, and how basely I had requited them.

Captain Rudstone led the way to the little room at the base of the watch-tower. We pushed through the crowd outside and when I was over the threshold I saw a pitiable sight by the glow of a lantern. Griffith Hawke lay partly on a blanket, with Andrew Menzies

109

supporting his head and shoulders. His face was ghastly pale, and there was blood on his lips and chest. The doctor, kneeling beside him, was preparing to give him a dose of spirits. Half a dozen sorrowing men stood about.

"His minutes are numbered," Captain Rudstone whispered in my ear. "He is shot through the lungs. They brought him here because it was the nearest place of shelter."

The factor looked up and saw me. He made a feeble gesture, and as I knelt by him the tears came to my eyes and a lump rose in my throat. I would have given anything to save his life; my sorrow was true and sincere.

"They tell me the fort is safe—that the Indians have retreated to the woods," he whispered faintly.

"Yes, they have been beaten off," I replied, "and with heavy loss."

"Thank God!" he murmured. "They will hardly make another attack. All will go well now. Menzies, have you sent for Miss Hatherton?" he added.

"Yes, she will soon be here."

The dying man lifted his head a little, looking at me with a smile. The doctor poured some strong liquor between his lips, and it instantly brought a brightness to his eyes and a tinge of color to his cheeks.

"That will keep me up for a time," he whispered. "I have something to say to Mr. Carew, and I wish it to be as private as possible. You and the doctor must remain, Menzies, but the rest—"

A spasm of pain stopped him, and while he writhed with it all the men who were in the room, save we three kneeling by him, stepped quietly outside. He grew more comfortable in a moment, glanced wistfully at the door, and put a cold hand in one of mine.

"Denzil, my boy, it is only a question of a few minutes," he said, in a low voice. "I am dying at my post, and without regret. It is better so. I nearly made a mistake, but I saw it in time. I know your secret— I suspected it days ago. You love Miss Hatherton—"

"It is true," I interrupted hoarsely. "Forgive me, my old friend, and believe that I would not for the world have wronged you in thought or deed. I would have left the fort long ago, had you given consent—"

110

"Hush! there is nothing to forgive," he murmured. "Mine was the mistake—mine the blame. It is only natural that you should have loved each other. I was too old to mate with one so young and fair. I had made up my mind to release her from her promise—to give her to you, Denzil."

He stopped again, and I saw a sudden change in his face. The doctor answered my questioning look with a grave nod, and just then the door was thrown open and Flora entered. She gave me a glance of startled surprise, and knelt on the opposite side. Shaking the snow from her furred cloak, she bent over the dying man; her eyes filled with tears of grief and pity, and her lips trembled.

"Griffith, tell me it is not true!" she cried; "Live for my sake!"

He looked from the girl to me.

"God bless you both!" he said weakly. "Do not grieve for me, Flora. I loved you, but it was more the love of a father for a daughter. Now I leave you a legacy of happiness—a husband who will cherish and protect you. Promise before I go that you will be Denzil's wife. I shall die the happier if I know that my mistake—is—atoned—"

The effort was too much for him. He gasped for breath, and his face turned the color of ashes, blood oozed to his lips. I was speechless with emotion, and Flora was weeping too bitterly for words; but I saw her lips move, and she suddenly stretched out her hand. I clasped it for a brief moment, and as I released it and looked at Griffith Hawke, he shuddered from head to foot and lay still, with closed eyes.

"He is dead," said Menzies.

"Yes, it is over," assented the doctor.

A silence fell on us all, broken only by Flora's sobbing. Overhead, the sentries spoke in low tones while they watched at their posts, and outside the wind howled a mournful requiem.

•   •   •   •   •

Through the remaining hours of that night the storm raged, heaping the snow in higher drifts, and keeping half a dozen men busily employed in clearing the entrances to the various outbuildings. That the Indians had taken shelter in the forest, and were not likely to attempt another assault, did little to lighten the general gloom and grief that pervaded the fort, for there was not a man but felt he had lost a friend in Griffith Hawke. As for myself, I had a heavy weight of responsibility upon me, and that prevented my mind from dwelling too much on other things. I gave a thought now and again to my new-born happiness, but the thrill of joy was as quickly stifled by bitter shame—by a vision of the dead man who had returned good for my meditated evil. Flora was in the care of Mrs. Menzies. Captain Rudstone had taken her back to the house, and I had no intention of seeking an interview with her until she should have partly recovered from the shock of the factor's death.

It was indeed a black and dreadful night—a night of horrors and anxiety, of gloom and mourning. For the outlook was by no means so bright as we had let Griffith Hawke believe. What the result would be if the savages rushed us a third time none of us dared contemplate. It was too much to expect that they would abandon the siege, with men of the Northwest Company among them to egg them on; and if they knew our weakness, as was likely, another desperate attack was certain to come sooner or later. Out of a total number of forty-six at the beginning of the trouble, no more than half were now fit for service, the rest were dead or disabled.

These were stern facts that weighed heavy on my mind and held me sleepless and occupied while the night wore on. I saw well to it that the sentries were alert and at their posts, that muskets and howitzers were loaded and ammunition within easy reach, that the stockade was secure at every point. I fought off drowsiness and fatigue with cups of hot coffee, with pipes of strong tobacco.

Two hours before dawn the weather thawed a little and the snow turned to a drizzling rainfall. In the gray flush of early morning when I made my last round, it was bitterly cold again; a crust was on the snow, and the leaden skies promised an early resumption of the storm. To north and east the drifts reached halfway to the top of the stockade.

Bluish curls of smoke, rising here and there out of the surrounding forest, told that the Indians were still in the vicinity. The frozen crust was an incentive to them to make a final attack, and I expected it during the day. I ate a hasty breakfast, and then Menzies summoned me to the factor's house, where he had called a meeting to consider the situation.

CHAPTER XXV.   A RAY OF HOPE.

In all five of us assembled—five low-spirited, grave-faced men: the others were Menzies and Captain Rudstone, Dr. Knapp and an old and experienced voyageur named Carteret, whose judgment was to be relied upon. A discussion of a few minutes found us unanimously agreed that it would be impossible to repulse the Indians should they make another attack in force; nor did we doubt that such a crisis would come sooner or later.

"There is no chance of the siege being lifted," said Captain Rudstone. "One or more disguised Northwest men are directing operations, and they must know —"

"I'll swear Cuthbert Mackenzie is the leader," I broke in. "He won't neglect such an opportunity as offers now."

"Right you are!" exclaimed Carteret, with a shrug of the shoulders. "It's temptation thrown in the way of the redskins. Talk about easy! A firm crust on the snow, and the drifts nearly up to the top of the stockade! Why, they could pour a hundred braves into the fort before we could shoot down ten of them!"

"And they will do just that," declared Captain Rudstone. "They know that we have lost heavily, and can't offer much resistance to a rush. I'll venture to predict that the attack is made late this afternoon, when the twilight begins to gather."

"It will mean the loss of the fort," said I. "We can't shut our eyes to that fact. We have a few hours of grace left; let us make the most of them."

"But what are we to do?" said Dr. Knapp.

"Ay, what?" Menzies echoed dismally. "There's no chance of help, you'll admit, and even if a messenger had got through in time, Fort York couldn't have spared us any men. As it is, they probably have no idea of what is happening here. Do you suggest that we lower our flag and surrender?"

"Never that!" said I.

"Then what other choice have we but to be slaughtered to a man?" continued the hard-headed old Scotchman. "Perhaps you will kindly explain, Mr. Carew, how we are to make the most of these few hours of grace."

Menzies spoke sneeringly, and with an aggravating touch of irony; but I kept my temper, hoping that he would shortly alter his opinion of my advice. In truth, I had been turning a matter over in my

113

mind while the discussion was going on, and I fancied I saw a way for some of us at least, to save both life and honor.

"If we surrendered, we should likely be slaughtered just the same," I replied. "So that is out of the question. But I have a plan, Mr. Menzies—a sort of a middle course—to offer in the event of the fort falling."

"Go on," said he, with a contemptuous sniff.

"I must ask you a question or two first," I replied.

"Dr. Knapp, how many wounded are in your care?"

"They are in Father Cleary's care at present," he answered. "But I have seven, Carew."

"And how many are fit to travel, on foot or on sledges?"

He reflected for a moment, looking at me with surprise.

"Two will die before night," he said, "and a third is in a bad way. The other four might make a shift on snowshoes."

"It is better than I expected," said I. "And now for my plan. This house, with its loopholes and heavy shutters, was constructed for such an emergency as the present. I suggest that we at once move in the wounded, three or four sledges, all the powder and ball and a quantity of provisions. If the attack comes, and we see that we can't repulse it, we will all take shelter here, and in time to withdraw the men from other points. The house is practically fireproof, and I am sure we can hold it for a week or more, if need be."

"It would catch fire from the outbuildings," suggested the doctor.

"The Indians won't burn those," said I. "They will save them for their own protection."

"And how is the siege of the house to end?" asked Menzies. "Do you expect the Indians to withdraw, or do you count on aid arriving?"

"I admit there is no chance of either." I replied. "My idea is this. The inside of the inclosure is already deep under a frozen drift, and from the look of the weather there will be more snow in plenty within a few hours. We will excavate a tunnel beneath it, starting from one of the little windows that give air to the cellar, and leading to some part of the south stockade. Then in a day or two, when the night is dark and other conditions favorable, what is to prevent us from making our escape unseen to the forest, and by quick traveling gain Fort York?"

"The Indians would break into the tunnel while prowling about," said Dr. Knapp.

"We won't make it high enough for that." I replied stoutly, "and, besides, the crust will be too hard."

"It's a sound plan!" exclaimed Captain Rudstone.

"Ay, I'm of the same mind," added Carteret. "It's well worth the trying. And it's that or a bloody massacre—there are no two ways about it."

"It seems a cowardly thing," grumbled Menzies, "to yield the redskins all but this house, and then slink away from that under cover of darkness and by a trick. A rich lot of the company's property will fall into their hands!"

"True enough," said I bitterly, "and the old flag will be hauled down for the first time in the records! But consider, sir; there is nothing else to be done! Carteret has given you the gist at the matter. And think of the women!"

The blunt old Scotchman was touched in a tender spot; his face softened.

"Ay, my poor wife!" he said, with a sigh. "And Miss Hatherton! They must not fall into the power of these red devils—or of Cuthbert Mackenzie. It's a level head you have on your shoulders, Denzil. I fear I spoke hastily—"

"As was your right," I interrupted. "It was presumptuous of me to offer advice. But I am pleased to think that you favor my suggestion."

"It is a last chance," he replied, "and we must cling to it for the sake of the women. Were it not for them I would hold out to the end. Ah, the pity of it! To think that Fort Royal will be lost!"

"It will rise again stronger than ever," Captain Rudstone said grimly, "when the Northwest Company has been crushed out of existence."

"May I live to see the day!" said Menzies fervently.

We held some further discussion, during which a number of minor details were arranged. Then Dr. Knapp returned to the hospital, and Captain Rudstone and Carteret set off to acquaint the men with the proposed plan, and to see to the removal of the wounded and the various supplies to the factor's house. Meanwhile, Baptiste having come in, he reported that there was no sign of any threatening movement on the part of the savages, and we fully expected none until evening.

I had promised my companions to take some sleep—which I stood badly in need of—but first I insisted on going over the lower

115

floor of the house with Menzies. We examined all the rooms, the doors and walls, the shutters and loopholes, and I was satisfied with the inspection. When we returned to the hall Mrs. Menzies hailed her husband from above. He went upstairs and as I passed the open door of the room in which we had held our gathering, on my way out, I caught the flutter of a woman's gown and heard my name pronounced in a whisper.

Stepping inside, I saw Flora. She was standing by the table, with a look on her sweet face that set my heart throbbing wildly. How it happened I scarcely knew, but the next instant she was in my arms, held close to my breast, and I was showering kisses on her unresisting lips and eyes.

"Denzil!" she whispered. "My hero—my own love!"

"At last, my darling!" I muttered. "You are mine! None can take you away from me. Say that you love me, Flora!"

"I do with all my heart!"

"And when will you marry me?"

"Some day, dear Denzil," she replied.

She gently released herself and gazed at me timidly.

"Oh, it must be wrong to feel so happy," she added with a little sob in her voice, "while he is lying cold and dead. How generous and noble he was! And think of it, Denzil, he intended to give me up! I am glad I was true to him."

"I wish I had been truer," I said bitterly. "But it is too late for regrets. A better man than Griffith Hawks never lived. He was worthy of you, Flora. Can I say more?"

"I will never forget him," she answered softly. "Oh, this cruel, cruel war! And they say the fort is in danger, Denzil. That is what I wanted to ask you."

"Don't believe it," said I. "There will be more fighting—perhaps a protracted siege—but our brave men will prove more than a match for the cowardly redskins. Trust to me, dearest. I will save you from, all harm and peril."

At that moment Menzies was heard returning. I caught the girl in my arms, kissed her twice, and hurried from the house. All was quiet as I crossed the yard, and I observed that fine flakes of snow were commencing to drop. Flora was mine! I could think of nothing else when I entered my quarters, but, for all that I was so worn out that I fell asleep the moment I threw myself on the bed.

116

CHAPTER XXVI.   AS TWILIGHT FELL.

For more than twenty-four hours I had taken no repose, and as nothing occurred to rouse me, I slept longer than I intended. When I opened my eyes languidly the room was so dark that I could scarcely make out a chair against the wall, and the window-panes were crusted with frost and snow. At once I was wide awake, and all the incidents of the morning flashed into my mind. I knew that this was the time when the attack was expected, and for a moment I sat up and listened anxiously, but I heard only a distant hum of voices.

"All is well so far," I thought. "I hope no precautions have been neglected, for when the storm bursts it will be sudden and fierce."

I threw off the blankets that covered me, and leaped out of bed. Hastily donning my fur capote, cap and mittens, and taking my loaded musket, I left the quarters without encountering any person.

I paused outside to look about, and the scene that met my eyes was a dreary one. The inclosure was shrouded in the murky gray gloom of twilight. It was bitterly cold, and snow was falling fast. The various outbuildings loomed dimly here and there between the narrow paths and high-banked drifts. The only ray of light visible was behind me, and shone from the window of Flora's room. As I turned from a brief contemplation of it, I saw a man passing and hailed him. He proved to be Baptiste.

"Why was I not wakened?" I demanded sharply. "Here is the night upon us, and I wished to be up at noon."

"Mr. Menzie's orders, sir," he replied. "He said you were not to be disturbed."

I questioned Baptiste further, and learned that there had been no alarm during the day, and that not an Indian had shown himself. He also relieved my mind concerning the preparations for holding the factor's house.

"They moved everything in," he said; "food and blankets, all the powder and ball, four sledges, and the wounded men."

"And the dead, Baptiste?"

"They are buried, sir—under the snow."

"Ah, then no time has been wasted," said I. "If the worst comes we shall be ready—"

"There is nothing more to be done, Carew," interrupted a voice at my elbow. "No step that prudence or forethought could dictate has been omitted."

117

The speaker was Captain Rudstone, who had approached unperceived.

"Has your sleep refreshed you?" he added.

"Very much," I replied. "I feel fit for another stretch of fighting. What is the situation now?"

"The calm before the storm, to my mind," he declared. "Sentries are posted to command a view from every side of the fort. Both towers will be abandoned at the first alarm, and all the men will rush to the quarter whence it comes, those are the general orders. If the redskins prove too strong for us, we will retreat to the factor's house."

"Ay, and hold it," said I. "The place is impregnable, Rudstone!"

"That remains to be seen," he answered. "Go and get some supper, Carew, while you have the chance."

"Then you think the attack is imminent?"

"Yes, it may come at any moment."

"But Baptiste tells me the Indians have made no sign all day."

"True enough," assented the captain, "and that's the worst of it. They are hatching some deep-laid deviltry, be sure! I have my suspicions, and I communicated them to Menzies. He agrees with me that the attack will probably burst upon us in the form of a—"

He never finished the sentence. The words were stifled on his lips by a tremendous explosion that seemed to shake the very ground, and rattled and thundered far away into the heart of the wilderness. A crash of falling debris followed, and then the night rang with shrill clamor and blood-curdling whoops.

"*Nom de Dieu!* we are lost!" wailed Baptiste.

"My God, what does it mean?" I cried, clutching Captain Rudstone's arm with a trembling hand.

"My prediction, Carew," he answered hoarsely. "It has come—it is what I expected. The devils have tunneled under the snow and planted a powder bag against the stockade. They have blown a breach."

"We'll keep them out of it as long as we can," I shouted. "Hark! the fighting has begun."

The captain and I had already set off on a run, and Baptiste was hanging at our heels. Shouting and yelling rose from all parts of the fort, and blended with the wild cheers of the savages. Dark forms loomed right and left of us as we sped on. Guided by the clamor and by the great column of smoke that was stamped blackly against the driving snow, we soon reached the scene of the explosion, which was the northeast watch-tower.

It is impossible to describe the sight that was revealed to us by the first rapid glimpse. All that day the redskins must have been burrowing a passage beneath the drifts from the woods to the fort. They had planted a bag or cask of powder at the very base of the tower, and blown it into a heap of ruins, out of which could be seen sticking the bodies of the two poor fellows who had been on duty there. As yet only a small force of Indians—those who had approached by the tunnel—were storming the breach, and these were being held at bay by a dozen of our men who had reached the spot before the captain and myself. Muskets were cracking, and tomahawks were flying through the air; the yells of invaders and invaded made a horrible din.

At the first I saw some hope of holding the sheltered place—of beating the enemy off. I plunged into the thick of the fight, emptying my gun into the breast of a red devil, and bringing the butt down on the head of another. We pressed close up to the sides of the tower, and gained footholds on the ruins. Hand to hand we fought desperately, shooting and striking at the Indians and keeping them on the outside of the fort. Not many of them had firearms, and so far as I could see, but one of our men had fallen.

"Stand up to it!" I shouted. "Hold your ground!"

"Hit hard!" cried Captain Rudstone. "Finish all you can before the main rush comes!"

Flushed with triumph, half-crazed by the thirst for blood, we did not pause to reflect that the scale must soon turn the other way. Face to face, weapon to weapon, we held the savages at bay, sending one after another to his last account. Meanwhile more men kept joining us, until, excepting a few who were on duty at other points, our whole available force was present. I heard Andrew Menzies giving directions. I saw Father Cleary on my left and Christopher Burley on the right, both striking at the painted faces behind the shattered walls.

"This is hot work, Carew," Captain Rudstone found a chance to shout in my ear, "and it's precious little use to keep it up. The devils will soon be at us in their hundreds. Now is the time to make a safe retreat to the house."

"I think the same," I answered, as I dodged a whizzing tomahawk; "and if Menzies don't soon give the command I will."

119

The words were scarcely out of my mouth when the clamor took a deeper, shriller pitch. We all knew what it meant—the tide was turning. Through the gaping holes in the watch tower stamped against the snowy mist, we saw a dark mass rolling forward—scores and scores of painted Indians.

CHAPTER XXVII.   THE SIEGE OF THE HOUSE.

They had started from the woods the moment the explosion occurred, and they would have arrived earlier but for the fresh snow that lay on the frozen crust.

"Stand firm!" cried Menzies. "Give them a raking volley at close quarters."

"And be ready to retire in good order," I shouted. "We can't afford to lose a man."

With that the living tide was upon us. Screeching and veiling like demons, the horde of savages struck the weakened northeast angle of the fort. There was no checking them, though our muskets poured a leaden rain. Some entered by the breach, dashing over the debris of wood and stone; others clambered to the top of the palisades and dropped down inside.

At the first we had to retire a little, so overwhelming was the rush. Then we made a brief stand and tried to stem the torrent. Bang, bang, bang! bullets flew thickly, from both sides and hissing tomahawks fell among us. I saw two men drop near me, and heard cries of agony mingling with the infernal din. We held our ground until the foremost of the savages were at arm's length, striking and hacking at us through the snow and powder smoke. Two or three score were already within the fort, and when a section of the stockade fell with a crash—borne down by sheer weight—I believed for a terrible moment that all was lost.

"Back, back!" I cried hoarsely. "Back for your lives, men! We can't do anything more here!"

"Ay, the inclosure is taken!" shouted Captain Rudstone. "Back to the house! Keep your faces to the foe, and make every shot tell!"

Menzies called out a similar order, seeing that any delay would imperil our last chance, and those of us who were left slowly began the retreat. We drew off into the narrow passage, with high banks of snow on either side, that led to the factor's house. The yelling redskins pressed after us, and for several moments, by a cool and steady fire, we prevented them from coming to close quarters again.

We kept firing and loading while we moved backward, and as it was next to impossible to miss, the Indians seemed disheartened by the heavy damage we inflicted on them. For ourselves, we lost three men in a brief time, and we would have lost more but for the shelter of the outbuildings, round some of which the path turned.

121

When we were halfway to the house, and had passed the quarters, we were joined by the sentries from the southwest tower. But now the savages plucked up courage, and made a rush that brought them within six yards of us. We stood at bay, and delivered a straggling fire. The Indians returned it as they pushed on doggedly. A voyageur fell at my side, and another dropped in front of me. There was a sudden cry that the priest was shot, and glancing to the right, I saw Father Cleary reel down in the snow and lie motionless.

"We must run for it!" shouted Captain Rudstone. "Make a dash for the house, men!"

"For God's sake, no!" I yelled hoarsely. "If we turn now we will be overtaken and butchered! Hold firm!"

Just then, when the situation was most critical, an unexpected thing gave us the opportunity we so sorely needed. In the retreat we had dragged one of the howitzers along with us, and we had forgotten until now that it was loaded. In a trice we put it in position and touched it off.

Crash! The heavy charge ploughed into the huddled mass of savages. To judge from the agonized shrieks that followed the loss of life must have been terrible, but we could see nothing for the dense cloud of smoke that hung between us.

"To the house!" cried Menzies.

"Quick—for your lives!" I shouted.

With that we turned our backs and made off, dashing along in some disorder and leaving the howitzer behind. We half expected to be overtaken, but by the time the Indians had recovered from their check and pushed on, the house was before us.

We staggered inside by twos and threes, and closed and barred the massive door. A respite for rest and breathing was badly needed, but we did not dare to take it. Half of our men went to the front loopholes, and as fast as they could load and fire they picked off the yelling wretches who were now swarming thickly before the house. In their frenzied rage they exposed themselves recklessly, sending volley after volley of lead against the stout beams and even hurling tomahawks.

I took no part in this scrimmage myself. With Menzies and several others I went over the lower floor of the house, and made sure that all was in right condition for a protracted siege. We placed

122

lighted candles in the hall, and opened the doors communicating with it, so that some light could shine into the various rooms.

Meanwhile the firing had dwindled and ceased, and when we returned to the front we found that the Indians had abandoned the attack and melted away; none were in sight from the loopholes, but we could hear them making a great clamor in the direction of the trading house and other outbuildings.

This relief gave us a chance to consult regarding our future plans, and to count up our little force. Alas! but sixteen of us had entered the house. That was our whole number; the rest of the forty odd had perished during the fighting of the past two days; and not the least mourned among that night's casualties was brave Father Cleary. Fortunately, none of us were disabled, though Christopher Burley had been grazed by a bullet, and Captain Rudstone and several others had been gashed slightly by tomahawks. The wounded transferred from the hospital, who were in a small room at the rear, were now reduced to five; two had died that morning, as Dr. Knapp predicted.

But there was no time for useless grief or idleness. We had no sooner served out rations, loaded all the guns and posted the men on the four sides of the house than the Indians showed a determination to crown their triumph by taking our stronghold. At first they kept to the shelter of the surrounding outbuildings, and blazed steadily away at the house, on the chance of sending a bullet through the loopholes or the chinks of the logs. Twice a little squad of savages rushed forward carrying a beam, with which they hoped to batter down the door. But we poured a hot fire into them—it was light enough outside for us to take aim—and each time they wavered and fell back, leaving the snow dotted with dead bodies.

After that came a lull, except for intermittent shots, and Captain Rudstone predicted that an unpleasant surprise was being prepared for us by the Northwest men whom we believed to be among the redskins.

"It may be all that," I answered him stoutly, "but the house is not to be taken."

A little later I took advantage of the inaction to go upstairs, whither Menzies had already preceded me. He was with his wife and Miss Hatherton in a back room with one small window, and that protected by a heavy shutter.

123

I drew Flora aside and explained to her, as hopefully as possible, the plan by which we expected ultimately to escape to Fort York. What else I said to her, or what sweet and thrilling words she whispered into my ear, I do not purpose to set down here; but when I returned to the lower floor my heart was throbbing with happiness, and I felt strengthened and braced to meet whatever fate might hold in store. I was strangely confident at the time that we should outwit our bloodthirsty foes.

Menzies followed me below, and almost at once the Indians renewed the attack, mainly on the front of the house and on the north side. They exposed themselves on the verge of the outbuildings, blazing away steadily, and drawing a constant return fire from our men. At the end of a quarter of an hour they were still wasting ammunition. They must have suffered heavily, and yet not one of their bullets had done us any harm. I wandered from room to room, taking an occasional shot, and finally I stopped in the hall, where Captain Rudstone and three others were posted at the loopholes right and left of the door.

"The Indians will run out of powder presently; if they keep up at this rate," said I. "They can't have much of a leader."

"Too clever a one for us," the captain answered, as he loaded his musket. "This is only a ruse, a diversion, Carew. There is something to follow."

"I hope it will come soon," I replied. "Then the savages will likely draw off and give us a chance to put a force of men to work at the tunnel. We should finish it by noon to-morrow, and escape through it at nightfall. If the snow keeps up—as it gives promise of doing—our tracks will be covered before we have gone a mile."

"I like the plan," said old Carteret, the voyageur. "It sounds well, and it's possible to be carried out under certain conditions. But if you'll not mind my saying—"

He paused an instant to aim and fire.

"One redskin the less," he added, peering out the loophole; "he sprang three feet in the air when I plugged him. As for your plan, Mr. Carew, I think the odds are about evenly divided. There's the chance that the varmints will suspect something of the sort, and watch the stockade on all sides."

124

"Likely enough," assented Captain Rudstone; "but it's not to that quarter I look for the danger. The Indians can take the house by assault in an hour if they choose to sacrifice a lot of lives."

"It would cost fifty or a hundred," said I. "They won't pay such a price."

"There is no telling how far they will go," the captain answered gravely, "with Northwest Company men to egg them on."

As he spoke there was a sudden and noisy alarm from the room on the right of the hall, which commanded the south side of the house. Half a dozen muskets cracked in rapid succession, the reports blending with a din of voices. Then Menzies yelled hoarsely: "This way, men! Come, for God's sake! Quick, or we are lost!"

The summons was promptly responded to. I was the first to dash into the room, followed by Rudstone and Carteret. I put my eyes to a vacant loophole and what I saw fairly froze the blood in my veins.

CHAPTER XXVIII.   THE END OF HOPE.

A body of Indians—nine or ten in number—were advancing at a run straight for the house, and each painted savage carried wrapped in his arms a mass of bedding from the abandoned sleeping quarters. I had no sooner caught a glimpse of the party and divined their alarming purpose, than a straggling volley was fired from the loopholes right and left of me. Crack! crack, crack!

Three Indians fell with their burdens, and one of them began to crawl away, dragging a broken limb after him. A fourth took fright and darted back, but the rest kept on. They were lost to view for an instant as they gained the very wall of the house and stacked the bedding against it. Then back they scurried to the shelter of the outbuildings, a single one falling by my musket, which I thrust quickly out and fired. Unfortunately my companions' weapons were empty.

"Load up, men, fast!" cried Menzies. "The devils intend to fire the house! They will be coming back with timber next!"

"God help us if they get a blaze started with bedding and dry wood!" said I. "The house will go—we won't be able to save it! I never counted on anything like this!"

"I was afraid of it from the first," replied Captain Rudstone, "though I hoped we should have time enough to dig the tunnel. Our only chance is to keep the redskins away from the wall."

"And that's a mighty poor one!" muttered Carteret.

"We must do it," groaned Menzies, "or it's all up with us. We can't get at the bedding; the fiends have put it too far off from the window."

A noisy clamor interrupted our conversation, as the men from other parts of the house poured into the room, drawn thither by Menzies' summons of a moment before. They were under the impression that a rush had been made and repelled; when they learned the truth they quieted down, and a sort of awed horror was visible on every face.

No time was wasted in words. At any instant the savages might return to complete their devilish task; the chance of beating them back, slight as it was must be made the most of. Our last card was staked on that, and we grimly prepared to play it. Eight men were assigned to the loopholes—there were four on each side of the shuttered windows—and five others, including Christopher Burley,

126

brought powder and ball, and set to work to load spare rifles. The rest were sent back to watch at their posts, lest a counter attack should be made in those directions.

It had all been so sudden, so overwhelming, that I felt dazed as I looked from my loophole into the murky, snow-flecked night. Across the crust, dotted with ghastly forms, the outbuildings loomed vaguely. Behind them hundreds of bloodthirsty redskins lay sheltered; but there was scarcely a sound to be heard save the pitiful whining of the husky dogs who were shut up in the canoe house.

"Fate is against us!" I reflected bitterly. "A few moments ago I believed we could hold out for days—I was confident that we should all escape; and now this black cloud of despair, of death, has fallen upon us! Flora, my darling, I pray Heaven to spare you! God help us to beat the savages off—to save the house!"

Just then I detected a movement in the distance, and I knew too well what it meant. My companions saw it also, and they broke out with warning exclamations:

"Here they come!" "Be ready, boys!" "Give the devils a hot reception!" "Keep the spare muskets handy!"

"Take sharp aim and make every shot tell!" Menzies cried hoarsely. "Fire at those nearest your own side. My God, look yonder—"

His voice was drowned by one blood-curdling screech poured from a hundred throats. Through the driving snow a dusky mass rolled forward, and when it was halfway across the space we made out no less than a score of Indians each shouldering three or four planks of short length. With reckless valor they came on, whooping and yelling defiantly.

"They've taken the cut timber that was stored in the powder house!" cried Carteret. "It's as dry as touchwood and will burn like wildfire!"

"We're lost!" exclaimed Menzies. "There are too many of the fiends; we shall never drive them back!"

"It's our last chance!" I shouted. "Steady, now. Fire!"

Bang! went my musket. Bang! bang! bang! rang other reports. The volley caught the savages at a range of twenty yards and as the smoke drifted up from the loopholes I saw the foremost, at whom I had aimed, sprawled on the snow. Three or four others were down, and two more dropped quickly. The rest darted on unchecked.

127

"Again!" I shouted. "Quick, let them have it! All together!"

We snatched spare guns from the men behind us, throwing down our empty weapons, and a second straggling volley of lead and flame blazed from the loopholes. But the smoke partly spoiled our aim, and the interval gave the redskins a terrible advantage. Half of them dashed on, under our very guns, and right up to the wall of the house, and the next instant we heard an ominous sound—the thump and clatter of the dried timbers as they fell against the logs.

"That's our death knell!" cried Menzies. "Heaven help us now! We are lost!"

Heaven help us indeed! That there was no hope save for the intervention of Providence, every man of us knew. Some cursed their hard fate, and some shrieked threats and imprecations. Others seized the guns as fast as the relief men could load them, and fired at the now retreating savages, who went back with more caution than they came; for they first crept along the base of the wall to the left angle, and then darted over the crust in zigzag fashion toward the outbuildings, where their comrades were howling and whooping with triumph.

"Two down!" cried Captain Rudstone.

"And one for me!" exclaimed Carteret.

I watched for a moment, but no more Indians appeared. The rest had escaped to shelter, and they must have been few in number; for I could count eight bodies lying about in the falling snow, amid scattered strips of planking, and four wounded wretches were trying to crawl away. Their attempt had succeeded, but at a terrible cost of life. With a gesture of despair. I turned round.

"Have they all gone back?" I asked.

"I think so," Menzies replied huskily. "They will rush us again directly, and fire the bedding and the wood. It's all up with us!"

Crack! A gun spoke shrilly from a loophole on the right, and Baptiste's voice shouted with elation:

"Bonne! bonne! another redskin! He ran out from beneath the window! He is dead now—I shot him in the back!"

"But why did he stay behind the rest?" Menzies asked suspiciously.

"To light the fire!" cried Carteret. "My comrades, it is Heaven's will that we perish!"

The old voyageur was right. As he spoke he pointed with one hand to the loopholes. We saw a red glare spreading farther and farther across the trampled snow crust, and heard a hissing, crackling noise. The dead Indian had ignited the heaped-up material, probably by means of flint and steel.

The flames leaped higher, throwing ruddy reflections yards away. They roared and sang as they devoured the inflammable mattresses, stuffed with straw, and laid hold of the dry timbers piled above. They spat showers of sparks, turned the falling snowflakes to specks of crimson, and drove curls of thick yellow smoke into the room through the chinks of the now burning logs. The house was doomed, and we who were caught there in the meshes of death, fated to perish by agonizing torture, looked at one another with white faces and eyes dilated by horror, with limbs that trembled and lips that could not speak. Outside, across the inclosure, the hordes of savages shrieked and yelled with the voices of malicious demons. From the hall, from the rooms beyond it, the rest of our little band came running in panic to learn the worst and share our misery.

Christopher Burley fell on his knees and clasped his hands in prayer.

"O, God, save us!" he cried. "Let me live to see London again."

"The fire is just to the left of the window," exclaimed Captain Rudstone. "If we had water—"

"There's only one small cask in the house," interrupted Carteret, "and if we had plenty we could do nothing. Fifty bullets would enter by the window the moment the shutter was opened."

With terrible rapidity the flames spread, roaring like a passage of a wind storm through treetops. Out in the snow it was as light as day, and one could have counted the streaks of paint on the faces of the dead savages by the awful red glare. The chinks between the logs were flickering lines of fire, and the smoke puffed through so thickly as to make us cough and choke, and fill our smarting eyes with water. The heat grew intense, and drops of perspiration rolled down our cheeks.

Crack! crack—crack—crack! The Indians suddenly began to fire at the loopholes, which were now distinctly outlined against the flame-lit wall. By twos and threes the guns went off, blending with a din of whooping voices, and the bullets pattered like hail. Menzies spun around and clutched at his right arm, which was bleeding above

129

the elbow. A ball whizzed by my ear and another struck Dr. Knapp just between the eyes; he fell with a crash and lay quite still.

It was clear that the savages had the range of the loopholes, and with one accord we fled from the room, taking the powder canisters with us. In the hall a candle was burning on a shelf, and by the dim glow I saw Mrs. Menzies and Flora coming hurriedly down the stairs.

CHAPTER XXIX.   THE SECRET OF THE FACTOR'S DESK.

I shrank from the encounter. The sight of the fair girl whom I loved so passionately made me a coward, and I felt that I could not speak the words of her doom and mine. So I lurked to one side while Mrs. Menzies rushed up to her husband and clutched him hysterically.

"The house is on fire!" she cried. "The smoke drove us downstairs, and—Oh, you are shot!"

"A mere flesh wound," Menzies answered huskily. "Tie it up for me with a strip of your skirt."

With trembling fingers she obeyed.

"The worse, Andrew!" she pleaded—"tell me the worst! I am a brave woman; I can bear it."

I did not hear Menzies' reply, for he quickly led his wife into a darkened room adjoining; but I had a glimpse of his face, and it seemed to have aged years in the last minute.

"Denzil!"

I recognized Flora's voice, and turning, I found her at my elbow. Her cheeks were white, except for a burning red spot in the middle of each. Her lovely eyes gazed into mine with a look of deepest affection, of heart-rending fear that she could not disguise.

"Come!" I whispered hoarsely.

I drew her past the little group of men to the far end of the hall, where the staircase screened us from the light of the candle. How to begin, what to say, I did not know. With one arm about her slender form, I pressed kisses on her lips and forehead.

"My darling!" I cried. "Oh, the pity of it—the pity of it!"

"Then it is true, Denzil?" she asked in faltering tones. "Don't deceive me at such a time. Is there really no hope?"

It would have been worse than folly to speak false words of comfort now, and with an effort I answered:

"No; all hope is gone. You must know the worst, my darling! We have but a little while to live. Heaven has deserted us. Oh, God, that it should be my lot to tell you this!" She crept closer to me, hiding her face on my breast. For nearly a minute she was still, while confusion and clamor, Indian yells, and musketry fire reigned round us. I could feel the agitated heaving of her bosom, the throbbing of her heart. Then she looked up at me bravely, with a sublime expression in her tear-dimmed eyes that brought to my mind the Christian martyrs of old.

"God is love and mercy, dearest Denzil," she said. "If it is His will that we die we must submit. We will find in heaven the happiness that is denied us on earth."

"It is a cruel, cruel fate!" I cried fiercely. "I would suffer ten deaths to save you—"

"It is better thus," she interrupted. "We shall not be separated! Promise me, Denzil, that you will not let the Indians take me alive!"

I tried to speak, but a sob choked my utterance. I nodded assent, and just then my name was called from the other end of the hall. I kissed Flora and led her forward, putting her in the care of Mrs. Menzies. The men were standing about in groups, some talking, some nervously loading guns, and others staring vacantly at the floor.

"We are considering what we had better do," said Captain Rudstone, "and we want your opinion, Carew. If we stick to the house it means death for all of us by suffocation or by flames. If we sally out there is a possibility that one or more of us may break through and escape."

"No chance of that," Carteret answered bluntly. "The devils will be ready for us, and we shall be hemmed in and butchered to a man. I prefer to die fighting myself; but think of the women! Suffocation will be the easiest fate for them."

I made no reply, for I did not know what to say—what alternative to choose. It was a horrible prospect either way, and I contemplated it with rage and despair, with such a whirl in my brain that I thought I should go mad. The musketry fire was dwindling a little, but the whooping and yelling of the exultant savages suddenly rose to a higher pitch, making such a din that the voices of my companions were quite drowned.

There was still an interval of time left in which to reach a decision—perhaps half an hour. By then, at the most, the house would be a furnace in which nothing could live. As yet owing to the snow on the roof, the flames were confined to the south side. But there they had eaten through the wall, and were roaring and crackling with fury as they devoured the thick beams and timbers. They had seized both angles of the house, and were licking their way into the room. We could see the ruddy glare under the closed door, and could feel the scorching heat. From cracks and crevices puffs of yellow smoke

132

darted into the hall; had a wind been blowing in our direction we should have been suffocated long before.

"Shall we stay here to perish like trapped beasts?" cried Andrew Menzies, his voice ringing above the infernal clamor of the savages. "Let us unbar the door, rush out, and sell our lives dearly! Take your muskets, my brave fellows! We will fight to the death, and kill as many of the devils as we can. And if no merciful bullets reach the women, we will shoot—them—with our—own—"

He could say no more. He stood with his hands clasped and his lips moving in prayer, while the men, almost unanimously shouted eager approval of his plan.

"Make ready, all!" cried Captain Rudstone, "we must be quick about it, for at any moment the heat or a spark may touch off the powder in yonder back room."

That the explosion might come that instant, and so insure us a speedy and merciful death, was my heartfelt wish as I leaned against the wall. I groaned aloud as I pictured Flora lying in the snow, her beautiful face and hair dabbled with blood. Just then a bullet, fired through a loophole at one side of the door, whistled within an inch of my ear. It gave me such a start that I lost my balance and reeled against an old desk of the factor's that stood under the shelf holding the candle. It yielded, and we came to the floor together.

I picked myself up and saw the desk broken open and a number of loose papers scattered at my feet. A word on one of them arrested my attention. I reached for it—it was a yellow document, faded with age, once folded—and on the outside, scrawled in big letters with a quill, I read the following:

"PLAN OF A SECRET PASSAGE FROM FORT ROYAL, 1762."

I fairly held my breath as I tore the paper open. Inside was a rude drawing that I recognized at a glance, and more writing below it. The latter I studied for a moment, and then my head turned dizzy with joy.

"Hurrah!—hurrah!" I cried, waving the precious paper in the air. "Thank God for His wonderful mercy! If this proves true we are saved—saved!"

My companions crowded round me excitedly, some thinking that I had suddenly taken leave of my senses.

"What is it?" they demanded. "What do you mean, Carew?"

133

"Look, look!" I shouted. "A secret passage from the fort—an underground exit built years ago—leading from the cellar to the very bank of the river! It opens from the east wall; the stone is marked with a cross!"

The paper was quickly passed from hand to hand, studied and read. The scene that followed—the transition from blackest despair to radiant hope—I am utterly unable to describe. Indeed, I saw but little of the behavior of the men. I ran to Flora, clasping her in my arms, and we mingled our tears of happiness together.

"Listen, men!" shouted Andrew Menzies. "I fully believe that this document is to be relied upon—that the passage exists. There was a rumor years ago that one of the forts was so provided when it was built, and that the tunnel was not repeated afterward on account of the vast labor; but I did not suspect it to be Fort Royal. Griffith Hawks alone knew the secret, and he died with it untold. We will proceed at once to verify this good news; there is not a moment to spare. Denzil, you and Captain Rudstone will come with me."

He turned to the others.

"There is much to be done," he added, "and it must be done quickly. Load a sledge with provisions, and get others ready for the wounded who are unable to walk. Let each may take a supply of powder and ball, and put on snowshoes. Helen, do you and Miss Hatherton prepare for a long and tiresome march."

There was, indeed, no time to be wasted. The entire side of the house was a mass of flames, and the hall was so scorching hot, so filled with smoke, as to be almost unendurable. The Indians were in a cordon around us, whooping at the top of their voices, firing occasional shots, and evidently expecting that the flames would drive us to meet death in the open.

Leaving the rest to execute Menzie's orders—Carteret volunteered to fetch the women their outdoor wraps from upstairs— the three of us procured a lantern and gained access to the cellar from the room at the end of the hall. Assisted by the plan, we quickly found on the east wall, a big square slab of stone marked by a faint cross.

"Here we are!" exclaimed Menzies. "Try to pry it out with axes."

Two minutes of work sufficed. The stone fell inward, and we shouted with delight when we saw a yawning black hole before us, large enough for two stooping men to walk abreast. Captain Rudstone hurried upstairs with the glad news, and meanwhile Menzies and I

134

ventured some distance into the passage, finding the air sweet and pure.

When we returned to the mouth all of our little party were assembled in the cellar, each man—and the women as well—carrying a pair of snowshoes. Flora and Mrs. Menzies were protected against the bitter weather by furred cloaks. Of the five wounded men one had died within the hour; the other four were able to hobble along temporarily with some assistance. For transporting these when we were safely away from the fort we had two sledges, not counting the one laden with food supplies.

As yet the redskins did not suspect that they were in danger of being cheated of their triumph; we could hear their frenzied cries faintly. Overhead the flames were roaring and hissing, and the cellar itself was hazy with pungent smoke.

CHAPTER XXX. A STRANGE DISCOVERY.

"All ready?" exclaimed Menzies. "Then forward. If no mishap occurs we shall be miles away before our escape is discovered."

He entered the passage first, flashing the lantern in front of him, and the others followed in double file. Captain Rudstone and I, who came last, took the precaution to replace the slab of stone as we had found it.

It was a strange experience to thread that underground corridor, built with herculean toil, when the fort was reared, for just such an emergency as it was serving now. We had to stoop low to avoid the raftered roof. The air was close, and not a sound reached us from outside. We groped along in semi-darkness for the lantern cast no light behind. It gave one a ghastly oppressive feeling of being buried alive.

The tunnel seemed longer than it really was. We were certain over and over again that we had passed under the fort yard and the outer clearing, yet still we went on. But at last Menzies stopped, and called in a low voice that he had come to the end. Captain Rudstone and I made our way up to him, and saw that further progress was barred by a slab of rock that fitted exactly across the passage.

"It will yield with a hard push," said Menzies.

"Wait!" said I. "Let us first blow out the lantern."

This was done, and the three of us put our weight to the stone. It grated like rusty iron, gave way slowly, and went down with a crunching noise. Ah, the happiness of that moment—the joy of that first glimpse and breath of the air of freedom! It was all we could do to keep from shouting and cheering.

The tunnel had brought us out on a narrow ledge midway down the steep and wooded bluff that rose from the edge of the river. A canopy of trees sheltered us overhead, and below us, through the evergreen foliage, the frozen, snow-crusted river gleamed against the murky background of the night.

A short time before we had stared death in the face; now the hope of life and safety thrilled our hearts with gratitude for a merciful and wonderful Providence. All the circumstances seemed in our favor.

Off behind us the Indians were still holding mad revelry in the fort yard, little dreaming, as they screeched and bowled, of the trick that had been played upon them. Not a sound could be heard close by; there was reason to believe that all the savages were gathered inside

136

of the inclosure. And the snow was falling so fast and thickly that it must cover our tracks almost as soon as made.

To put some miles between ourselves and our bloodthirsty foes was our first thought, and we did not lose an instant by delay. Creeping down to the foot of the bluff, we strapped our snowshoes to our feet, and fixed the four wounded men comfortably on the two empty sledges. As we started off—twenty-one of us in all—the factor's house seemed to be wrapped in flames, to judge from the increasing glare that shone around us. We traveled rapidly to the south, up the river's course, and closely skirted the timbered shore nearest the fort. Gradually the whooping of the Indians died away, and the reflection of the fire faded, until it was only a flickering glow on the dark and wintry horizon. In the excitement of leaving the fort we had given no thought to our future plans; but now, as we hurried along the frozen bed of the river, we discussed that all-important matter. It had been commonly understood in a vague way that we should strike direct for Fort York. However, on reflection, we abandoned that plan. If the Indians should discover our escape, as was only too likely, they would suspect that Fort York was our destination, and make a quick march to cut us off.

"We must look after the interests of the company as well as our own lives," said Menzies, "and I think I see a clear way to do both. The rising of the redskins and the Northwest people may be checked by prompt action; it is probably not yet known beyond Fort Royal, nor have there been attacks elsewhere. So I suggest that we split into two parties. I will command one, take the wounded with me, and push on to Fort Elk, which is about eighty miles to the southeast. You will command the other, Denzil, and strike for Fort Charter. It lies rather more than a hundred miles to the south, and your shortest route will be by way of old Fort Beaver. If we both succeed—and the chances are in our favor—two forts will be put on the alert, and couriers can be sent to other posts."

This plan commended itself to us all, and was ultimately decided upon. There was little danger of pursuit, or of meeting hostile Indians in the directions we proposed to go. We made a brief halt at a small island about five miles from Fort Royal, and separated our party into two. Menzies, having the shorter journey, insisted on taking less men, and I reluctantly yielded.

137

Including himself and wife, and the four wounded, his party numbered eleven. I had eight men in mine, as follows: Captain Rudstone, Christopher Burley, an Indian employee named Pemecan, two voyageurs, Baptiste and Carteret, and three old servants of the company, by name Duncan Forbes, Malcolm Cameron, and Luke Hutter. Flora, of course, went with me, and she had made me radiantly happy by a promise to become my wife at Fort Charter, if the ceremony could be arranged there. One of the sledges, with a quantity of supplies, was turned over to us.

It was a solemn parting, at the hour of midnight, by that little island on the frozen river. The women embraced and shed tears; the men clasped hands and hoarsely wished each other a safe journey. Then Menzies and his companions vanished in the forest on the right bank of the river, and through the driving snow I led my band of followers to the south. Flora was beside me, and I felt ready to surmount any peril for her sake.

It was well toward noon of the next day, and snow was still falling, when we ventured to halt in a desolate region near the headwaters of the Churchill. We rested a few hours, and then pushed on until night, camping in a deep forest and not daring to light a fire. Of what befell us after that I shall speak briefly. The weather cleared and grew colder, and for two days we marched to the south. We made rapid progress—Flora rode part of the time on the sledge—and saw no sign of Indians, or, indeed, of any human beings. We all wore heavy winter clothing, so suffered no hardships on that score; and the second night we built huge camp fires in a rocky gorge among the hills. But our stock of provisions was running short, and this fact caused us some uneasiness.

As the sun was setting that second day—it was the third day's journey in all—we glided from the depths of the virgin forest and saw what had been Fort Beaver on the further side of a shallow clearing. I had been thinking with strange emotions of the past since morning— since we began to draw near the neighborhood—and at sight of my old home, close to which both my father and mother were buried, my eyes grew dim and a choking lump rose in my throat.

"I have never been this way before," remarked Captain Rudstone, "but I know the place by repute. It was of importance in its day; now it is a mass of crumbling ruins."

"Is this really where you were born, Denzil?" Flora asked me.

138

"Yes," I replied; "here I spent my early years and happy ones they were."

"Ah, this is interesting," Christopher Burley said, thoughtfully. "And here your father, Bertrand Carew, lived from the time he left England until his death?"

"Until a treacherous Indian killed him, sir," I said. "And the murderer was never discovered. It is too late to go any further, men," I added, wishing to turn the subject. "We will put up here for the night, and enjoy resting between walls and beside a fireplace."

We crossed the clearing, and entered the stockade by the open gateway, which was half filled in with drifted snow. We went on, past crumbling outbuildings, to what had been the factor's residence. The house was in a fairly good state of preservation, and a push sent the door back on its hinges.

We were on the threshold of the main room, where I so well recalled my father sitting musingly by the great fireplace evening after evening smoking his pipe. Now the apartment was dreary and bare. Snow had filtered in at the windows, and the floor was rotting away. There were ashes in the fireplace, and near by lay a heap of dry wood—signs that some voyageur or trapper had spent a night here while journeying through the wilderness.

"This is like civilization again," said Christopher Burley, with a sigh.

"We are sure of a comfortable night, at all events," replied Captain Rudstone.

"The first thing will be supper," said I. "Baptiste, you and Carteret unpack the sledge. And do you build us a roaring fire, Pemecan."

I went into another room for a moment—it had been my own in times past—and when I returned the Indian had already started a cheerful blaze. As I walked toward the fireplace, intending to warm my hands, a loose slab of stone that was set in at the right of it was dislodged by the shaking of the floor. It toppled over with a crash, breaking into several fragments, and behind it, on the weatherworn stratum of plaster, I saw a number of hieroglyphics. On pulling down some more plaster I found more lines of them, and they were doubtless an inscription of some sort. The odd-looking characters were carved deeply into the wall, and I judged that they had been made years before.

"How strange!" cried Flora, coming to my side.

The rest also drew near, scrutinizing the mysterious discovery with eager eyes and exclamations of surprise.

"It looks like a cryptogram," said Captain Rudstone, and his voice seemed to tremble and grow hoarse as he spoke. "What do you make of it, Carew?"

"Nothing," said I. "You know as much as myself—I never saw it before."

"Was it put there in your father's time?"

"Perhaps," I answered, "but I am inclined to think that it belongs to a much earlier date."

The captain shook his head slowly. He stared at the hieroglyphics with a thoughtful face, with his brow knitted into tiny wrinkles over his half-closed eyes.

CHAPTER XXXI.   A CRY IN THE NIGHT.

We all, more or less, shared Captain Rudstone's curiosity. For a minute we gazed in silence at the strange marks—the company men stolidly, the two voyageurs with disdainful shrugs of the shoulders. Pemecan touched the spot with something like awe, and Christopher Burley followed his example.

"This is a very odd thing," he muttered. "I wish I could take the plaster just as it is back to London with me."

"I've seen nothing like it," declared Luke Hutter, "and I've lived in the wilderness, man and boy, for nigh onto fifty years."

Naturally Fort Beaver having been my home, the rest looked to me to throw some light on the mystery of the cryptogram—if such it was; but I was no wiser than they, and they questioned me in vain. I remembered the fireplace as being always in sound condition, and as my father had never spoken of the matter, I judged that the marks had been cut years before his time—perhaps during the youth of my maternal grandfather.

"It may be so, Mr. Carew," said Christopher Burley; "but to my mind the work is of more recent date. I should say the stone had been purposely removed, and then put back after the hieroglyphics were carved on the plaster. I would take a copy, but unfortunately I have no material at hand—"

"It would be a useless waste of time, sir, if you had," Captain Rudstone interrupted, almost fiercely. "The characters are meaningless. I'll warrant 'tis but a jest on the part of some crack-brained hunter or trapper, or possibly one of the laborers who built the fort. And surely we have more serious matters to think about!"

"Ay, that is true!" I assented, wondering meanwhile at the captain's earnestness. "Cryptogram or not, we'll leave it for wiser heads than ours! Come, reset the stone!"

Baptiste and Carteret lifted the fragments of the slab, and fitted them into place again. That done, I ceased to think of the mystery, and it was not subsequently referred to.

It was a great relief, after the hardships at the fort and the exposure of the long march, to have a shelter over us once more. The danger of pursuit was a specter that had faded behind us, and we counted on reaching Fort Charter at the end of another day's journey. We found some rickety stools and benches, and drawing them around the roaring fire, we ate our simple meal with thankful hearts. Flora sat beside me, and I watched her lovely face, now pensive, now radiant with happiness and love, as the flickering glow of the flames played upon it. I held myself a lucky man to have won such a treasure.

But we were devouring almost the last of our food; indeed, when supper was finished nothing remained but a sack of cornmeal and half a pound of dried fish. It was necessary to provide for the next day, since we would march but poorly on empty stomachs and so we arranged a plan that we had partly settled on that morning.

The suggestion was mine. About five miles to the east, in a hilly and timbered bit of country, a spring bubbled up, so cold and swift that it never froze near its source. The deer and other game knew it, and came to the place by day and night to drink, and there I proposed to guide one or two of my companions.

"We are certain to be back before midnight," I said, "for we can make the round trip in less than three hours. And I'll promise venison for breakfast—or perhaps moose meat."

"Will it be safe to use firearms?" asked Christopher Burley.

"I don't think there is any risk," I answered. "There are no Indian villages within many miles, and as for our old enemies, they are probably searching for us in the neighborhood of the trail to Fort York."

To this Carteret and some of the other men assented. They were all eager to go with me.

"I wish you would stay behind, Denzil," Flora said wistfully.

"But I alone know the exact spot where the deer drink," I answered. "Have no fear; I will return safely."

"At least let me sit up until you come," she pleaded.

"I am afraid I must say no," I replied. "You need sleep and rest too badly. And here, between these walls, you will be as safe as if you were in Fort Charter."

Flora yielded without further words, but there was an appealing, anxious look in her eyes that I remembered afterward. Twilight had turned to darkness, and no time was lost in preparing for the start. I chose to accompany me Carteret and Captain Rudstone; and I fancied the latter was ill pleased at his selection though he spoke otherwise. We donned coats and caps, strapped our snowshoes on our feet, and looked to the loading and priming of our muskets.

As a matter of precaution, I decided to set a watch outside the fort while we were gone—and indeed through the night—and Malcolm

142

Cameron volunteered for the service. On pretense of showing Flora something I found an opportunity to snatch a kiss from her lips and to whisper a few foolish words into her ear. A little room to one side had been reserved for her, and a comfortable bed made of blankets. The rest were to sleep around the fireplace.

The moon was shining from a starry sky and the air was still and cold when the three of us started away. We waved our hands to Cameron, who was at the stockade gates, and plunged eastward into the forest. I led off, and Captain Rudstone and Carteret followed in single file.

At the first I was troubled by a vague premonition of coming disaster, which, in default of sound reason, I set down to Flora's ill-concealed solicitude for my safety. But when we had gone a mile or so this feeling wore off, and I enjoyed the exhilaration of striding on snowshoes over the frozen crust, through the silent solitudes of the wilderness, by rock and hill and moonlit glade. Never had the spell of the Great Lone Land thrilled me more deeply. Watchful and alert, we glided on from tree to tree, our shadows trailing behind us, and the evergreen recesses of the wood stretching on all sides like black pits. Birds and beasts were still; the only sound was the light crunch of our feet, the crackle now and then of a fallen twig.

Not a word was spoken until we came to a gap between two mighty hills, a short distance beyond which, on the verge of a flat of marshland, lay the spot we sought. Then I briefly explained to my companions what we must do.

We made a detour in a semicircle, working our way around to the right side of the wind, and so approached the spring. The cover of bushes and trees ended fifty yards short of it, and with the utmost caution we progressed that far. Crouching on the hard crust, scarcely daring to breathe, we peeped out.

I had expected to see several head of game, at the least, and I was disappointed. Only one was in sight—a fair-sized buck. He was drinking at the source of the spring, and the moonlight glistened on his pronged antlers and on the bubbling water.

"We have but a single chance," I said in a whisper. "We must run no risk of losing it. I take it you are a good shot, Captain Rudstone?"

"I have twice killed my man in a duel," was the curt reply.

"Then you and I will fire together," I continued, "when I count three. And do you reserve your ball, Carteret, if by any chance we both miss. Ready now!"

"All right," said the captain, as he took aim.

"One—two—three!" I whispered.

Bang! The two reports were simultaneous. Under the rising powder smoke the buck was seen to spring in air and then topple over in a quivering mass, dead beyond a doubt. The crashing echoes rolled away into the depths of the forest. We were on our feet instantly, ready to run forward with drawn knives; but before we could do so an unexpected thing checked us. Up the valley behind us, from a point no great distance off, rang a shrill, wavering call. As we listened, staring at one another with alarmed faces, we heard the sound again. And now it was a plain call for help.

"What man can be in this lonely spot?" exclaimed Carteret. "Our ears deceive us. It is the scream of a crafty panther we hear."

"No; it is a human voice," muttered the captain. "I'll swear to that. But I am afraid of a trick."

"If enemies were about they would have no need to lure us," I replied.

"Come, let us see what it means."

I started in the direction of the sound, and my companions followed me.

144

CHAPTER XXXII.   THE TRAVELER FROM ALASKA.

Although the cries for help had now ceased, and were not repeated, our search was crowned with success in a brief time. Pushing up the valley for about five hundred yards, amid trees and thickets, we came suddenly upon a little camp. A lean-to of spruce boughs was rudely built against the base of the steep hill on the right, which towered upward above it to a dizzy and remote height, its alternate patches of timber and snow traced out by the moonlight.

The front of the lean-to was open, and inside, by the glow from a handful of smouldering embers, we saw a strange sight. In the far corner, apparently sleeping, lay an old man. On a small sledge near him were a powder horn, and bullet pouch, a musket and a few pelts.

There was no reply to our sharp greeting, and we ventured closer. Carteret found some bits of dry wood and threw them on the fire. He knelt down and blew them quickly into a blaze, which enabled us to see more distinctly. The old man was breathing heavily, and it needed but a glance to tell us that he was near to death from starvation or some illness. His head rested on a pillow of skins, and he was rolled partly in blankets, which were pushed off enough to show his tattered and travel-worn clothing. His cheeks were deeply sunken, his gray hair was long and matted, and his tangled beard reached nearly to his waist.

"There is not a sign of food," said I.

"It's a clear case of starvation," replied Captain Rudstone. "Poor old chap!"

Just then, roused from his stupor by our voices, or by the warmth of the fire, the stranger opened his eyes and looked about him wildly. He clawed at the air with skinny fingers, and tried to speak. I had a little rum with me, and I poured it between his lips. This brought a tinge of color to his cheeks and a brightness to his glazing eyes, but he was too weak to lift his head.

"Who are you?" he muttered faintly. "Friends? Ay, thank God! White faces once more—after all these months! I heard the shot, and judged that Indians or trappers were near. I called as loudly as I could, but—but —"

"The exertion was too much for you and you fainted," said I. "But we heard your cries, and found you. How long have you been here?"

"Three days," he answered—"three days and nights without food. I ate the last bite when I reached this spot, and a fortnight before I had fired my last charge of powder and ball. I was too ill to go further. I built this shelter to die in, and from time to time I crawled out for fuel to keep up the fire. But the end is close now. Don't leave me—let me die with white faces round me."

"Cheer up, my friend," said Captain Rudstone. "You are going to live."

"We have a deer yonder," I added. "We will make you a venison broth, and then take you to the fort, where the rest of our party await us."

But Carteret, who had the keener eye, shook his head gravely.

"It is no use," he whispered.

The old man heard him.

"Ay, you are right," he said. "I am past help. I feel death stealing over me. Months of privation have worn out my rugged frame—this frightful wilderness has drained my life blood. Comrades, I have journeyed on foot from the far province of Alaska."

Carteret shrugged his shoulders, and the captain and I exchanged incredulous glances. Doubtless the stranger's mind was wandering.

"You think me mad," he said hoarsely. "But no; I will prove otherwise. Listen to my story. It is the last service you can do me, and you will find it well worth hearing."

His manner was so earnest that we began to believe a little in spite of ourselves. We crouched on the blanket alongside of him, and in a voice that was barely audible—he was failing fast—the old man proceeded. The earlier part of his narrative, which was the least interesting, I will set down briefly in my own words.

His name was Hiram Buckhorn, and he was now sixty odd years of age. Half of his life had been passed in New York State and the Lower Canadas, and then he had gone across the continent to San Francisco. From that port he sailed with a dozen adventurous companions two years previously to explore the almost unknown territory of Alaska and prospect for gold. They sailed hundreds of miles up the mighty Yukon, and when their vessel was wrecked they journeyed some days inland on foot.

"And we found what we sought," he continued, with sparkling eyes—"riches such as were never dreamed of! Gold? Why, men, it was as plentiful as the sand and gravel! The streams were paved with

146

nuggets; it was everywhere under the soil! Our camp was near a tributary of the Yukon, and within a square mile was gold enough to purchase a dozen empires; but many a year will pass before men lay hands on the treasure. It is a terrible country—almost impossible to reach, and there is scarcely any summer season. And then the savage Indians! They fell upon us suddenly and treacherously, and butchered every one of my comrades. For some reason they spared my life and held me a prisoner."

The old man paused a moment, breathing heavily. "After a month of captivity, during which my sufferings were terrible, I managed to escape," he went on, in a weaker voice. "I could not return through Alaska, so I headed to the southeast through the Hudson Bay Company's territory. I had musket and powder and ball—which I recovered from the Indians—and I built myself a rude sledge. This was thirteen months ago and since then I have been on the way. Ay, I have plodded more than fifteen hundred miles, through all seasons, over rivers, mountains, and plains. And to what end? To fill a grave in the wilderness! I had hoped to reach civilization, but the task was too great."

Such was Hiram Buckhorn's narrative, and when it was finished we looked silently at him with awe and amazement, with the deepest pity. His exploit had far surpassed anything in the annals of the pioneers of the Northwest. Fifteen hundred miles, on foot and alone, through an untrodden wilderness that even the Hudson Bay Company had never dreamed of tapping! It bore the stamp of truth, and yet it was so incredible a thing that we wavered between doubt and belief.

He noted this, and a grim smile flitted across his face.

"You shall see!" he whispered. "Reach under my head! Be quick!"

I gently thrust a hand beneath the pillow of skins, and drew out a small but heavy bag fashioned of rawhide. At his bidding I placed it beside the old man. With a hard effort, he loosed the mouth and turned the big upside down. Out fell on the fold of a blanket a mass of golden nuggets of the purest quality. There were not less than fifty, of large size, and they gleamed dull yellow in the rays of the fire. The sight almost took our breath, and we gazed with greedy, wondering eyes.

"Look! I spoke the truth," said Hiram Buckhorn. "There is the evidence! Millions like them are to be dug in the region of the Klondike! But put them back—their glitter is no longer for me!"

I hurriedly gathered the nuggets into the bag and thrust it deep under the skins again. The old man watched every movement and heaved a faint sigh.

"The gold is yours, my friend," he muttered. "Take it and divide it when you have put me beneath the snow. And one other favor I crave. Send word at the first opportunity to San Francisco, of the fate of those who sailed with me. They were trusty comrades! As for myself, I have no kith or kin—"

His voice suddenly dwindled to a whisper, and a spasm shook him from head to foot. His glassy eyes closed, he lifted one hand and dropped it, and then his heaving chest was still.

"Is he dead?" I exclaimed.

"Ay, that was his last breath," replied Carteret. "He went quickly."

"The excitement finished him," said Captain Rudstone. "But listen! What is that?"

We looked at one another with startled faces. Far, far above us we heard a roaring, grinding noise, increasing each second. And we knew only too well what it meant!

"A snowslide—an avalanche!" cried Captain Rudstone. "It has started at the top, and will carry everything before it down the hill."

"Run for your lives!" shouted Carteret. "We're in the track, and will hardly escape as it is!"

In a trice we were out of the lean-to, panic-stricken and alarmed, thinking of nothing but our lives; for of all perils of the Great Lone Land, the snow slide, with its speed and destructive power, was the most to be dreaded. We forgot the dead man—the gold under his pillow. We sped down the valley as though on wings, not daring to look up the hillside, where the avalanche was cleaving its way with a deafening noise, with the crash of falling trees, the grind of dislodged bowlders, and the roar of tons and tons of loosened snow. And the monster seemed to be reaching for us!

Flora's dear face took shape before me in the frosty air, and I fancied I could hear her voice pleading with me to remain at the fort. Should I ever return to her arms again? The thought lent me speed, and I out distanced my companions. The next instant I tripped in a

148

clump of bushes and fell headlong, and plump on top of me came Carteret and Captain Rudstone.

We were all three so tangled together that our efforts to extricate ourselves only led to worse confusion. We broke through the crust and floundered in soft and powdery snow. As we struggled hard—we had fled but a short distance—the avalanche struck the valley close behind us. There was first a mighty crash that made the ground tremble, next a long, deafening grind like a hundred thunderpeals in one, and then the hissing rush of a few belated rocks.

Silence followed, and we knew that we were saved. With grateful hearts and trembling limbs we scrambled out of our pit and regained the firm crust.

"Thank God!" I exclaimed.

"We had a close shave of it, comrades," Carteret said huskily, as he wiped the perspiration from his brow.

We turned back and were pulled up short within twenty feet. For in front of us, stretching two-thirds of the way across the valley, was a lofty barrier of snow, trees and bowlders; its track down the hillside was marked by a clean, wide swath, the beginning of which we could not see. And deep under the fallen mass, covered by tons and tons of compact debris, was the crushed body of Hiram Buckhorn.

"He could not have a better grave," said Captain Rudstone. "No men or beasts will ever despoil it."

"Peace to his bones!" replied Carteret, reverently taking off his cap. "He deserved to live, after what he did."

"But the gold!" I cried. "It is buried with him!"

"And there it will stay," Captain Rudstone said coolly. "Even when the snow melts in the spring, it will be covered deep by rocks and trees that no man could drag away."

The old voyageur appeared equally unconcerned. Money meant little to him, and I could understand the captain taking as easy a view of the loss. But with myself it way different, I confess. I looked forward to marriage, and for Flora's sake I longed for my share of the precious nuggets. But there was nothing to be done—nothing further to be said. With a heavy heart I turned and followed my companions down the valley. We quickly cut the deer apart, burdening ourselves with the choicest haunches, and then set off on our return to the fort.

CHAPTER XXXIII.   A CONVIVIAL MORNING.

It must have been an hour past midnight when we broke from the forest into the clearing, and as we strode across toward the stockade we noted with relief that all was still and peaceful. Malcolm Cameron greeted us at the gate, and we passed on to receive a hearty welcome at the house. With the exception of Pemecan, our comrades were all awake, sprawled about a blazing fire, and at sight of the meat we carried they set up a great shout.

"Hush! you will rouse Miss Hatherton!" said I, for I saw that she had retired.

However, I doubt if she had slept a wink; and no sooner was there a lull in the conversation than she called from the little room adjoining, in a hesitating voice:

"Have you returned, Denzil?"

"Yes," I replied. "I am back, safe and sound, and with a fat deer for breakfast. But go to sleep at once; it is very late."

"I will," Flora answered. "Good-night, Denzil."

"Good-night," I responded, and then my face grew hot as I saw Captain Rudstone regarding me with half-veiled amusement.

"You are a lucky chap, Carew," he said; "but you have well earned your happiness."

I never quite knew how to take the captain's words, so I merely nodded in reply. We were all sleepy, and without delay we completed the preparations for the night. Two men were chosen for sentry duty at the gate—Luke Hutter and Baptiste, and the latter at once relieved Cameron and sent him in. Carteret and I had a look about the inclosure, and then, after putting a great beam on the fire, we rolled ourselves in our blankets and laid down beside our companions.

I must have fallen asleep as soon as my eyes closed, for I remembered nothing until I was roused by a hand on my shoulder. Luke Hutter was standing over me, and from head to foot he was thickly coated with snow. The gray light of dawn glimmered behind the frosted windows, and I heard a hoarse whistling noise. The fire was blazing cheerily, for Baptiste had replenished it when he came off duty. Several of the men were stirring; the others were sound asleep.

"A bad day to travel, Mr. Carew," said Hutter.

"What do you mean?" I asked.

For answer he led me to the door, and as he opened it a fine cloud of snow whirled into the room. I cried out with astonishment, for one

150

of those rapid changes of weather so common in northern latitudes had taken place during the night. A storm of wind and snow, much like a blizzard, was raging violently. The cold was intense, and it was impossible to see more than a yard or two in front of one's face.

"It began several hours ago," said Hutter, "and it is good to last until night. If we set out for Fort Charter we shall lose our way, sir, and perhaps become exhausted and freeze to death."

I agreed with Hutter, and after some reflection I hit upon a plan that afforded me no little pleasure. My companions were by this time awake and up, and I called their attention to the storm. As to the danger and impossibility of proceeding on our journey, they were all of one mind.

"We need a rest," said I, "and here is a chance to take it, with a bit of recreation and enjoyment thrown in. There is not the slightest risk of an attack by Indians. We can spare a day, and we have snug quarters and enough to eat. The storm will doubtless abate by to-morrow morning, and then we will push on. What do you say, men?"

They assented readily, even with enthusiasm, and I saw that they entered fully into the spirit which had prompted me to make the proposal.

"I'm thinking it will be like old times," said Cameron. "It was a happy life at Fort Royal, on the whole, sir. There's one thing we'll be lacking for the day's pleasure—a stiff glass of grog all round."

"We'll manage to get along without it," I replied. "And now let's finish up the work; there is plenty to do."

First of all we made a kettleful of warm water by melting snow, and I handed a pannikin of it in to Flora, whom I had heard stirring for some time. She bade me a sweet good-morning, and showed me a glimpse of her pretty face round the corner of the door. Then some of us began to prepare breakfast—we had found an ample supply of dish ware in the fort—and others demolished a part of the stockade and brought the timbers in for fuel. Captain Rudstone and I busied ourselves by making the crevices of the door and windows secure against wind and sifting snow. For once we dispensed with sentry duty, thinking it to be unnecessary.

As breakfast was ready to be served, Flora tripped out of her little room looking radiantly beautiful. When she learned that we were to stop at the fort that day her eyes glowed with pleasure, and what I read in them set my heart beating fast. Seated about the fire on

151

benches and rickety stools, we attacked the delicious slices of venison, the steaming coffee, and the crisp cakes of cornmeal. Then, the dishes washed and the room tidied a bit, we heaped the fire high and settled ourselves for a long morning. Outside the wind howled and the whirling snow darkened the air; inside was warmth and cheer and comfort.

Looking back to that day over the gulf of years, I can recall few occasions of keener enjoyment. The security and comfort were in such strong contrast to what we had lately suffered, that we abandoned ourselves wholly to the pleasure of the passing moment. We forgot the tragedies and sufferings that lay behind us, and gave no thought to what the uncertain future might hold in store. For me the horizon was unclouded. Flora was by my side, and I looked forward to soon calling her my wife.

Luckily, we had plenty of tobacco, and wreaths of fragrant smoke curled from blackened pipes. Baptiste and Carteret sang the dialect songs of the wilderness; Duncan Forbes amused us with what he called a Highland fling, and Pemecan, to the accompaniment of outlandish chanting, danced an Indian war-dance. Captain Rudstone and Christopher Burley, who were rarely anything but quiet and reserved, showed us sides of their characters that we had not suspected before; they clapped their hands and joined in the laughter and merriment. And in Flora's unfeigned happiness and light spirits I took my greatest enjoyment.

"Comrade, it's your turn," said Forbes, addressing old Malcolm Cameron. "Maybe you'll be giving us your imitation of the skirl of the bagpipes."

"Man, it's too dry work," Cameron replied. "If I had a wee drop of liquor—But it's no use asking for that."

"By the way, Carew," said Captain Rudstone, "as I was overhauling that heap of rubbish in the cellar this morning, I pulled out a small cask. Could it contain anything drinkable?"

I was on my feet like a shot.

"Come; we'll see!" I cried. "Lead the way!"

I followed the captain to the cellar and we found the cask. I quickly broached it, and to my delight it, contained what I had scarcely ventured to hope for—a fine old port wine.

"Where did it come from?" asked the captain, smacking his lips.

"My father used to have it sent to him from England," I replied, "and this cask must have been mislaid and covered up."

"Your father?" muttered the captain: and he gave me one of those strange looks that had so mystified me in the past.

"Yes, he was a judge of wine, I believe," I answered. "Come, we'll go up. Cameron can wet his whistle now, and we'll all be the better for a little sound port."

When we returned to our companions with the cask, and told them what it held, they gave us an eager and noisy welcome. We rummaged about until we found a sufficient number of cracked glasses and cups, and then we filled them with the fragrant, ruddy beverage.

"Miss Hatherton shall drink first," said I, as I sat down beside her and handed her a glass.

My own I held up with a little nod, and she partly understood me. Such a roguish look twinkled in her eyes that I carried out my purpose.

"Attention!" I cried, standing up. "A toast, comrades! to my promised wife!"

With an earnestness that I liked, the men drank, one and all, and Flora smiled very prettily through her confusion and blushes.

"Ah, she's a bonnie lady," old Malcolm Cameron said bluntly.

"And with the spirit of a man," added Luke Hutter.

I acknowledged these compliments with a bow as I sat down. Most of the drinking vessels were emptied and passed to Carteret to be filled. That done, at a sign from me he carried the cask to a closet at the other side of the room. Some of the men were bibulously inclined, and for Flora's sake I had to be cautious.

Of a sudden Captain Rudstone rose, his handsome, stern face almost transformed by an expression of genial good will.

"Mr. Carew," he began, "on such an occasion as this I feel that I must say a word. Indeed you have won a prize. 'Tis an old proverb that a man married is a man marred, but in you I see an exception. Were I a few years younger I should have ventured to enter the lists against you. I have knocked about the world, and I can pay Miss Hatherton no higher compliment than to say that she is equally fitted to be queen of a London drawing room or mistress of a factor's humble house. But enough. I wish you every prosperity and happiness, and a long career in the service of the company."

153

The captain was evidently sincere, and I had never liked him so well as now, though I must confess that I felt a spark of jealousy when Flora made him a smiling courtesy.

He was no sooner down in his seat than Christopher Burley stood up. The law clerk's face was flushed, and his eyes had an unwonted sparkle. He had drunk but two glasses of port, yet he was a different man to look at.

"Mr. Carew and Miss Hatherton, my compliments," he said. "I shall think of this convivial gathering when I am back in London—in that crowded, bustling heart of the world, and I hope some day to have the pleasure of seeing you there—of seeing all of you, my friends. I will take you to my favorite haunt, the Cheshire Cheese, in Fleet Street, where the great and learned Dr. Johnson was wont to foregather. But I have much to do before I can return to England. The task that brought me to this barbarous country—this land of snow and ice—is of a most peculiar and difficult nature. I will take the present opportunity to inquire—"

"Enough!" suddenly interrupted Captain Rudstone in a harsh voice. "Your tongue is rambling sir. I am doing you a service by requesting you to sit down."

"Sir, do you mean to insinuate—" began Christopher Burley.

But at that instant voices were heard outside and the door was thrown open.

CHAPTER XXXIV.   ON THE WAY.

A visitor of any sort was the last thing we could have expected, and the reader can imagine what a surprise and scare the interruption gave us. We leaped to our feet with such haste that several of the benches wore knocked over, and Christopher Burley, who was in the act of sitting down at the time, landed on the floor with a heavy crash. But there was no occasion for alarm—no need to rush frantically for our muskets. The intruder was not an Indian, not an enemy. In the open doorway, framed against the whiteness of the storm, stood a big, bearded man clad in the winter uniform of the Hudson Bay Company.

And the moment I saw him I recognized an old acquaintance—a hunter who had of late years served at Fort Charter.

"Tom Arnold!" I cried gladly, as I hurried forward to greet him.

"By Jupiter, if it ain't Carew!" he shouted, clasping my hand. Turning round, he called loudly: "Come in, boys, it's all right!"

At the bidding five more men stamped noisily into the house, shaking the snow from their clothing, and dragging a well-laden sledge behind them.

"I left these chaps outside, not knowing who might be in the fort," Tom explained; "but when I listened a bit I reckoned it was safe to enter. I heard a couple of voices that sounded kind of familiar. And no mistake either! We're in luck to find friends and shelter at one stroke. What a snug place you've got here!"

A scene of merriment and excitement followed, and hands were clasped all round; for the most of our party and of the new arrivals were acquainted with one another, even Captain Rudstone finding a friend or two.

After a generous glass of wine, Tom Arnold lit his pipe, stretched his feet to the blazing logs, and volunteered explanations, which we had been waiting anxiously to hear. He and his party, it seemed, had left Fort Charter on a hunting trip three days before. On the previous night they had chosen a poor camping-place—it afforded little shelter against the storm, and so, in the morning, they determined to try to reach old Fort Beaver.

"That's my yarn," Tom concluded, "and now let's have yours, Carew. What are you doing in this part of the country, and with a pretty girl in tow?"

As briefly as possible I related all that had happened, from the swift beginning of trouble at Fort Royal to the night when we escaped

155

by the secret passage. Every word of it was new to Tom and his companions, and they listened with breathless interest and dilated eyes, with hoarse exclamations of rage and grief. And when the narrative was finished a gloom fell upon all of us.

"So the country is quiet down your way?" asked Captain Rudstone.

"Yes, as far as Fort Garry and the Red River," Tom replied. "We had dispatches within a week, and though they mentioned bad feeling and a few rows in which men were killed on both sides, there has been no general outbreak. As for the trouble up north, we hadn't an inkling of it."

"Apparently, then," said the captain, "the attack on Fort Royal was a private grudge—an act of revenge instigated solely by Cuthbert Mackenzie, who stirred up the redskins to help him. There was motive enough, you know, for a man of his nature."

"It's likely as you say," Tom answered, "but at the same time I'm afraid the Northwest Company knew what was on foot, and will declare open war as soon as they hear of the fall of Fort Royal. The Indians may have gone north to attack other forts on the bay, or possibly they will march to Fort Charter next. We must lose no time in getting back and giving the alarm. This is the worst of news."

"I am sure there is no danger," I said hurriedly, noticing that Flora looked disturbed and anxious. "The Indians must have gone toward Fort York to cut us off; if they had come this way you would have heard of them long ago."

"Yes, that's right," assented Captain Rudstone. "It will be time enough to start in the morning, when the storm will likely be over. If you set off now, you have ten chances to one of perishing in the snow. You can't do better than share our cozy quarters."

"I'll think about it," Arnold answered doubtfully. "At all events, we'll have a jolly good feed together, and then we'll see what the weather promises. I ought to be back at the fort long before to-morrow morning."

By this time the dinner was ready. Carteret had found a packet of cornmeal that had been overlooked before, and our visitors contributed freely from their own ample store of food. So our spirits brightened a little, and while we ate and drank we chatted of more pleasing things than Indians and warfare. But Christopher Burley was in a sullen mood and showed a very curt manner to Captain Rudstone.

156

Why the latter had cut the law clerk's speech short so brusquely, and why he had been disturbed by it, were mysteries to which I could find no solution. Indeed, I felt keenly disappointed, for I knew that Burley had been on the point of explaining the task that had brought him out to the Canadas.

The meal over, a surprise was in store for us. We observed that more light shone through the frosted window panes, and Tom Arnold rose and opened the door. He gave a shout that drew most of us after him, and we were amazed to see the change that had taken place in so short a time. Of the howling storm there was not a trace, save the fresh snowdrifts. It was still blowing a little, but no snow was falling, and through the clear air the clouds gave signs of breaking.

"Hurray! We can start now!" cried Tom.

"Yes, if the calm lasts," added Captain Rudstone.

"What do you think of it?" I asked of Carteret, who was considered an authority on the weather.

The old voyageur sniffed the air for a moment.

"It's hard to tell in this case, sir," he replied. "The clouds may break and clear away for good; and then ag'in, the storm may come on as bad as ever, within the hour. But it's worth risking the chance."

Some held Carteret's opinion, and others were in favor of waiting till morning. But in the end the latter were won over, and we decided to start at once. For a little while there was bustle and commotion as the men repacked the sledges, donned their furred coats and snowshoes, and looked to the priming of their muskets.

In less than ten minutes we were ready, and with a last lingering look at the room which had sheltered us so well, we left the house. I saw Captain Rudstone glance keenly at the spot where the cryptogram was hidden, and he muttered something under his breath as he turned away. We passed across the inclosure, out at the ruined gates, and struck off in the direction of Fort Charter. We were soon in a heavy forest, where it was necessary to march two or three abreast. Tom Arnold, Captain Rudstone and another led the way. I was in the next file of three, with a couple of Fort Charter men for company. Flora was a little distance in the rear, strapped to our half-empty sledge, which Baptiste and Carteret were drawing. From time to time I glanced back for a sight of her pretty face looking out from a dainty headdress of fur.

157

The storm did not recommence, though the clouds, instead of breaking, hung low and heavy over us. We marched as rapidly as possible through the wilderness, gliding over the drifts and dislodging miniature avalanches of snow from the drooping limbs of the trees.

At about three o'clock in the afternoon, when we had covered some six or seven miles, we were filing along a deep and narrow valley, over the bed of a frozen stream. The snow covered the undergrowth and rocks, making a fairly good road. On both sides of us rose mighty hills, densely covered with timber, and seared with granite crags. Of a sudden, from a point slightly ahead on the left, rang the dull report of a musket.

"I'm shot!" cried Tom Arnold, clapping a hand to his arm.

CHAPTER XXXV.   RETRIBUTION.

Our first thought was that we had blundered into an ambuscade and that the bluffs to right and left of us swarmed with redskins. Our little column stopped short, confused and panic-stricken, and for a brief instant we stood huddled in the narrow valley like sheep. Our muskets were lifted, but no foes were insight; we expected a withering fusillade to be poured into our ranks.

"They've got us, boys!" cried Tom Arnold, who was staring in all directions while he held his wounded arm.

But the silence remained unbroken—and I began to hope that our alarm was groundless—at least, so far as an ambuscade was concerned. Just where the shot had been fired from I could not tell, for the wind had quickly drifted the smoke away; but as I watched alertly I detected a slight movement in the evergreen-clad face of the hill on the left, at a point some distance ahead, and about twenty feet from the ground.

"There is only one redskin," was my instant reflection, "and he is loading for another shot."

My gun was at mid-shoulder, and I did not hesitate a second. Taking swift aim at the spot, I pulled the trigger. The loud report was followed by a screech; then the bushes parted, and an Indian pitched out headforemost, landing with a thud in the soft snow.

"Good shot!" cried Arnold. "One red devil the less! But what can the others be about?"

"It's doubtful if there are any more," said I.

"By Heavens, Carew I believe you are right!" shouted Captain Rudstone. "We've had a scare for nothing. This follow was certainly alone, or his comrades would have blazed away at us before this. I fancied I saw him stir just now—if he's not dead, we may get some information out of him."

With that the captain started toward the fallen Indian, keeping his musket ready and darting keen glances right and left. I would have followed him, but at sight of Arnold's pale face I changed my mind. His left arm was bleeding profusely below the shoulder, and three or four of his men were standing about him.

"Is the bone hit?" I inquired anxiously.

"No; it's only a flesh wound," Arnold replied. "But I can't afford to lose much more blood. Fix me up, some of you fellows."

159

Just then Christopher Burley pushed in among us, his countenance agitated and frightened.

"Is the danger over?" he cried.

"Are there no more Indians in the hills?"

Before I could answer him I was tapped on the shoulder, and turning round I saw Flora; she had left the sledge, and her eyes looked into mine calmly and fearlessly.

"Do not be alarmed," I said. "It seems there was but one Indian."

"I was afraid we were going to be attacked," she answered; "but I am not a bit frightened now. See, my hand is steady. Let me bandage this poor man's wound, Denzil."

The plucky girl did not wait for permission, but took a knife from one of the men and began to cut away Arnold's shirt sleeve. I had a large handkerchief in my pocket, which I produced and gave to her. Meanwhile I glanced forward to Captain Rudstone, who was kneeling beside the Indian, with his back turned to us. I saw him look quickly and furtively over his shoulder, and his hands seemed to be actively engaged. I noted this, as I say, but at the time I thought nothing of the incident.

A moment later the captain rose to his feet and turned round. He met my eyes, and his own dropped; for a passing second he looked slightly confused.

"Here's a queer go, Carew," he called. "You've killed your man, and I fancy there is something on him that will be of personal interest to you."

I hurried to the spot, in company with half a dozen others. The Indian lay dead on his side—an elderly, wrinkled savage with a feathered scalp-lock, dressed in buffalo robe, leggings and beaded moccasins. His musket was clutched in his hand, and blood was oozing from a wound in the region of the heart.

"What do you mean, Rudstone?" I asked.

He pointed silently to the redskin's throat and bending closer, I saw a necklace of the teeth and claws of wild beasts. Something else was strung with it—a tiny locket of smooth gold—and the sight of it made my heart leap. With a single jerk, I tore the necklace loose, and the locket fell in the snow. I picked it up, looked at it sharply, and suspicion became a certainty.

160

"This is the working of Providence!" I cried hoarsely, "I have committed an act of just retribution. Look: the Indian killed my father nearly six years ago, and now he has died by my hand."

"I suspected as much," said Captain Rudstone. "I remembered your speaking of a locket that your father always carried, and that was missing from his body."

"This is the locket," I replied. "I know it well! And here lies the murderer! Thank Heaven, I have avenged my father's death!"

"There is doubtless something in it," suggested the captain. "Most likely a miniature portrait."

He looked me straight in the eyes as he spoke, and with an expression of calm curiosity.

"It is the use to which such trinkets are usually put," he added. "I am glad you have recovered it, Carew. It is a memento to be prized and treasured."

By this time all of the party were gathered around me; Arnold's wound had been tightly and deftly bandaged, and the flow of blood checked. A whisper of my strange discovery ran from mouth to mouth, and Flora pressed my arm in silent sympathy. There was a solemn hush, and every eye was on me as I fingered the locket in search of a spring, for I knew it opened that way. I must have touched the spot by accident, for of a sudden the trinket flew open. But the inside was quite empty. I could not repress a little cry of disappointment.

"Strange!" muttered Captain Rudstone "I was sure the locket held something! You say you never knew what your father kept in it, Carew?"

"No, he never spoke of it," I replied. "It was rarely I caught a glimpse of it, though I knew that he always wore it."

"Have you reason to believe that he kept anything in it?" asked Christopher Burley.

"To tell the truth, sir, I have not," I answered.

"Ah, that lets light on the matter," said the captain. "The trinket is probably treasured for itself—for the sake of some old association connected with it."

"That is very likely," I assented. "At all events, it is empty now."

Christopher Burley begged to be allowed to examine the locket, and after a close scrutiny he handed it back to me.

"This is a very curious case, Mr. Carew," he said, speaking in dry and legal tones. "It resolves itself into two issues. In the first place, the locket may have been empty when your father wore it. In the second place it may have contained something. But if we take the latter for granted, what became of the contents? It is extremely unlikely that the Indian could have found the spring, or, indeed, suspected that the bit of gold was hollow."

"Which goes to prove," put in Captain Rudstone, "that the trinket has been restored to Mr. Carew in the same condition in which it was torn from his father's body. The redskin prized it merely as a glittering adornment to his barbaric necklace."

"I agree with you," said I, "and I think it is time we closed so trivial a discussion. Justice has been done and I am satisfied."

With that I thrust the locket deep into my pocket.

"There is another thing," said Captain Rudstone; "why did the Indian fire on us? He may have been scouting in advance of a hostile force."

"I do not think we are in any danger," I replied. "Indeed, I can offer a solution to the mystery. After my father's death the murderer was sought for, but his own tribe spirited him away, and I believe he fled to the far West. His relatives declared at the time that he had gone crazy on account of a blow on the head, and believed he had a mission to kill white men. This was likely true. And now, after a lapse of five years, the fellow wandered back to this neighborhood and fired on us at sight."

Such was my earnest conviction, and for the most part the rest agreed with me. But Tom Arnold was inclined to be skeptical, and shook his head gravely.

"You may be right, my boy," he said, "but I'm a cautious man, and I don't think overmuch of your argument. Leastways, the chances are even that your dead Indian belonged to the party who took Fort Royal, and that the whole body is marching on Fort Charter. So off we go for a rapid march, and let every man put his best foot forward."

"Under any circumstances," I replied, "whether we are in danger or not, we ought to reach the fort as soon as possible, and at the best we can't make it before midnight."

So a little later we were traveling south again, surmounting by the aid of snowshoes, all the rugged difficulties of the wintry wilderness. Flora was strapped on the sledge as before, and we had left the dead

Indian—for whose fate I felt not the least compunction—lying where he had fallen.

We marched on for two hours, and then our fear of the weather proved to be well founded. A furious snowstorm came on suddenly, and a violent wind whirled the flakes into our faces; the cold grew intense, and we could not see a yard ahead of us. A more terrific blizzard we had none of us known in the past.

For a little while we floundered on resolutely, blinded and half-frozen, becoming more exhausted each minute. The storm seemed to be getting worse, and we encountered great drifts. There was not a sign by which we could steer in the right direction, and we could not be sure that we were not traveling in a circle.

"Hold on, boys; this won't do!" Tom Arnold cried at last. "We can't go any farther. We must find shelter and lie close until the morning, or until the weather takes a turn."

CHAPTER XXXVI.   A PAINFUL MYSTERY.

But how and where should we seek shelter? Each man, I am sure, asked himself that question uneasily, and the quest grew more hopeless as we groped our way on for a quarter of an hour, our faces set against the stinging cold wind and the biting snowflakes. Arnold was leading, and I was some distance back, trudging alongside of Flora, and trying to keep up her spirits.

But good fortune befell us when we least expected it. Exhausted and half-blinded, we suddenly emerged from the tangled forest on a bit of an open space. Before us was the bed of a frozen stream, now filled up with drifted snow, and from the farther side of it a hill towered steeply, affording almost complete protection from the violence of the wind. A short distance on our left, nestled at the base of another hill, was a little Indian village, long since deserted—a dozen tepees half-buried in the snow, a couple of canoe frames protruding from a drift, and some worn-out snowshoes hanging from a tree.

"By Jupiter! I know the spot," cried Tom Arnold, in a tone of consternation and astonishment. "I remember the village and the stream! Why, men, we are away out of our reckoning—on the wrong tack altogether. This shows how easily a fellow can get lost in a blizzard, no matter how old a hand he is."

"We're in luck, anyway," said I. "Here is decent shelter, and the hills keep off the worst of the storm. We are safe for the night."

"And Fort Charter twenty miles away!" grumbled Arnold. "We've got to reach it to-morrow, come good weather or bad. All hands to work," he added sharply. "We'll make things as snug as possible."

We set to with a will and the exercise soon warmed our sluggish blood. Some dug out the canoe frames and broke them up for fuel; others cleared the loose snow from half a dozen of the huts, and we were delighted to find them dry inside, and in sound condition. We did not hesitate to build a roaring fire, for we knew that the light could not be seen at any distance, and that if any hostile Indians were in the vicinity the storm would have driven them to camp.

Twilight was falling when we found the abandoned village, and the evening was well advanced by the time our preparations were completed. We cooked and ate supper, and then sat smoking for awhile about the fire. The best of the tepees had been assigned to

164

Flora, and she retired immediately after the meal. The storm was still raging and the snow falling thickly, but our camp was so sheltered by the two great hills that we were almost as comfortable as we had been at Fort Beaver. Yet only a short distance away, to right and left, we could hear the wind shrieking and howling through the open wilderness.

"We had better be turning in, so we can make an early start," Tom Arnold said finally. "My arm is stiff and sore, and I can't sit up any longer. How about sentry duty?"

"We mustn't neglect that," replied Captain Rudstone. "I volunteer for the first watch."

The matter was quickly settled. There were to be three watches, Carteret following the captain, and a Fort Charter man named Humphrey taking the last turn. The orders were to pace a short distance right and left of the camp at intervals, and to keep up the fire; each sentry was to rouse the next man at the proper time.

We smoked a last pipe, and turned in leaving Captain Rudstone on guard. We were divided into batches of four, and those who shared my tepee with me were Christopher Burley, Luke Hutter and Duncan Forbes. We huddled close together, wrapped in blankets, and I for one was so tired out that I fell asleep instantly.

I remember nothing more until I was roused, after what seemed a short interval, by a husky shout and a spluttering of angry words. The noise was enough to waken the whole camp, and indeed it did so with amazing rapidity. I rushed outside in alarm, followed by my companions. The gray dawn was breaking, and the air was free of snow. The rest of the men were pouring from the tepees, rubbing their drowsy eyes and fumbling with their muskets. I saw Flora's face, flushed and frightened, peeping from the little doorway of her hut. We all gathered round Tom Arnold, who was pointing to a heap of dead ashes—what was left of the fire.

"We might have been murdered in our sleep!" he cried savagely. "Who's to blame for this cursed carelessness? I turned out a minute ago, and look what I find! Nobody on guard, and the fire burned to ashes! Humphrey, you scoundrel, you had the last watch! What have you got to say for yourself?"

"I—I wasn't roused, sir," stammered Humphrey. "It was Carteret's place to do that."

"How could I do it when I wasn't wakened myself?" exclaimed Carteret. "Naturally I slept sound, thinking I would be called in time."

"Just my case," added Humphrey in an aggrieved tone.

"Then Captain Rudstone is the man!" cried Arnold. "Where is he?"

Where indeed? We suddenly became aware that the captain was not among us. We shouted and called his name, but no answer came back. We looked into all the tepees, and found them empty. It was a deep mystery, and our alarm and wonder increased. We glanced at one another with startled and anxious faces. None could throw light on the matter; we had all slept soundly through the night. I questioned Flora, but she was no wiser than the rest of us.

"It's the queerest thing I ever heard of," said Arnold. "The man can't have been spirited away."

"Perhaps an Indian crept up and tomahawked him," suggested Malcolm Cameron, "and he's lying yonder under the snow."

"No; that is out of the question," said I. "Captain Rudstone could not have been caught off his guard."

"It's my opinion," declared Arnold, "that he heard some noise in the forest and went to see what it was. He wandered farther from camp than he intended, and got lost in the storm—you can see by the depth of the snow that the blizzard didn't hold up till near morning— and ten to one he's lying stiff and dead under a drift. We'll search for him till the middle of the morning, and if we don't find him by then, we must be off to the fort while the weather permits."

Arnold's reasoning was not very sound, but no one could offer a more plausible solution to the mystery. While breakfast was preparing some of us fruitlessly explored the vicinity of the camp, and a little later, having fortified ourselves with food and hot coffee, we set off on a more extended search. Christopher Burley and three other men stayed behind with Flora; the rest, divided into four parties, went in as many different directions.

To cut a long tale short, our efforts proved of no avail. One after another the search parties returned—the last one arriving an hour before noon—and all had the same story to tell. The ground had been carefully gone over within a radius of several miles from camp, but Captain Rudstone had disappeared without leaving a trace behind him. That Arnold's theory was correct—that the unfortunate man lay dead under one of the mighty drifts that had formed while the storm

166

raged in the night—we all believed. That he could have voluntarily deserted us was out of the question.

"It would be no use to hunt any longer," said Arnold, "even if we had the time to spare. Perhaps next spring, when the snow melts, some trapper or hunter will find the body and give it decent burial."

So, after a sad and hurried dinner, we packed up and resumed our journey. The weather held good, and about midnight we arrived safely at Fort Charter.

I will make but brief mention of our stop at the fort, where we were received and treated with the utmost kindness. As for Captain Rudstone, I need only say that I had grown sincerely attached to him, and felt his loss deeply. Not a scrap of news was waiting for us on our arrival. No couriers had come in, and what was taking place in the North, or whether Andrew Menzies and his party had reached Fort Elk, were matters of conjecture. One keen disappointment I had. Contrary to expectation, there was no priest at Fort Charter, so my marriage with Flora had to be put off indefinitely, as I feared at the time.

But something happened shortly to raise my spirits. The factor of the fort decided to send word down to Fort Garry of the Indian rising and the loss of Fort Royal, and I gladly consented to be his messenger. Moreover, since an attack was far from improbable, and the post was weak, two of the officers seized this opportunity to dispatch their wives to the South, believing from the reports they had heard that the country was safe in that direction.

Preparations were pushed forward, and just three days after our arrival we started on our long march of five hundred miles to Fort Garry through the dead of winter. We numbered fifteen in all, including Flora, and two other women. Christopher Burley, Baptiste and Carteret, and Luke Hutter were of the party. We were well provided with all that was needful—sledges and dogs, provisions and firearms.

CHAPTER XXXVII.   REST AND HAPPINESS.

Rat, tat, tat! Thump, thump! Bang!

So noisy and persistent an assault on my door roused me at length from a delicious slumber. I sat up, rubbing my blinking eyes.

"Who's there?" I called in a drowsy tone.

"It's nine o'clock, sir," responded the voice of Baptiste. "I thought you would wish to know it," he added, and with that he went shuffling down the corridor.

Nine o'clock! And I had slept several hours over my usual time of rising! This was the result of sitting up so late the night before. I was wide awake instantly. I sprang out of bed, broke the thin crust of ice on my basin, and plunged hands and face into the bitter cold water. A brisk rubbing with a towel put me all aglow, and I felt what a good thing it was to be alive. The past, with its perils and hardships, was behind me like a dim dream, and the future was rose-colored in spite of the grim spectre of war that it held over us in those days.

This was to be an eventful morning, in a way, for I had a happy piece of news to impart to Flora; I thought of it constantly as I dressed—an operation to which of late I devoted much care and attention. From regions downstairs—I was in the factor's house— came the rattle of dishes and a murmur of voices. Out of doors the frosty air was filled with the hum of busy human life.

But I forget that I owe the reader an explanation. The day of which I write was the 9th of January, 1847, and just one week after we entered Fort Garry and exchanged the harsh monotony of travel for the comforts of this nourishing post in the western wilderness.

I need dwell but briefly on the interval. The journey from Fort Charter had been severe and trying, protracted by furious storms that held us in camp for days at a time. But we were not attacked on the way—indeed, we saw no signs of Indians—and every one of our little band had come safely down from the North, through the heart of the Great Lone Land. It had been a disappointment to spend Christmas in the wilderness, but our trials were forgotten when we reached the fort.

But of these matters enough for the present. I must return to where I left off, and continue the narrative. When I had finished dressing that morning I went downstairs to the factor's living room, meeting no one on the way except Christopher Burley, who was too absorbed in thought to return my greeting.

I opened the door softly, and beheld an attractive picture. The sunlight shone on rugs and easy-chairs, on walls hung with tastefully chosen prints, on a table spread for two, with snowy linen and white china. To my relief, the room had but one occupant, and that was Flora. She was standing by the window, and as I entered she turned round quickly. She looked radiantly beautiful in a frock of some pink material with her rich hair coiled in a new and becoming fashion.

"Denzil, how late you are!" she cried, with a roguish pout. "They have all finished breakfast long ago. But I waited for you, sir, and am nearly famished. You do not deserve—"

She got no further, for by this time I was at her side, and had stopped her pretty lips with a kiss—nay, a shower of them.

"Darling, I have news for you," I said, a moment later.

"Well, what is it?" she asked, blushing as she spoke.

"I had a long talk with Mr. Macdonald last night," I replied. "A better fellow never lived. I told him all, and—and he is anxious to have a wedding at Fort Garry."

"Is he?"

"Yes, that's what he said. It will sort of cheer up things, you know, and—"

"But he has one wife already."

"Don't be stupid," said I. "Listen: he is going to send a man off to-day for the priest, who is visiting a little settlement fifty miles to the south. In a week, if you are willing, we can be married."

"In a week!" she cried, with mock consternation.

"I am serious," I replied. "Do not play with me. Think how long I have waited. Say that you will be my wife in a week's time."

"You foolish boy!" She nestled closer to me, adding, in a different and tremulous voice: "I am yours, dearest. I will marry you whenever you wish."

Our lips met, and then I held her at arm's length, looking into her big, purple eyes, soft and shining with the light of love.

"I am the happiest man in the world," I said hoarsely.

"You deserve it," Flora answered.

"And I am glad to feel that we are carrying out the wishes of Griffith Hawke. Poor fellow! he was a true friend; and so was Captain Rudstone. I often think of his sad fate."

"I never liked Captain Rudstone," said Flora. "I feared and mistrusted him. And I have seen him looking at you so queerly sometimes, Denzil."

"Have you?" I replied. "I have noticed the same thing myself. But I can't believe—"

"Hush! we won't talk of the past," Flora interrupted. "But the future worries me, dearest. I am afraid of war breaking out—"

"The cloud will likely blow over," said I; "but if trouble does come the Northwest Company will quickly get the worst of it. And I forgot to tell you, darling, that Mr. Macdonald has promised me a good post here at Fort Garry."

"How lovely," exclaimed Flora. "I don't want to return to the North, with its bitter memories."

Just then footsteps were heard approaching, and we drew apart in some confusion. The next instant the door opened and the factor himself appeared, flourishing a paper in one hand.

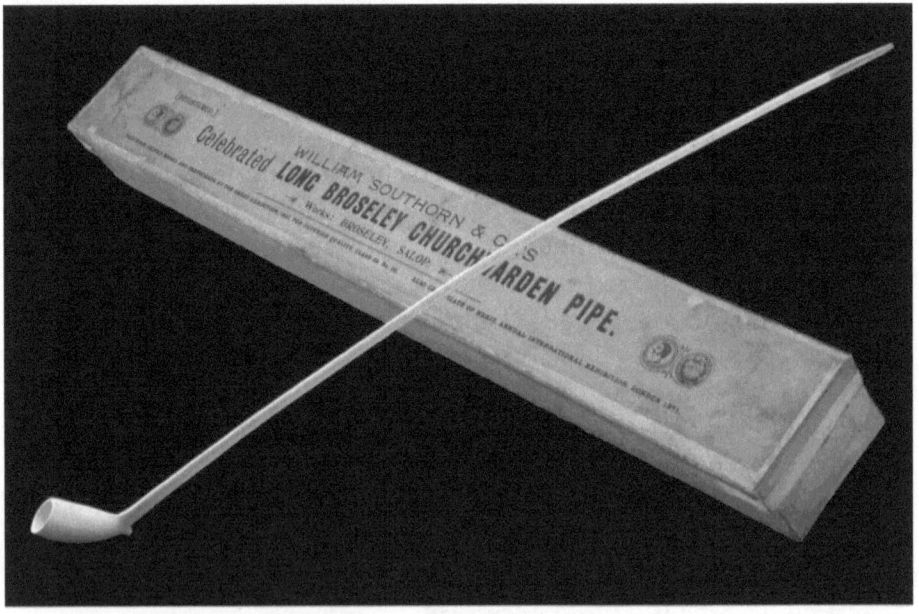

CHAPTER XXXVIII. GOOD NEWS.

Colin Macdonald, I have omitted to state, was rather more than sixty years of age; a stalwart, bearded, well-preserved Scotchman, who had grown gray in the service of the Hudson Bay Company. He was an old friend of mine, as I had visited Fort Garry on previous occasions.

"Good-morning, Carew," he began. "Overslept yourself—eh? Miss Hatherton would insist on waiting for you—lucky dog that you are! But here is something that will interest you."

"Dispatches?" I exclaimed eagerly.

"Right you are."

"From Quebec, I presume?"

"No; from the North. But sit down and have breakfast, man. You must be half-starved."

Curbing my impatience, I seated myself at the table. Flora sat on the left and poured out the coffee. The factor remained standing.

"I must be off directly," he said. "I knew you would want to hear the news. A special courier came in at daybreak—splendid fellow!— all the way from Fort Charter—left three weeks after your party."

"From Fort Charter?" I cried. "And what is the news?"

"I hope it is good news," said Flora.

"Well, yes, what there is of it is good," replied Macdonald, "and that's not so much after all. The dispatches come from Fort Charter, and contain information received there from Fort York and other northern posts. For one thing, my prediction was right. The Indians, instead of continuing on the war-path, have disbanded as mysteriously and swiftly as they assembled. A small force, collected from the different forts, has started out to pursue the scattered parties of the enemy."

"I hope they will succeed," said I. "Anything about Cuthbert Mackenzie?"

"Yes. That infernal ruffian was the leader, according to Indian spies who arrived at Fort York. But there is little hope of catching him. He is supposed to have fled south with a few followers. By Heaven, sir, if he comes back to the Red River, I'll arrest him at once! The whole North West Company shan't hinder me!"

"I'm sorry he escaped!" exclaimed Flora, with flashing eyes. "But tell me, Mr. Macdonald, is there any word of Mr. Menzies and his party?"

171

"They are all right," replied the factor. "They reached Fort Elk in safety, and then went on to Fort York. So you see that the North is quiet again."

"But that won't avenge the burning of Fort Royal," I said bitterly, "or the death of so many brave men."

"The work of retribution will come later," declared Macdonald; "be assured of that. The governor will leave no stone unturned to seek out and punish the murderers. I wish Lord Selkirk were here; he is the very bones and sinews of the company. I understand that he contemplates an early visit to the Canadas, and this outrage may hasten his arrival. And now I must be going, Carew. When you have finished your breakfast—"

"One moment, sir," I interrupted. "I suppose there is no news of Captain Rudstone? It is foolish to ask—"

"Oh, but there is! Bless me, I quite forgot to speak of it. Let me see; there was a reference to the matter in the dispatch from Fort Charter. What did he say? Wait—I have it!"

Running his finger down the page of thick yellow paper, covered with scrawly writing, he read as follows:

"... and tell Mr. Carew that we made a further search the next week for his friend Captain Myles Rudstone. A party set out under Tom Arnold and were gone three days. But they found no trace of the unfortunate man, and there can be no doubt that he perished in the storm, and is buried deep under a drift."

"Poor fellow!" said I. "I hoped he might turn up, but there is no chance of it now."

"It is a strange case," replied Macdonald. "I was familiar with Captain Rudstone's name, but I can't recall every having met him."

With that the factor looked at his watch, gathered up his papers, and hurried from the room. Left to ourselves, Flora and I discussed the welcome tidings we had just heard, as well as some matters of a more personal nature. Then, breakfast finished, I reluctantly departed to my day's work, and a few moments later I was seated at a desk in the clerk's quarters, with ink, quill, and paper before me; for I was writing a detailed account of the siege and capture of Fort Royal, which to be forwarded to the officials of the company at Quebec.

· · · · ·

The breakfast room again; the time nine o'clock that same night. After laborious toil with brain and hand, I was enjoying a well-earned

172

rest. Supper was over long since, and the ladies had retired a few minutes before. A snugger, more cozy place could scarcely have been found in Quebec itself. Two lamps shed a soft light, and a mighty fire roared in the huge stove.

Macdonald and I sat in easy-chairs at opposite sides of a table that was littered with books and papers, glasses, a bottle of whiskey, and a canister of tobacco. He was smoking a long churchwarden, I a stubby and blackened short one. At a small table at the other end of the room three officers of the fort were playing cards with the silence and attention of old-world gamesters.

"Nearly done with your report?" asked the factor.

"I think another day will finish it," said I.

"It's a trying task, no doubt."

"I would rather be fighting Indians," I replied. "The work is better fitted for Mr. Burley."

"Quite so," assented Macdonald. "By the bye, where is your legal friend to-night?"

"I'll warrant he's in the men's quarters, as usual," I answered, "on the hunt for information."

"He's a queer chap, but sound-headed," said the factor. "He spoke to me of the matter that brought him to the Canadas, but I couldn't give him any assistance; I never heard the name of Osmund Maiden. I'm afraid it's a useless search—so many years have passed since the man disappeared.

"I agree with you," I replied. "But he is a plucky fellow, and sticks on in spite of failure. He deserves to win. I don't suppose he told you what he wants with the man?"

"No; he was close-mouthed about that, Carew. Fill up your glass again. That rare old Scotch I get straight from Edinburgh, and the tobacco is the best crop of the Virginias. You see, we try to live up to the mark here in the wilderness."

"Royally," said I. "I have tasted no such tobacco or whisky since I was in Quebec last."

We smoked for awhile in silence, and then Macdonald suddenly blurted out:

"If the Northwest people make trouble, my supplies will be cut off."

"Any news to-day?" I asked.

"A little," he replied. "It may mean nothing—or much. Certainly our enemies are growing bolder. Last night a lot of half-breeds marched through our colony, making murderous threats and singing war songs."

"And a week ago two swivel guns and a howitzer were stolen," said I; "and a week before that there was a brawl up at Isle-a-la-Crosse, in which a man was killed on either side. Mr. Macdonald, the situation is becoming intolerable. How will it end?"

The factor brought his fist heavily down on the table. "In a general fight—perhaps in a war spread over the whole territory," he declared. "By Heaven! sir, if I had authority from Governor Semple, I would take stern measures at once—I would make the Northwest people show their hand, and then attack and crush them. We have borne insults and affronts too long."

"I hoped that I was done with fighting," I replied.

"Ay, you have had more than your share of it. I am sorry for you, Carew. I will hurry on your marriage—I sent for the priest this morning—and then I would advise you to send your wife to Quebec. We shall win in the end, and uphold the supremacy of the company, but not without a struggle, I fear."

The thought of parting from Flora—of sending her hundreds of miles away from me—made me feel very blue; and the factor's keen eyes observed this:

"Cheer up," he said. "We are discussing events that may never occur. Come, what do you say to a little diversion—to a hand at cards?"

"With all my heart," I assented gladly.

But just then the door slowly opened, and Mr. Christopher Burley slowly entered the room. He was neatly attired in black, and after looking about him he made a low bow.

"I trust I am not intruding," he said in a dry, precise voice. "I desire to see you particularly, Mr. Macdonald. I have been conversing with some of the older employees of the fort, and I find that through ignorance I overlooked a most important matter during the interview you granted me several days ago."

"Indeed!" replied Macdonald. "And to what do you refer? Go on; you may speak freely in front of Mr. Carew."

174

CHAPTER XXXIX. A MESSAGE.

I think Mr. Burley would have preferred a private audience with the factor, but he made no verbal objection to my presence. He looked rather glum, however, as he came near and seated himself. He first took a pinch of snuff from an enameled box, and blew his nose vigorously; then, stretching his long legs under the table and resting an elbow on each arm of the chair, he interlocked his lean fingers.

"If I remember rightly, Mr. Macdonald," he began, "you informed me that you had been a resident of this fort, in various capacities, for the space of thirty-two years?"

"That is quite true, sir."

"And during that period—indeed for some years prior to it," continued the law clerk, "I understand that travelers stopping at Fort Garry on their way to the far north were in the habit of leaving their trunks and other luggage behind them here for safe keeping."

"Certainly—certainly! You have not been misinformed, Mr. Burley."

"And some of these travelers never came back—never returned to claim their belongings?"

"Alas! too many of them," replied Macdonald. He shook his head sadly as he filled the bowl of his pipe. "You have stirred up a host of buried and half-forgotten memories," he went on, in a reminiscent tone, puffing out clouds of smoke. "I recall dozens of poor fellows—hunters, trappers, and explorers—who set out with hopeful hearts to conquer the perils of the wilderness, and have not been heard of to this day. Their trunks and boxes are still in the fort—their bones are scattered in the solitudes of the Great Lone Land. Of course a greater number turned up again, and it is quite likely that some of the missing ones are alive. You see, their property may not have been worth sending for."

I began to see the drift of Mr. Barley's questioning.

"You knew these men?" he asked.

"Yes; at the time."

"And you have no recollection of Osmund Maiden? He would have been a young man of about twenty—handsome and spirited, well educated."

"I have told you before, sir," replied the factor, "that the name is strange to me. I should probably recall him if he had passed through the fort, for I have a very keen memory."

175

"Twenty-nine years is a long time—long enough for much to slip the mind," said Mr. Burley. "I have been in the Canadas for the better part of a year, sir, and I have made not the slightest advancement in the matter that brought me from England. It is strange that a man should vanish with leaving a clew behind him, and I will not confess that I am beaten. My task, gentlemen, is to find Osmund Maiden alive, or to discover clear proof of his death. And it occurred to me to-night that he may have been one of those luckless travelers who passed through Fort Garry to tempt fortune in the wilderness."

"It is not impossible," replied Macdonald. "I could not swear to the contrary."

"It seems like enough," said I. "At that period few went to the far north except by way of Fort Garry."

Mr. Burley gave me a grateful glance, and regaled himself with a second pinch of snuff.

"I will come to the point, Mr. Macdonald," he resumed. "These unclaimed trunks and boxes—you say they are in the fort?"

"Yes; they are stored in an upper room of this very house—at least, the greater part of them. All that were deposited here during the last five or six years are in another building."

Mr. Burley's relief and satisfaction were visible on his face.

"I presume that a record was kept of such deposits?" he asked.

"Yes, from the first," the factor answered. "It was done in a business-like way. Every man who left a trunk or a box here was given a receipt. Then his name was entered in a book and numbered, and his number was marked on his property."

"And that book?"

"A new one was started a few years ago," replied Macdonald. "The first one went to pieces with age, and had to be put aside."

"And what became of it?" the law clerk cried eagerly. "It was not lost?"

"Lost? Of course not, sir. I have it stored away in some place."

"Ah, that is fortunate! I beg you to produce it, Mr. Macdonald. It will be very easy to ascertain if I am right or wrong. If Osmund Maiden passed through Fort Garry, and left any luggage behind him, his name will appear in the record."

"Quite true," assented the factor; "but I am sorry that I can't—"

He stopped suddenly, and put his head to one side.

176

"I fancy I heard a shout yonder—off by the gates," he added. "Did you hear anything, Carew?"

"No." I replied; "it must have been the wind."

Macdonald turned to the law clerk.

"I was about to remark," he continued, "that I can't put my hands on the record-book to-night. But I will search for it to-morrow morning, and give you the satisfaction of examining the entries."

"You are very kind, sir," replied Christopher Burley. "And I trust I shall find—"

He was interrupted by a quick, imperative rap on the door.

"Come in!" cried Macdonald.

At the summons a clerk entered, holding a sealed envelope in his hand.

"From the settlement," he said. "Very urgent, sir! It came by messenger a moment ago."

The factor silently opened the envelope, drew out a letter and glanced over it briefly. Then his deep-sunken eyes flashed with rage.

"The daring scoundrels!" he cried. "Listen! This is from Walker, my right-hand man in the colony," and in a hoarse voice he read aloud as follows:

"I have just learned, through a trusted Indian spy, that some Northwest men captured a traveler twenty miles up the river this morning. The prisoner is said to be a Hudson Bay Company courier, bound for Fort Garry with important dispatches from the north. He is held on a trumped-up charge of some sort, and before daylight to-morrow he is to be hurried round the fort and the settlement and conveyed down the river to the Northwest Company's main post. His captors number seven, and to-night they are putting up at Lagarde's store. This is reliable, and I have kept it quiet so far. I wait your commands, and will execute them promptly."

Having finished, the factor crumpled the letter into a ball, and poured some whisky with a steady hand. I sprang to my feet, heated by excitement and indignation. The three officers had been listening; they dropped their cards, and hastened across the room to us.

"Can this be true?" I cried.

"I believe it," said Macdonald. "It's bad news, and I only hope it won't be the spark to fire the blaze. But my duty is clear all the same, and I intend to act promptly. Not through Walker and the colonists, though; we must strike direct from the fort. Let me see; Lagarde's store is eight miles from here—six north of the settlement. There is no time to lose, for it is past midnight. The messenger has not gone, Stirling?"

"No, sir; he is waiting," replied the clerk.

"Start him back at once," directed the factor. "Bid him tell Walker to do nothing in the matter—that I have taken it into my hands. And he is to be careful that not a word of the affair gets out. I don't want anything known until it is all over. I can't trust the colonists; they are too hot headed and reckless."

"Very good, sir."

"You may go. Be quick."

The clerk hurried off, and Macdonald turned to the officers.

"Lieutenant Boyd, I am going to put this mission into your hand," he said, "and I hope you understand its delicate nature. Take twenty men armed and mounted. Follow the road that swings off to the left of the settlement, and then ride straight on to Lagarde's; the night is dark, and the crust is in fine condition for horses. These are your orders: First make sure that the ruffians have a prisoner; then compel them to deliver him up. But let there be no fighting or bloodshed, if possible. Don't fire a shot unless you are fired on yourselves."

"I understand, sir," replied the officer. "I will do my best. With your permission I will take McKay and Nicoll"—pointing to his fellow-officers. "And perhaps Mr. Carew would like to come?"

"With all my heart!" I exclaimed eagerly; for the adventure promised to be to my taste.

A moment later, Macdonald, having added a few words of instruction, we were out of the house and hastening toward the men's quarters.

CHAPTER XL.   A STARTLING CHANGE.

We found a few men up, but most of them had turned in, and thus some little time was lost in selecting and rousing them. As quietly as possible—for we did not want to alarm the whole fort—the horses were led out and saddled. Then the twenty of us mounted, filed through the gates and rode off to the north. Among those chosen—it was my suggestion—were Luke Hutter and Carteret. I was up in front, with Lieutenant Boyd and his fellow officers.

Our destination, Lagarde's store, was a stoutly-built log house standing quite by itself, and near a lonely trail that led into the wilderness. It had been erected a few years before, and served the Northwest people for a small trading post until they constructed larger ones. Then it was turned over to Pierre Lagarde, one of their own men, who ran it as a combined supply store and lodging house for passing voyageurs and hunters. It was a rough place in these times of ill feeling, and was avoided by Hudson Bay Company men. I knew a good bit about it myself, and what more there was to know Lieutenant Boyd vouchsafed as we rode along.

"It was natural that the ruffians should break their journey there," he concluded. "They will probably be sleeping, and I don't anticipate any trouble in getting the prisoner into our hands. As for Lagarde, he is a blustering fellow, but a coward at heart."

"They won't show light if they are seven to twenty," said I. "But do you really believe they have dared to capture one of our couriers?"

"They would dare anything, these Northwest Company scoundrels," replied the lieutenant. "And Walker's information, I assure you, is always accurate."

By this time we had left Fort Garry a couple of miles behind us, and far off to our right a couple of twinkling lights on the horizon marked the little settlement. On we went at a rattling pace, the hoofs of our horses ringing on the hard, frozen snow. The night was dark and bitterly cold; the stars shone in the steely vault of the sky, but there was no moon.

Presently we dipped into a heavy forest, which made the road gleam whiter by contrast. When we had come within a mile of our goal, we settled down to a trot, and a little later the word to halt and dismount was passed along the line in a whisper.

"I don't want to give the rascals any warning," the lieutenant explained. "It will be far the wisest plan to take them by surprise,

179

before they can show fight. We are less than a quarter of a mile from the store now."

The men were quickly out of the saddle, and three of them were told off to guard the horses, which we tethered to saplings by the side of the road. Then the rest of us—seventeen in number—looked to our muskets and started forward on foot. We moved as silently as possible, and soon reached the edge of the forest, where we halted in the deep shadow of the trees.

Before us was a spacious clearing, fifty yards across which stood Lagarde's store. Smoke was pouring from the chimney and a ray of light was visible under one of the shuttered windows; but not a sound could be heard, and not a moving object could be seen on the white snow crust.

"It's all right," said Boyd. "They have turned in for the night, and I don't suppose they have set a watch; Lagarde keeps no dog."

"We had better make sure," suggested Nicoll. "I'm light on my feet—if you say the word I'll have a closer look about."

I offered to accompany him—I was keenly curious about the prisoner—and the lieutenant consented.

"Go on, then," he said, "but don't let them catch you spying, and get back as fast as you can. It's too cold to wait about long."

So off we went, Nicoll and I, and we crept across the clearing with scarcely more noise than a cat would have made. A hum of voices grew on our ears as we approached, proving that Boyd's surmise was wrong.

The conversation, and the light under the windows, came from the room in the nearest angle of the house. But there were no crevices between the logs, and the shutters fitted so tightly that we could see nothing.

We heard little more. A number of men were talking in low tones, and after listening a minute we gathered that they had a prisoner and intended taking him down to the Northwest Company's fort in the morning. We made a circuit of the house finding the other rooms dark and silent, and then safely rejoined our party and communicated our discoveries to the lieutenant.

"Up and awake, are they?" he muttered. "And it's a sure thing about the prisoner! Well, they won't have him long. I'll surround the house and induce them to open the door by craft. If that don't work—?"

180

"Look here," interrupted Nicoll. "I didn't tell you that I recognized the voice of one of those fellows in the room."

"Ah! Who was it?"

"Ruthven!"

"Are you sure, man?"

"Yes; positive!"

"Then there is all the more reason for acting with promptness and decision," the lieutenant said emphatically. "Ruthven is a dangerous man," he added to me. "He is an official of the Northwest Company, and is said to have stirred up the half-breeds against us. But I'll get the upper hand of him this time."

A moment later, Boyd having given the force sharp and precise instructions, we sallied out from the woods and across the clearing. As stealthily as panthers we gained the house, and a dozen of our men quickly surrounded it. Five posted themselves before the door—the lieutenant, Nicoll and McKay, Carteret and myself. We held our weapons ready for use.

"If they don't let us in at once," Boyd whispered, "we'll force an entrance. It's not a case for parleying."

With that he rapped on the door—by no means lightly. There was a sudden hush inside, then a cautious approach of booted feet, and then a gruff voice demanded:

"Who's there?"

"A friend," answered the lieutenant.

"What do you want?"

"I have an important message for Jim Ruthven."

"From the fort?"

"Yes, from the fort. Open, Pierre!"

An instant of hesitation. Creak, creak! Bolts were being withdrawn. Next the door swung open, and we dimly saw the bearded, rum-bloated face of Pierre Lagarde. The lieutenant's ruse had thoroughly deceived him, and at sight of us he was struck dumb. Before he could give an alarm we had jammed him back between the door and the wall, and dashed past him into the room.

"Don't stir!" cried Boyd in a ringing voice. "The first one of you that moves, or reaches for a weapon, I'll shoot like a dog!"

And he leveled a pistol in each hand.

It was the neatest piece of work I had ever seen done. We had surprised the enemy at a moment when they believed themselves in

181

perfect security, and they were powerless to offer any resistance. Seven men surrounded a table littered with cups and bottles, all hunters or voyageurs save one—a better-dressed, crafty-featured man, whom I took for Ruthven. They sat staring at us with savage faces and flashing eyes, trembling with rage, muttering deep curses. Their muskets were stacked on the wall behind them, and they dared not reach for knives or pistols.

"I've got you trapped," the lieutenant added. "You can't help yourselves. Three times your number are outside. But I mean you no harm. My business can be settled without bloodshed—"

"Do you think you are acting in your rights, sir," Ruthven broke in defiantly, "when you invade the property of the Northwest Company and threaten its servants?"

"You scoundrel!" cried Boyd, "were you acting in your rights when you waylaid and captured a courier of the Hudson Bay Company?"

"It's a lie!"

"Come, we know better," said I. "The prisoner is in this house and we want him at once."

"And who are you, my young cock-of-the-walk?" snarled Ruthven.

"Denzil Carew," I replied, on the spur of the moment, "formerly of Fort Royal."

By the sudden pallor of the man's face I knew that the shot had struck home—that he knew all about the burning of the fort, and his companions looked no less disconcerted and alarmed. He changed the subject instantly.

"Lieutenant Boyd, I command you to leave," he said hoarsely. "You forget there is such a thing as law in the Canadas."

"It is you who forget that, sir," retorted the lieutenant, "as you will learn to your cost before many days. But to business! Produce the prisoner."

"I admit that I have one," said Ruthven, "but my claim to him overrides yours. He is a murderer; he has killed a Northwest Company man in cold blood."

"Who?"

"Cuthbert Mackenzie!"

I could scarcely believe that I had heard aright. I exchanged significant and wondering glances with my companion. Could it be

182

possible that Cuthbert Mackenzie had paid the last penalty for his crimes?

"It's a good job, if it's true!" muttered Carteret.

CHAPTER XLI.   BACK FROM THE DEAD.

Lieutenant Boyd was silent for an instant, and I saw that he was a little staggered by the bold daring of the accusation. Then, looking Ruthven straight in the eyes, he said, in a curt and significant tone of voice:

"I am glad to have found some one who can give information concerning Cuthbert Mackenzie, and I will remember you when certain investigations now pending are taken up by the Hudson Bay Company. Shall I make my meaning clearer?"

"As you please," muttered Ruthven, with an air of forced calmness.

"It is needless; I think we understand each other," the lieutenant continued. "As for the prisoner, and the charge you have made against him, I won't enter into that matter at present. Did you arrest him with a warrant?"

"No."

"Then you can't hold him. Set him at liberty, and I will guarantee that you will find him at Fort Garry when you are ready to serve the proper papers on him."

"It's likely I'll believe that," sneered Ruthven. "I tell you the man is guilty. I have witnesses—proofs of the murder."

"I don't care what you have," cried the lieutenant. "I want the man at once—I've parleyed with you far too long. If you don't produce him I'll search the house."

Ruthven sat glowering like a tiger at bay. He scanned our resolute little party, and looked helplessly at the sullen, scowling faces of his own men. "I yield to force of arms," he said hoarsely; "but I protest against this unjustifiable outrage. Lagarde, bring the fellow out!"

The storekeeper had meanwhile returned to the room, and now, at Ruthven's bidding, he entered an apartment in the rear and partly closed the door behind him. For a brief interval we waited in silence, hearing only an indistinct murmur of voices. Then Lagarde reappeared, followed by the prisoner.

At sight of the man my heart gave a wild throb, and a cry of amazement was forced to my lips, for there before me, as dashing-looking as ever, but with cheeks slightly sunken and blanched from illness, stood Captain Myles Rudstone.

"You!" I gasped. "Back from the dead!"

"It's the captain, sure enough!" shouted Carteret.

184

I half expected to see him vanish in thin air, but my doubts were dispelled when he came quickly forward and clasped my hand.

"Don't stare at me as though I was a ghost," he said laughingly. "You see I am real flesh and blood, my dear Carew. I have turned up again, like a bad penny."

"I never dreamed that the prisoner could be you!" I exclaimed. "We believed you dead—buried under the snow."

"It was a natural supposition," the captain replied, as he shook hands with Carteret and Lieutenant Boyd.

"My good fellows, I am greatly indebted to you for this service—for your timely rescue. I was awake when you arrived, and overheard the little discussion, but as I was both gagged and bound, I could do nothing in my own behalf."

With that his face darkened, and striding to the table, he struck it a blow with his fist that set the bottles and cups rattling, and caused Ruthven and his evil crew to shrink back in their seats.

"You and I will have a reckoning at a later time," he cried, addressing Ruthven. "Be assured that it will come!"

"A word with you, Captain Rudstone," said Boyd. "I must warn you that you are charged with a grave crime, and that I have given a pledge for your safe keeping at Fort Garry."

"What is the accusation?"

"The murder of Cuthbert Mackenzie!" Ruthven blurted out savagely.

The captain shrugged his shoulders, laughed insolently, and gave me a meaning and reassuring glance.

"I reserve my defense," he said. "I will say nothing at present as to the truth or falsity of this charge. Certainly I have done nothing that I would willingly undo—quite the contrary."

"I am sure of that," I said warmly.

"As for your pledge Lieutenant Boyd," the captain continued. "I give you my word I shall wait Mr. Ruthven's pleasure at Port Garry, and I defy him to bring his witnesses before a competent tribunal. Indeed, I court and desire a full investigation of the act with which I stand charged." As he spoke he glared at Ruthven, and the latter's eyes fell.

"Well said!" exclaimed the lieutenant. "I perceive you have grasped the delicate nature of this affair, Captain Rudstone. By the

185

way, I understand you are the bearer of dispatches. Do you still retain them?"

"That is a misapprehension, sir," was the reply. "I have no dispatches; nor did I stop at any of the company's forts on my journey from the north. I am bound for Fort Garry on a private and personal matter."

"You shall accompany us there at once," said Boyd. "I think we have finished here." Turning to Ruthven, he added: "We are going now, sir. Let me warn you to keep your men under control—to see that no shots are fired treacherously."

"When we want to shoot it will not be behind your backs," Ruthven replied significantly, and in a voice that trembled with suppressed passion. "You will be sorry for this night's work!"

Without further words we left the house, gathered up our men outside, and crossed the clearing to the woods. We pushed on more rapidly to the horses, and one of the men gave his steed to Captain Rudstone and mounted behind a companion. As we rode on a trot toward the fort, the captain, who was in front, between Boyd and myself, related to us in confidence the thrilling story of his adventures. He spoke in low tones, for it was not advisable that the rest should hear a narrative which ought properly to have come to the factor's ear first.

"I shall spin the yarn briefly and without going into details," he began. "My disappearance on that night when we encamped near Fort Charter was a very simple thing. I was on duty, you will remember, and I either heard—or imagined I heard—the report of a musket within half a mile. Hoping to learn what it meant, I ventured too far from camp. The result was that I lost my bearings, and for several hours wandered about in the blinding storm. I shouted at intervals, and fired a couple of shots. At, last, when I was nearly exhausted I came across a recess under a mass of rocks. I crawled into it—it was warm and tight—and there I slept as I have never slept in my life before. I wakened to find that I was snowed up—many hours must have passed—and with tremendous toil I dug myself out of the huge drift. It was then late in the afternoon of the next day. I had no idea of my bearings, and after tramping aimlessly until twilight I stumbled upon a small camp in the wilderness, and found myself Cuthbert Mackenzie's prisoner."

"And did you really kill the scoundrel?" I asked.

186

"Wait; I am coming to that," replied the captain. "Mackenzie had half a dozen Indians with him, and was on the way south. He knew me, of course, and he swore that he would shoot me at daybreak. We held some conversation, during which he virtually admitted that he had instigated and led the attack on Fort Royal. He meant to kill me— I saw that clearly—and I felt pretty blue when I was bound fast to a tree."

"You worked your bonds loose, I suppose?" inquired Boyd.

"No; I was saved in another way," said the captain—"by your old friend Gray Moose, Carew. It seems that he and a dozen redskins had been following Mackenzie up on account of some old grudge—some act of false dealing—and that night they surprised and attacked the camp. They cut me loose first, seeing that I was a prisoner, and I took part in the scrimmage. I grappled with Mackenzie and overpowered him, and to save my own life I had to stab him to the heart—"

"He deserved it," said I. "It was a just retribution. And how did the fight turn out?"

"Two of Mackenzie's party escaped, and the rest were killed," Captain Rudstone answered. "I knew little of it at the time, for I was shot through the shoulder and fainted from loss of blood. Gray Moose and his braves carried me to an Indian village some miles to the west, tended me until I was recovered, and then supplied me with a sledge and food for the long journey South. And it ended, as you know, in my falling into the hands of those Northwest Company ruffians a few miles from my destination."

"But how do you suppose Ruthven knew of the affair?" asked Boyd.

"From the two Indians who escaped," replied the captain; "they must have pushed right on down country. I'll tell you more of my story at another time. Yonder, if I am not mistaken, are the lights of Fort Garry."

187

CHAPTER XLII.   TRUNK 409.

At three o'clock the next afternoon Christopher Burley and myself might have been found in the factor's private office, waiting expectantly for the door to open, and gazing meanwhile at the desk littered with papers and maps, the shelves stacked with musty documents and old account books. I had not been up long, having slept till past noon. It had been daylight when I retired, and Captain Rudstone was then closeted with the factor. I had seen neither of them since.

"Mr. Macdonald has evidently been detained," said the law clerk as he looked at the huge silver watch he had carried through all his adventures. "He told me to find you and bring you here, and promised to join us almost immediately."

"He must have a great many things on his mind to-day," I replied. "But, tell me, why did he request my presence?"

"It was my suggestion, Mr. Carew. You have always shown a keen interest in the matter, and I thought you would like to see if this last straw to which I am clinging amounts to anything."

"You are quite right," said I. "It was thoughtful of you to remember me, and I am very anxious to know the result of your search."

This, I must confess, was a polite evasion of truth. I had much rather have been with Flora, whom I had seen for only a few moments since the previous evening.

"I am by no means sanguine of success," the law-clerk resumed. "There is but a meagre chance. And yet I feel a sort of presentiment that—Ah, here he comes now!"

As he spoke the door opened, and Macdonald entered the room. I saw at a glance, and with some surprise, that he was in good spirits.

"Sorry to have kept you waiting for me," he began. "I had some urgent matters to attend to. I turned in long after you, Carew, and slept but two hours. Have you seen anything of Captain Rudstone?"

"No," Mr. Burley and I answered together.

"He is doubtless in bed yet, he needed rest," said the factor. "I had his whole story from him this morning."

"He gave me an outline of it last night," said I. "It was a most thrilling narrative."

"Yes, and one that I was heartily glad to hear," replied Macdonald. "Even if Cuthbert Mackenzie had been killed otherwise

188

than in a struggle his death would have been a simple act of justice; for it seems that he admitted and boasted of his part in the capture of Fort Royal. As for the charge of murder, it is ridiculous!"

"Then you think the affair will blow over?" I cried.

"I am sure of it, under the circumstances," declared the factor. "I understand that Lieutenant Boyd spoke plainly last night, intimating that our people suspected the Northwest Company of complicity in the attack on Fort Royal, and that they would hear from us shortly. So it is unlikely that Ruthven or his superiors will take any steps to apprehend Captain Rudstone. Indeed, since they can't tell what evidence we have—or have not—they may be frightened into adopting a more peaceable policy than heretofore."

"I hope so, with all my heart," said I.

"Time will tell," replied Macdonald. "We shall continue to prepare for the worst at all events. It is possible that the rescue at Lagarde's store may drive the half-breeds, or the more hot-headed of the Northwest Company men to some desperate act."

With that the factor turned to Christopher Burley, who had been waiting with visible signs of impatience for our conversation to terminate.

"Now, sir, I am ready to attend to your business," he said. "I can't spare much time, for I have promised an interview to Captain Rudstone this afternoon. I believed some personal matter—I have not the least idea what—is connected with his visit to the fort."

"I trust I shall not detain you long," replied the law clerk. "I sincerely regret that—"

"Oh, it's all right," interrupted Macdonald. "I am glad to be of service to you. A few minutes will settle the question in one way or another."

He seated himself at his desk, glanced over a row of account books, that were shelved within reach, and finally took down a small leather-bound volume that looked to be on the point of falling to pieces.

"Ah, this is it!" he exclaimed. "I thought I could lay my hands on it promptly."

Christopher Burley and I stood behind his chair looking over his shoulders, as he turned the faded, musty-smelling leaves one by one. The law clerk's cheeks were slightly flushed, and a rapt and expectant expression was on his face.

"1780," muttered the factor—"'83—'85—'87—was that the year?"

"He left England in the year 1787," Christopher Burley replied eagerly, "in the month of June. Try September to start with."

"It's rather too early," said Macdonald. "There are only five entries in September," he added, as he glanced rapidly down two pages, "and a smaller average for the remaining months of that year. Now we come to 1788. I have not found your man yet. Let me see—January, February, March—they are unlikely months, and contain scarcely an entry."

The search was growing doubtful, and I felt sorry for Mr. Burley.

"We are not through yet," I said cheerfully.

"Perhaps, sir," suggested Macdonald, "Osmund Maiden took another name when he came to Canada."

"No, no," the law clerk exclaimed sharply. "I hope not. He could have had no reason for doing such a thing."

"It's not uncommon," the factor answered dryly. "Ah, here we are at April! Half a page of entries at the least! Massingham, Clarke, Bent, Duvallard—"

He paused with an exultant little cry, and Christopher Burley, bending further over him, noted where his finger rested near the bottom of the page.

"Osmund Maiden!" the law clerk shouted in a tone of wild excitement. "It is he! it is he! There, you can read it! plainly! Success at last!"

"You are right, sir!" exclaimed Macdonald. "Here we are; 'April the 19th, 1788—Osmund Maiden, one trunk, marked 409.' Doubtless this is your man."

It was a thrilling moment, and I felt a sudden and keen interest in the discovery, which I had by no means expected. I stared at the faded inscription on the brown page, written there nearly twenty-eight years before. Then I looked at Christopher Burley. I had never seen him so deeply stirred. He was rubbing his hands together, drawing quick, short breaths, and examining the book with an expression of mingled triumph and anxiety.

"But how is this?" he asked hoarsely. "Look: a line is drawn through every name on the page except that of Osmund Maiden."

"His name is not erased," replied the factor, "because he never came back—because the receipt for his trunk was never presented."

190

"Ah, I see!" muttered the law clerk. "He never came back. Twenty-eight years in the wilderness! I fear he is dead."

"That is the most reasonable way to look at it, sir."

"And yet he may be still alive, Mr. Macdonald. Surely if he stopped at Fort Garry he made some mention of his future plans."

The factor shook his head.

"The entries on this page are not in my handwriting," he replied. He opened his desk, took out a small book and glanced at it. "At that time I was absent from the fort," he added. "From the end of March to the beginning of May, 1788, I was in Quebec."

"But are none of the old employees here now?"

"No; not one. There are a few who have served a long time, but not prior to 1790."

"Failure at every point!" exclaimed Mr. Burley, with a gesture of disappointment. "But I will not despair. This clew must lead to others. I cannot return to England without proofs of Osmund Maiden's death."

"I do not know where you will get them," said Macdonald. "The man has been missing for nearly thirty years."

"And you made constant inquiries for him in the north," I added.

"But he may not have remained in the wilderness," cried the law clerk. "Perhaps he went south again by another road. It is even possible that he claimed his trunk and that by mistake this name was not erased."

"We never did business here in that loose way," replied the factor a little sharply. "Come, Mr. Burley, I will give you a final satisfaction. It would be useless to search the file of receipts, for I am positive that Osmund Maiden's is not there. But I will readily show you his trunk—trunk 409. Will you please to follow me, gentlemen?"

CHAPTER XLIII.   A DRAMATIC INTERRUPTION.

It need not be said that Christopher Burley and myself accepted the factor's invitation with alacrity, though, indeed, the mere sight of the missing man's trunk promised to be but poor game. On the contrary, should the trunk not be found, it would amount to a certainty that Osmund Maiden had returned to claim his property, but I did not look for this contingency, which would throw the law clerk off the trail once more.

On the way from the office we had occasion to cross the house, and in the lower hall we came upon Flora, attired in her outdoor costume of furs. She looked at us with some surprise, standing so that we could not pass her.

"I am going for a short walk, Denzil," she said, "and I hoped you would accompany me."

"Yes, if you will wait just few moments," I replied. "We are on our way to the room where the unclaimed trunks are stored. It is a matter of some importance to Mr. Burley and I wish to see the end of it myself."

"Oh, has Mr. Burley's search been successful at last?" Flora exclaimed eagerly. "He was telling me of his fresh hopes this morning, and I was deeply interested."

"Yes, Miss Hatherton, it seems that I was on the right track," the law clerk replied. "Osmund Maiden passed through Fort Garry nearly twenty-eight years ago. He left a trunk here—"

"And you are going to look for it?" Flora interrupted. "How curious! Please take me with you, Denzil, if Mr. Macdonald does not object."

"Not in the least," the factor answered gallantly. "Come with us, if you like, but I warn you it will be a dusty undertaking."

"I am not afraid of dust or cobwebs," Flora said laughingly.

She slipped a hand under my arm, and as we followed Macdonald and Burley upstairs I told her in a few hurried words what we had discovered.

"It is not much," she replied. "And what good can the trunk do Mr. Burley unless he can open it?"

"I'm afraid the factor won't permit that," said I. "He could do it only with a legal order of some sort."

By this time Macdonald had led us through two empty rooms on the upper floor, and now he stopped at the door of a third.

192

"This is the place," he said fitting a key in the lock.

An instant later the door swung open, revealing darkness within, and letting a musty, ancient odor escape. Christopher Burley stumbled over the threshold, and the rest of us followed him.

"This is worse than the underground passage at Fort Royal," said Flora. "The room needs airing badly. Are you going to give us any light, Mr. Macdonald?"

"At once," the factor replied.

He groped his way into the darkness, fumbled a moment at a closed window, and flung the shutters wide open. The cold wintry air blew in our faces, and the rays of the sinking sun brightened every nook and corner. It was a good-sized room, and on three sides of it—except where a space was left for the window—trunks and boxes were neatly stacked to the ceiling. Dust and cobwebs lent a disreputable and ruinous effect to them.

"All unclaimed," Macdonald said significantly, "and none of recent date."

For a moment the four of us stood in silence, as though under the influence of a strange spell. It was indeed an impressive and a thoughtful sight, this array of boxes and trunks, chests and cases, of all sizes and all kinds. Could these mute witnesses only have spoken! As we stared at them we wondered what had been the fate of their owners—of the daring men, young and old, who had gone forth years ago into the untrodden wilderness and never been heard of since.

"Where is his trunk?" demanded Christopher Burley, breaking the spell. "Show it to me! I don't believe it is here!"

"We shall find it presently, I assure you," the factor answered.

With that we fell to searching, two of us at one side of the room and two at the other. Its proper number was painted in white on each box or trunk, but as the numbers were not in order, and some of them were partly obscured by dust, we were not successful at once. When we came to the stack at the end of the room, however, Flora's sharp eyes quickly discovered what we were seeking.

"There it is!" she cried, "Number 409!"

Yes, there it was—the fateful characters staring us in the face from the end of a small black trunk, next but one to the top of the heap, I felt a pang of disappointment, I had half-hoped that this mysterious Osmund Maiden had returned to claim his property, and that by an oversight the black line had not been drawn through his

193

name. But here was evidence that strongly suggested his death in the wilderness.

"Get it down," Christopher Burley said hoarsely. "Let me see it!"

Macdonald assented half-reluctantly. I helped him to drag the trunk from the one resting on top of it, and we placed it on the floor. It was a small affair and it seemed very light. It was low and narrow, brass-bound, and covered with decaying leather. In addition to being locked it was wrapped about with rope.

"Nothing in it but spare clothing, I should say," remarked the factor. "It's a common enough type and was made and sold in Quebec. I know the brand."

"You are right, sir; the trunk did not come from England," said the law clerk.

"But you will surely open it, so that all doubt may be set at rest."

"I shall do nothing of the sort," Macdonald answered curtly. "Your request is impossible. I have no right to touch the trunk. How do I know that Osmund Maiden is not alive—that he will not turn up with the receipt some day?"

"I admit the possibility of that," said Christopher Burley. "Indeed, I prefer to take that view of the matter myself. But consider my perplexing situation, sir. I have reason to think that the trunk contains papers—not only documents to prove Osmund Maiden's identity, but a statement of what his future plans were when he left Fort Garry. And by that means I will learn where to search for him— how to trace his afterlife. I can't return to England until I have either proved him dead or found him alive."

Macdonald shook his head.

"I must be true to my trust," he replied. "Only legal measures can empower me to open this trunk, and you can take steps to that effect if you please. You know better than I if such a remedy is within your reach. In the eyes of the law I admit Osmund Maiden would probably be accounted dead."

"But my dear sir, the plan you suggest would involve a journey to England and back, not to mention the delay in the Quebec courts."

"It is the only course, Mr. Burley. And you must remember, for my side of the case, that you have not let me into your confidence. Why are you searching for this man?"

"I could speedily satisfy you on that point," the law clerk said slowly; "but this is not the time to do so. I am acting for my

194

employers—Parchmont & Tolliver, of Lincoln's Inn, London. They are a well-known and honorable firm of solicitors, and it is of importance to them that Osmund Maiden should be found."

"Then find him," the factor replied. "Find him, but don't ask me to break into this trunk."

Mr. Burley agitatedly wiped his brow.

"Sir, I beg of you to reconsider your determination," he pleaded. "Permit me to see what is in the trunk. Open it in my presence, let me hastily examine the contents, and then seal it up intact. It is a simple matter for you—a most important one for me."

At first Macdonald made no reply, but he was clearly moved by the law clerk's earnestness and importunity. He hesitated a moment, and then said coldly:

"I will do this much for you, sir: I will take the rope from the trunk and if it can be picked open without breaking the lock, well and good; if not, you must be content."

"Try it, sir, at once," exclaimed Mr. Burley.

Taking a knife from his pocket, the factor knelt beside the trunk. He began to sever, one by one, the tightly-knotted strands of rope; they had been tied so many years that they could not be picked open. The law clerk fairly trembled with excitement as he bent over him; Flora and I watched the operation calmly.

Just then we heard soft footsteps, and looking up we were surprised to see Captain Rudstone standing within a yard of us. There was a peculiar gleam in his eyes, and a half-amused, half-mocking expression lurked on his inscrutable features. His glance swept about the room, then settled keenly on our little group.

"Pardon me for interrupting you, Mr. Macdonald," he said in well-modulated tones. "I heard you were here, and as my business happened to lie in the same direction, I took the liberty of following you uninvited. I could not have arrived at a more opportune time. I think that is my trunk you are trying to open. May I relieve you of the trouble?"

"Your trunk, sir?" gasped the factor, letting the knife drop from his fingers.

"Yes, mine. I am Osmund Maiden!"

CHAPTER XLIV.   THE RIGHTFUL CLAIMANT.

Imagine, if you can, the effect this amazing assertion had upon us. We were stupefied—struck speechless; we could only stare breathlessly, with dilated eyes, at Captain Rudstone. Had we heard aright? Was he really the missing Osmund Maiden? Folding his arms on his breast he returned our scrutiny with a cynical smile.

"He is mad—mad!" gasped Christopher Burley.

The law clerk pointed with trembling hand, and the veins stood out on his forehead like whipcords. His face was of a purple hue.

"Captain Rudstone, is this a jest?" cried the factor, as he rose from his kneeling position. "On my word you will find it a sorry one—"

"It is not a jest, sir."

"What, do you insist that you are speaking the truth?"

"Certainly," was the haughty reply. "I repeat it. I am Osmund Maiden!"

"And this is your trunk?"

"I have told you it was."

"Bless my soul, I never knew the equal of this!" exclaimed Macdonald. "But you can't expect us to accept such a statement without clear proof."

"Yes, he must prove it!" Christopher Burley cried hoarsely. "His word is not sufficient; I fear the captain trifles with us. I demand the proofs—quick!"

"They are easily produced," said Captain Rudstone.

We watched him expectantly as he thrust a hand into an inner pocket of his coat, I with a growing conviction that the right man was found, while on Flora's face was an expression of aversion and mistrust. He drew out a yellow slip of paper and gave it to the factor.

"I claim my property, sir," he said curtly.

"The receipt!" cried Macdonald, after a hasty glance. "'April the 19th, 1788; trunk No. 409'!"

"Is it correct?" exclaimed the law clerk.

"Yes, quite so. Mr. Burley. I know the signature."

"Perhaps you would like further satisfaction gentlemen," said the captain; "though, indeed, I think the receipt is all that is called for. But, with your permission, I will open my trunk."

"Do so, I beg of you," replied the law clerk. "Show me more proof—more proof!"

196

"Mr. Burley, did you ever see Osmund Maiden?" asked the captain.

"Only a portrait of him, sir—painted before he left England."

"Then look sharply at me!"

The law clerk came forward a little, and stared for a moment into Captain Rudstone's face.

"Good Heavens!" he cried. "I see it—I see it now! You are much changed, but the features are the same. And you have Osmund Maiden's eyes!"

"Are you satisfied?" said the captain, with a short laugh. "But, wait; I will open the trunk. Do you admit my right to it, Mr. Macdonald?"

"I do, sir. It is certainly your property."

Captain Rudstone took a small key from his pocket, and knelt beside the trunk. He fitted the key to the lock, turned it, and threw open the lid, revealing to our eager gaze some articles of clothing, and a few letters and papers tied in a packet. He opened the bunch, selected one of the letters, and handed it to the law clerk.

With trembling hands Christopher Burley took the inclosure from the envelope, and glanced over it briefly.

"Written in 1785," he exclaimed, "to Osmund Maiden by his mother, when he was at the University of Oxford! Gentleman, my quest is at an end. I have found the missing—" His face suddenly turned deathly pale. He staggered, and would have fallen, but for Macdonald, who caught and supported him. "It is nothing," he muttered faintly. "The excitement—the shock; I shall be better in a moment."

Just then I happened to glance at Flora, and was startled by her appearance. She was gazing at the letter, which was still in the law clerk's hand; her cheeks were deeply flushed, and her expression was one of incredulous amazement.

"What is the matter?" I said anxiously.

"Don't be foolish, Denzil!" she replied, turning her eyes in another direction, and making an effort to speak calmly. "I thought I saw—No, I was mistaken."

The words were so low that none heard them but myself. I attached no meaning to them at the time, thinking that she was slightly unnerved by the dramatic scene we were witnessing.

197

But Captain Rudstone—as I remembered afterward—seemed to notice Flora's agitation. At all events he quickly recovered the letter from the law clerk and restored it to the packet. That he tossed into the trunk, closing and locking the lid, and putting the key in his pocket. Then he rose to his feet.

"I think," he said, "that I have fully proved my claim"—to which undeniable statement Macdonald and I nodded assent.

"And in the future we are to call you Mr. Osmund Maiden," said Flora, with a mocking flash in her eyes.

"Yes, he is Osmund Maiden," hoarsely declared Christopher Burley. "But do you know all—all, sir?" he inquired eagerly.

"I think I do," replied the captain.

"When we first met in Quebec, months ago, Mr. Burley, I suspected what had brought you to the Canadas. Your own words, you will remember, gave me the clew. I can assure you that I have managed to keep an eye on the London papers for years past. No news of importance has escaped me."

"But—but why did you not—"

"Why not reveal myself before, you would say? I had a reason, Mr. Burley—one that might have kept my lips sealed indefinitely. But that reason ceased to exist about a month ago, and I was free to follow you to Fort Garry—free to disclose the truth. Are you satisfied, sir?"

"I am content and I am grateful," replied the law clerk. "I have accomplished the difficult task that brought me across the seas. In this moment of triumph my arduous labors—my wanderings in a barbarous land—count for nothing. They are forgotten."

With that Christopher Burley rolled his eyes till the whites, showed, and a look of vast importance grew on his smug and shaven face. Then, to my astonishment, he made a low and cringing bow before Captain Rudstone.

"My lord, I congratulate you," he said proudly. "I greet you as the Earl of Heathermere, of Heathermere Hall, in Surrey—as the heir to an old and honored title, to a vast and rich estate!"

"I greet you as the Earl of Heathermere, of Heathermere Hall, in Surrey—as the heir to an old and honored title, to a vast and rich estate!"

198

CHAPTER XLV.   FORGING THE LINKS.

Never had I experienced such excitement. The scene was beyond my wildest thoughts, though I confess that I had expected the captain to prove to be the heir to some property. But to find him a British peer—this man who had been my friend and comrade for so many months—it fairly took my breath away!

Yet there could be no doubt that Captain Rudstone and Osmund Maiden were one and the same, and with sincere and heartfelt pleasure I offered him my congratulations. Macdonald followed my example, but Flora held aloof, and had nothing to say.

"Thank you, my dear Carew," the captain cried heartily, as he clasped my hand. "I dare say this is a big surprise to all of you. But if it is quite true—I am the prodigal son come into his own again, and I can assure you I am glad of it."

"The story is not complete yet," suggested the law clerk. "With your permission, my lord—"

"You have it, sir," interrupted the captain. "Give these gentlemen a full explanation. It will come most fittingly from you."

"The narrative is a very brief one," commenced Christopher Burley, turning to us. "It starts properly in the year 1787. At that time Hugh Cecil Maiden, third Earl of Heathermere, was a widower with three sons, by name Reginald, Bertie, and Osmund. The latter was the youngest son and was not a favorite with his father, if I may take the liberty of saying as much. One day he quarreled bitterly with the old earl and vowed that he would leave home and begin a new life in another country. That vow he kept. He was scarcely twenty years of age then, but he sailed from England for the Canadas with a small sum of money in his pocket. And in all the years that followed nothing was heard of him.

"I now pass over a long period. In the year 1814 the eldest son Reginald died; he left a wife but no issue. Three months later the second son was thrown and killed while hunting. In consequence of this double shock the old earl was stricken with paralysis. He lingered for months speechless and helpless, and early in the following year he, too, died. Having no blood relatives—save the missing younger son—the title was threatened with extinction. The estate, of course, went into Chancery."

As the law clerk paused for a moment there flashed into my mind an incident that had happened long before at Fort York—the sudden

199

agitation exhibited by Captain Rudstone while reading a copy of the London *Times*, and the paragraph I had subsequently found relating to the Earl of Heathermere. It was all clear to me now.

"There is but little more to tell," resumed Christopher Barley. "The disappearance of Osmund Maiden in 1787 was not generally known, but it came to the knowledge of my employers, Parchmont & Tolliver. They determined to take the matter up on speculation, and accordingly they sent me out to the Canadas to search for the missing heir, or for his issue in case he had married and died, and I trust you will remember, my lord, that they incurred very heavy expenses on a slim chance of success."

"There are several things I should like to ask you," replied Macdonald. "I infer from your own statement that you were aware months ago of the death of your father and brothers, and of the fact that Mr. Burley was in Canada seeking for you?"

"That is correct, sir."

"And yet you kept silence—you did not reveal your identity?"

"Yes. I had a reason, as I mentioned before."

"It must have been a very important one!"

"My lord, I agree with Mr. Macdonald," broke in the law clerk. "Looking at it from a legal standpoint, I feel that an explanation should be forthcoming."

"You shall have it in the presence of these gentlemen," declared the captain. "There is nothing now to prevent me from speaking openly, though I must admit that the story is not one I like to tell. To be brief, I was under the impression that I had killed a man, and that a charge of murder rested against me. The affair happened in Montreal in February of 1788, a few months after I landed in Canada. I was in a gambling den with a companion, and another man at our table, with whom I was playing cards, deliberately cheated. When I accused him of it he reached for his pistol, and to save my life I fired first. I saw him fall, shot in the chest. Then some one put out the light, and in the confusion that followed I managed to escape. Before morning I was a fugitive from Montreal, heading for the wilderness."

The captain paused a moment, his head bowed in an attitude of sorrow.

"That, gentlemen, is the reason why I hid my identity all these years—during more recent months," he continued. "I preferred to lose title and riches rather than bring shame and dishonor on one of

200

England's proudest names—not to speak of the danger of arrest and conviction."

"Who was the man you shot?" the factor demanded eagerly. "His name—quick!"

"He was a Frenchman—Henri Salvat."

"Ah, I thought so!" cried Macdonald. "He did not die—he recovered from the wound. And as he did not know your name, you were not suspected of the deed, I was in Montreal shortly afterward, and heard of the affair."

"And I learned the truth but a few weeks ago—when I was coming down country," Captain Rudstone replied huskily. "I met an old trapper who had been in Montreal at the time, and by adroit questioning I drew from him what you have just told me. I need not say what a relief it was. I determined at once to find Mr. Burley and reveal all. Does the explanation satisfy you?"

"You were certainly justified in keeping silence," Macdonald answered. "The reason was sound. But there is one little point I would like to have cleared; Why, when you believed yourself a fugitive from justice, did you use your real name at Fort Garry?"

"Simply because there was no alternative," said the captain. "The first person I met when I entered Fort Garry in April of 1788 was a man who had known me as Osmund Maiden in Quebec a few months before; so I had to leave the trunk in that name. At the time, of course, no word of the affair at Montreal had reached the fort—I came here by rapid marches. But fearing that the clew might be followed up, I abandoned my intention of going north, and went south instead, ultimately crossing the border into the United States. I remained there for twelve years."

"And afterward, Captain Rudstone, I think you visited England—your native land?" Flora exclaimed at this point. "At least, I have heard you say so."

The captain gave her a sharp glance, and I fancied I read a hidden menace in his eyes. Then he shrugged his shoulders and smiled.

"You are quite right, Miss Hatherton; I did say so," he replied. "I had earned some money in the States and in 1801 I sailed for England. I lodged in London for some months, avoiding all who might have known me; then I crossed to the Continent, where I lived for six years in various towns. In 1807, older and much changed, I ventured back to the Canadas. I need not speak of my record from that time. I joined the Canadian Volunteers, and subsequently entered the service of the Hudson Bay Company, in which I rose to a position of trust. I may say that I have not been in Montreal since 1788."

"I beg your pardon, captain—I mean, my lord," said Flora, with a pretty blush. "It was presumptuous of me to question you."

The law clerk shouldered the trunk and marched from the room. The rest of us followed, and the factor closed and locked the door.

That same evening, feeling restless, I left the house to take a stroll in the fort inclosure. It was a relief to be away from the red-hot stove and from the chatter of my companions.

I was in low spirits, I confess—which was one reason why I had come out. Flora had been unlike herself at supper, very quiet and thoughtful—a rare thing for her—and I had not seen her since she left the table. I feared that she was feeling ill, and, of course, lover-like, I evolved all sorts of dread possibilities from this. I had in mind, besides, another and more vague cause of anxiety, which was as yet too intangible to grasp.

For an hour I must have tramped here and there about the inclosure.

At last, wretched and miserable, I returned to the factor's house. I entered the sitting room and was glad to find it empty and dark. I lighted a lamp, and coaxed up the dying embers of the fire with fresh wood. I was in no mood for sleep, and for a long time I sat by the stove, smoking pipe after pipe of strong tobacco, and staring gloomily at the flames.

When a distant clock struck twelve I roused from my stupor. I felt in better spirits, for I had reasoned myself into the belief that Flora still loved me, and that her strange actions sprang from another cause. I blew out the lamp and, lest I should waken any of the sleepers in the house, I took off my boots and carried them in one hand.

I went softly upstairs in the darkness, and threaded a long, narrow hall. Two-thirds of the way along this I passed the door of Flora's room, and I was careful not to disturb her by the slightest sound. At the end of the hall a window admitted the silvery glow of the moon, and here a cross passage turned to the right. Twenty feet away a thin bar of light shone from a room that I knew was Captain Rudstone's, and beyond that lay some empty apartments. My own room was one of the first. I slipped into it, put my boots on the floor and began to grope for a light.

202

But before I could find the candle I was startled to hear footsteps—very faint, but unmistakable—approaching without. I crept noiselessly to the door and looked down the passage. Good Heavens! did my eyes deceive me? Did I actually see a ghost—an apparition?

But a ghost in black? Impossible! Now I beheld more clearly. A woman, gliding on slippered feet, was coming toward me. The moonbeams shone on the long cloak of fur that enveloped her from head to foot—on the loosened hair and silver-hued face. And it was the face of Flora Hatherton!

For an instant the hot blood rushed to my brain; I felt a sharp pang at my heart. Then I stepped suddenly out—out into the flood of moonlight—and confronted her. She gave a little scream, and choked it as quickly on her lips.

"Denzil!" she gasped.

"Flora!" I said sternly. "What does this mean?"

"Hush!" she whispered. "We shall be heard! You—you said you would trust me. Is this keeping your word?"

"Where have you been?" I demanded hoarsely.

"I will tell you—again. Oh, be merciful, be patient!"

I saw that Captain Rudstone's light had vanished. A madness sprang up in my breast.

"Where have you been?" I repeated. "Speak, for God's sake! Only two rooms are occupied on this passage—mine and—and his."

I would have given my life to recall the hot words when I saw the horror, the pitiful look of agony that shone from Flora's eyes.

"Denzil, can you think that—that?" she asked. "Do you believe that I have come from his room? Oh, merciful Heaven! that is too much! Say that I have not read your thoughts aright!"

"Forgive, darling!" I whispered. "God help me, I knew not what I said! No, no, I will never believe that! Flora, my wife——"

"I am trying you cruelly," she interrupted. "But I am innocent— my heart is all yours! Trust me, dearest, to the end. And now go—go! Think what it will mean to be found here together!"

With that she slipped by me, passed quickly to the end of the passage, and vanished from sight. I reeled like a drunken man into my room, closed the door noiselessly, and threw myself on the bed.

CHAPTER XLVI.   THE ALARM.

That sleepless night—I shudder as I recall it. For hours I tossed on the bed, rent by conflicting emotions, ashamed one minute of my ignoble thoughts, plunged the next into a black abyss of doubt. At the first flush of wintry dawn I dozed off into slumber; the sun was shining when I awoke, and the moonlight encounter seemed more a dream than a reality.

As I dressed I considered the matter as calmly as possible, and I made two resolves—that I would hold fast to my faith in Flora, and would patiently wait her own time for explaining the mystery. But the demon of mistrust still lurked within me; I was as miserable as only a jealous lover can be, and I dreaded unspeakably the ordeal of hiding my feelings through the day.

What a memorable day it was to be! Its every incident is etched on the curtain of the past with sharp and unfaded lines. The beginning was commonplace enough. I was too late for breakfast, and I sat quite alone over my coffee and fried fish. Flora I did not see. I exchanged a few words with Captain Rudstone and Christopher Burley and then went off to the clerks' quarters, where I assisted with the work until dinner time.

At that meal I was forced to pretend to be in good spirits, and I found it a hard task. Captain Rudstone, whose identity was known to but the four of us, told a laughable story of one of his experiences in the States. But I observed, to my discomfiture, that he kept a close watch on Flora. She sat opposite to me, joining in the conversation with a ring of merriment that I detected as false, and as much as possible she avoided meeting my eyes.

After dinner she left the room with Mrs. Macdonald, but first she found an opportunity to slip a scrap of paper into my hand.

I walked to the window and opened it, and the few words that it contained made my heart beat rapidly:

"If you love me, Denzil, trust me. All will come right in the end."

As I thrust the paper into my pocket, feeling both comforted and puzzled by the message, the factor called me.

"I am going to the settlement," he said, "on a matter of business. Do you care to ride along with me, Carew?"

Any occupation promised to be a relief, and I gladly accepted the invitation. Half an hour later we were off, mounted on good horses. The object of our visit was to examine several secret agents—spies, to

204

speak plainly—who had come in with reports concerning the Northwest Company. For obvious reasons, Macdonald did not wish them to be seen entering the fort.

It proved to be a lengthy business, and we were detained all afternoon and part of the evening. As to what we learned, that may be dismissed in a few words: but the news was more satisfactory than it had been for a long time. The half-breeds were comparatively quiet, presumably because of a warning hint from headquarters. And the truculent officials of the rival company had taken no steps to call our people to account for the attack on Lagarde's store, nor did they appear to have any intention of demanding the person of Captain Rudstone. Doubtless they thought it best to let sleeping dogs lie. Of course this altered situation caused the factor and myself no little relief.

We had supper at the settlement, and rode back by moonlight. We put our horses away, and entered the house. It was then half-past ten o'clock, and we found Christopher Burley in solitary possession of the sitting room, hugging the stove closely and reading an old newspaper. Every one else, he informed us, had turned in for the night, Captain Rudstone having left only a few minutes before.

"I'm not sleepy," Macdonald said to me. "Are you?"

"Not a bit," I replied.

"Then we'll have a sociable hour, Carew. I'm just in the humor for it."

He took tobacco and whisky from a closet, and after filling our glasses and lighting our pipes, we joined the law clerk round the stove.

"It has been a tiresome afternoon," the factor said finally, "but the prospect looks bright—very bright. You will be glad to hear, Mr. Burley, that his lordship—ahem! I mean your client—need not remain at Fort Garry any longer than he wishes. At least that is my opinion."

"I am indeed relieved, sir," the law clerk replied. "I feared grave complications. I admit that I am anxious—if I may say so without putting any slight upon your gracious hospitality—to start for England as soon as possible. There is much to be done—many legal matters to be attended to—and it is important that the new Earl of Heathermere should lose no time in claiming his title and property."

"Lucky fellow!" said Macdonald. "And in what a cool, matter-of-fact way he takes his good fortune!"

"He is a man of the world—that accounts for it," said I.

"It is purely a matter of breeding," Christopher Burley replied stiffly. "Blood tells always. His lordship is a worthy descendant of an ancient family."

"Then you won't admit that I, or Carew here, would be as well fitted to fill the position?" Macdonald asked laughingly.

What reply the law clerk would have made will never be known, for just then from the upper part of the house rang a woman's shrill scream.

"My God, that is Flora's voice!" I cried.

"Come with me, gentlemen!" shouted the factor.

He led the way, with Burley and I at his heels. In a trice we were upstairs, and dashing along the hall.

"Help—help! Be quick!"

The summons guided us straight to Captain Rudstone's room, from the open door of which streamed a yellow light. I was the first to pass the threshold, and I shall never forget the sight that greeted me— Flora holding a twisted paper in one hand and with the other pointing a pistol at Captain Rudstone, who stood six feet from her, with his back to a glowing stove; his face was very white, but his bearing was defiant.

"Seize him!" Flora cried, when she saw us.

Macdonald and Burley grabbed the captain, who did not resist. I caught hold of Flora, and she thrust the paper into my hand.

"Take it, Denzil," she said faintly. "I saved it—"

206

CHAPTER XLVII.   CONCLUSION.

By this time the other inmates of the house, including Mrs. Macdonald, had assembled in the doorway in various stages of attire, in a state of consternation and alarm. I had no inkling of what the affair meant; my first thought was to revive Flora. I placed her in a big chair, and the factor hurried off for brandy. Meanwhile Captain Rudstone had waved off the detaining hold of the law clerk. He stood with folded arms, pale to the lips, regarding me with an expression of half-veiled scorn.

Macdonald returned with the liquor, and a small portion of it, forced between Flora's teeth, quickly brought her round. She insisted on rising, and clung to me for support.

"Has he escaped?" she asked eagerly. "No, there he is!" she pointed to Captain Rudstone. "Liar, thief, impostor!" she said, half-hysterically. "You are unmasked at last—and by a woman! Denzil, the papers!"

"See, I have them!" I replied.

"Then read them—quick!"

"But what does it mean? Explain, Flora!"

"The papers—they will tell all!"

"Wait!" interrupted Captain Rudstone. "Permit me, gentlemen, to end this little comedy with a word. It is very simple. I have played my game, and I have lost—a woman was too sharp for me. I yield to necessity, and throw up my cards. Mr. Carew, I congratulate you. My lord, you are the rightful Earl of Heathermere!"

What foolish words were these? I could only stare, dazed and speechless, at those around me—at the mocking face of Captain Rudstone. And he had called me Earl of Heathermere!

"It is true!" cried Flora, breaking the spell of silence. "I knew it."

"It is madness!" shouted Christopher Burley, whose countenance had turned the color of Parchmont.

"Look at the papers, Carew," suggested Macdonald.

I examined them with shaking fingers, having first let go of Flora. One was the certificate of marriage of Bertram Carew with the daughter of the factor of Fort Beaver; another was the proof of a birth—my birth. I glanced at the third and largest, and I caught my breath as I saw the first few words. I read on—read to the very end—like a man in a dream. Then I handed the document to the factor.

"I can hardly realize it," I said, "but it is all there—written plainly. Read it aloud!"

Macdonald did so, and those in the room, Captain Rudstone not excepted, listened with rapt attention. I need not give the contents of the paper word for word, but it meant that my father, Bertram Carew, had been Osmund Maiden—that I was Osmund Maiden's son and heir. It was all revealed in the letter, which was addressed to me, and was written by my father. In it he told of the family quarrel in England years before, of his voyage to the Canadas in quest of adventure and fortune, of his meeting and subsequent friendship with a young man named Myles Rudstone, of the dispute in the Montreal gambling den, and the shooting of the Frenchman Henri Salvat.

Then followed an account of the flight and journeying of the two—Osmund Maiden and Myles Rudstone—how they traveled in haste from Montreal to Fort Garry, from the fort to the northern wilderness, where they were attacked by a party of treacherous Indians. My father was struck down and left for dead, and was found by the factor of Fort Beaver, who nursed him until he was recovered. Of Myles Rudstone no trace was discovered, and he was believed to have been carried off a prisoner by the Indians. The conclusion of the narrative dealt with my father's subsequent life up to shortly before his death. From the time he met the factor he took the name of Bertrand Carew, and carefully preserved the secret of his identity. He did this, of course, through fear of the consequences of the Montreal brawl, the result of which he could never have learned. There was also in the letter a reference to the cryptogram at Fort Beaver, and to the receipt for the trunk left at Fort Garry. I omit some personal instructions that would be of less interest to the reader.

Macdonald, having finished reading the paper aloud, returned it to me.

"Bless me, I don't know what to make of it all!" he exclaimed. "It is bewildering; it beats anything that one reads in fiction!"

"The proofs, Mr. Carew, if you please," said Christopher Burley.

He spoke in a quick, anxious voice.

I handed the three papers to him and a very brief scrutiny of them seemed to satisfy him.

"They are indisputable," he declared. "They leave no room for doubt."

He made me a low bow.

208

"My lord, pray accept my sincere congratulations," he added. "I am convinced that you are the real Earl of Heathermere."

I tried to thank him, but the words faltered on my lips. I was beginning to comprehend the amazing, wonderful truth.

"As for this man," went on the law clerk, pointing to Captain Rudstone, "this detected impostor—"

"I am that no longer, sir," interrupted the captain. "You will please to remember that I have renounced my claim."

"But why did you conceive such a daring scheme in the first place?" asked Macdonald. "It will be better for you to make a full confession."

"I am quite willing to do that," replied Captain Rudstone. "I will not try your patience long—it is a short story. My first meeting with Osmund Maiden was in Quebec, a few days after his arrival from England. There was a certain resemblance between us, and we took a fancy to each other; we decided to cast our fortunes together. Unluckily, however, we had that row in Montreal—it was I who shot Henri Salvat—and this started us off to the wilderness in a hurry. But you are already aware of these facts, of our brief stop at Fort Garry, and of our adventure with the Indians. I was a prisoner among them for months, and finally I escaped to the south, believing that Osmund Maiden was dead. After that I lived, as I have told you, in the States, England and on the Continent.

"And now," he continued, "I will take up the thread of my narrative in Quebec a few months ago, where I made the acquaintance of Denzil Carew and Christopher Burley. I was struck at once by the remarkable likeness the former bore to Osmund Maiden as I remembered him. As for the law clerk, I suspected what his errand was, and from that time I began to consider the chances of passing myself off for Osmund Maiden. We had been of the same age, not unlike each other, and he had told me every incident of his early life. The thing seemed impossible at first, but when I learned from a paper at Fort York that the Earl of Heathermere and his two elder sons were dead, I was more than ever set on gaining the rich prize.

"And a strange fate played the game into my hands later, as you shall see. You remember the cryptogram at old Fort Beaver, Carew. Well, that gave me something to think about—I had an inkling of the truth then. And soon afterward I found the key to it. How? you will ask. I will tell you. It was in the locket worn by the Indian you shot—

209

the Indian who had killed your father years before. I managed to take it out and conceal it—"

"You stole it!" I cried bitterly.

"Call it that, if you like," he answered, with a shrug of the shoulders. "I tore up the key, but here is a translation of the cryptogram."

He handed me a slip of paper, and I read aloud the following:

"To my son, Denzil Carew: To discover secret of my birth, search for papers in North Tower, behind third stone above door. Your father.

"BERTRAND CAREW."

"That same night," resumed Captain Rudstone, "when I was on guard at the camp, I slipped away into the storm. I reached Port Beaver the next day, read the cryptogram, and found the papers; with them were the receipt for the trunk at Fort Garry and the key. I was now in possession of proofs which I believed would secure for me the title and estates of the Earl of Heathermere. But I need say no more— you know the rest. I have failed in the hour of triumph, and I accept my defeat with the philosophy that has ever been a part of my nature. If I felt any scruples, Carew, they were on your account. You are a good fellow, and I am glad you have come into your own. As for me I suppose I must pay the penalty of my misdeeds."

With that the captain finished his story and stood regarding us with an impassive, cynical look on his handsome face. I confess that I pitied him from my heart, as I thought of his wasted talents, of the months of comradeship we had spent together. Indeed, I had never liked him more than I did at that moment, and yet he would have robbed me without compunction of my birthright.

"This is a serious matter, Captain Rudstone," Macdonald said sternly. "You have confessed to a great crime. I will decide to-morrow what is to be done with you. For the present I must keep you in safe custody."

"Quite right, sir," the captain assented, and a moment later he left the room, walking erect between the factor and Lieutenant Boyd.

"Now for your story," I said, turning to Flora. "I have not the least idea how—"

"Let me see that ring, Denzil," she interrupted—"the one you showed me once before."

210

I took it from my pocket—the seal ring that had belonged to my father—and the moment he saw it Christopher Burley cried out:

"The Heathermere crest!"

"Yes, the same that was on the letters Captain Rudstone took from the trunk!" exclaimed Flora. "It was this discovery, made at the time, that roused my suspicions. Instead of saying anything about the matter, I determined to watch Captain Rudstone. I crept last night to an empty room adjoining his and observed him through a hole in the wall. He had the papers out, and was talking to himself; but he could not make up his mind to destroy them. To-night, when I heard him pass my door, I slipped to the room again. I was just in time, for he had made a fire in the stove. I knew he was going to burn the papers. I dashed into his room, snatched them from him, and held him at bay with a pistol. I think I fired at him in my excitement, but I fortunately missed. And then—then you came to my assistance."

"My darling, can you ever forgive me?" I said to her, in a low voice. "You have given me riches and a title, and how basely I repaid your efforts in my behalf! To think that I could have suspected you for a single moment!"

"Hush! it is all forgotten and forgiven," she replied. "But we had better give each other up, Denzil. You don't want me for your wife— you, a peer of England, with a long line of noble ancestors!"

My answer satisfied her scruples—the others had meanwhile left the room, and as she lay trembling in my arms, I felt how unworthy I was of all the gifts Heaven had bestowed upon me.

It is time to write Finis. A few more words and the curtain will drop on the story of my life. That night, to my secret delight and to the factor's great relief, Captain Rudstone effected his escape. He dropped from the window of the room in which he was confined, scaled the stockade and vanished in the wilderness. No search was made for him, and I have heard nothing of him from that day to this. I often think of him, and I would give much to see him once again. He is probably dead, for if he were living now he would be more than eighty years of age.

But to return to Fort Garry. Within a week Flora and I were married, and a fortnight later we started for Quebec, accompanied by Christopher Burley. We reached England toward the close of the summer, and my case was so clear that in a comparatively short time I was in full possession of my father's birthright—the title and estates of the Earl of Heathermere. The years rolled on, rich in happiness for my wife and myself, until now three decades separate us from the early life of the Canadas—of that life which we recall so well and love dearly to talk of.

In conclusion, I may say a word or two about the rival companies. In June of 1816 a sharp conflict was fought at Fort Douglas, near Fort Garry, Governor Semple, of the Hudson Bay Company, and twenty-two of his men were killed by the Northwest Company's force, who themselves suffered little loss. The next year Lord Selkirk came to Canada, raised a force, and arrested most of the leading officials of the Northwest Company, sending them to Quebec for trial. And how the Hudson Bay Company held its own against rivalry and intrigue, how it protected its rights, the reader will find set down in the records of history.

THE END.
[79100 WORDS]

www.ingramcontent.com/pod-product-compliance
Lightning Source LLC
Chambersburg PA
CBHW020949180626
46814CB00003B/1007